Praise For The Alford

"If you like your Canadian history fast and furious, a crisis on every page, you will enjoy this film-on-paper by director Paul Almond. This story is entertaining and heart-throbbing."
—*The Globe and Mail*

"Moving, fascinating, informative, and involving ... readers are in for an extraordinary treat."
—*The Gaspé Spec*

"The Alford Saga may well go on to become one of our more important literary oeuvres, considering both the epic and historical nature of the subject matter, as well as the easily accessible prose style employed by its nationally prominent author."
—*The Westmount Examiner*

"Can you talk about thrill-a-minute Canadian history? You can now. Paul Almond has worked for many years as a TV and film director, and his skill shows in the drama and pacing of this first-rate read."
—*Carole's BookTalk*

"I believe this one should be placed into the hands of every young student learning the history of Canada... "
—*Mrs. Q Book Addict*

Also by Paul Almond

THE ALFORD SAGA

The Deserter: Book One

The Survivor: Book Two

The Pioneer: Book Three

The Pilgrim: Book Four

The Chaplain: Book Five

THE GUNNER

Book Six of The Alford Saga

Paul Almond

Red Deer Press

Published in Canada by Red Deer Press, 195 Allstate Parkway, Markham, Ontario L3R 4T8
Published in the United States by Red Deer Press, 311 Washington Street, Brighton, Massachusetts 02135

10 9 8 7 6 5 4 3 2 1

Red Deer Press acknowledges with thanks the Canada Council for the Arts, and the Ontario Arts Council for their support of our publishing program. We acknowledge the financial support of the Government of Canada through the Canada Book Fund (CBF) for our publishing activities.

Library and Archives Canada Cataloguing in Publication
ISBN 9780889955127
Cataloguing data available from Library and Archives Canada

Publisher Cataloging-in-Publication Data (U.S.)
ISBN 9780889955127
Data available on file

Design by Daniel Choi
Cover image courtesy of: Clive Prothero-Brooks, The RCA Museum CFB Shilo

Printed in Canada by Friesens Corporation

For Joan, as always,

Cousin Ted,

And in memory of my father
and his brave companions in
the Canadian Field Artillery
And for Canada's soldiers
who sacrifice so much on our behalf.

Lieutenant Eric Almond, 1919

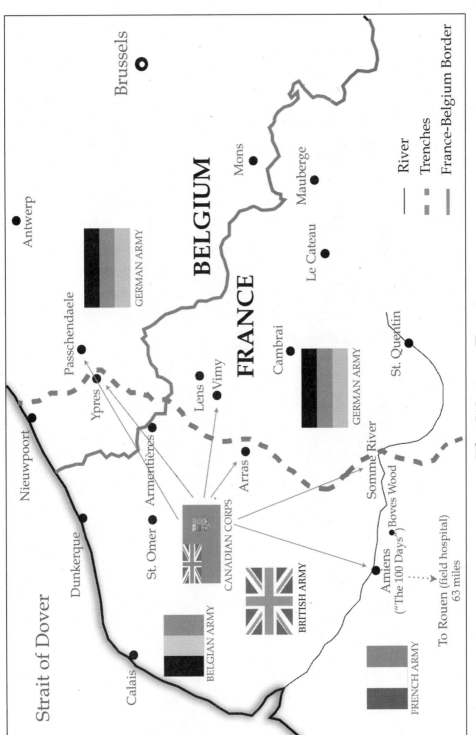

The Western Front

A NOTE ON USAGE

I have adopted the usage of the diaries and reminiscences of WWI Gunners. So you will find fuze for fuse, SOS for S.O.S., MO for M.O. and so on. The military fashion of the time capitalizes Wagon Lines, Gunners, Drivers and other ranks, and the branches of the Military, such as Infantry and Artillery. Also, we English on the Gaspe never used the accent, so: Gaspe (sic). A Glossary of Military Ranks is added at the end.

PART ONE

Four Seasons on the Gaspe Coast

CHAPTER ONE

August 5, 1914

"That there Kaiser, he wants war!"

War! I looked at Mr. Byers in astonishment. No talk of war on the Coast that I heard. Furthest thing from our minds; Old Poppa and me were heading for New Carlisle with a shovel in the back: we planned on sticking up a cross on the grave of my grandfather. He'd been in wars all right — as a sailor fought under Nelson at Trafalgar, and in Alexandria, no stranger to war, for sure.

"He may want it, but is he gonna get it?" Poppa relaxed the reins and wiped his face; that rain was driving in on us.

I stared at Mr. Byers who pointed to the oilskins covering the bag beside him on the sulky. "These here newspapers, they say England's gone and declared war. So Canada's in, too." He'd just come galloping down the Station Lane with the mail.

I glanced sideways at Poppa. His eyes darkened and grew serious in those boney features, lean from long years in the wind and rain. With his Old Poppa, another James Alford, the one who deserted the *Bellerophon* over a hundred years ago, he'd built our Old Homestead from wilderness into one of the best farms on the whole Gaspe Coast, centred as it was between Gaspe and Matapedia.

"I heard them fellas in Europe might be gittin' all riled up. But who'd a thought it'd come to war?" He peered at our mail-driver over his greying moustache.

Mr. Byers shook his head. "The station master, his telegraph tells of men already jinin' up." The railway had come through to Gaspe six or seven years ago, so now we got pretty up-to-date news.

"Bad business," groaned Poppa. "Thank ya, James. Guess we better be gettin' on."

"I'll leave yez a spare *Quebec Chronicle* at the post office." Off he trotted.

"The best!" Poppa hollered, while my thoughts spun: Canada at war! Not again!

Thwack went the reins and back I skipped to a few years ago.

I'd been in the loft after a hen I'd heard: she'd been proclaiming her laying loudly and I wanted her eggs. I had hurried forward over the hay to the huge, broad-axed beam, rested my elbows on it and looked down onto the threshing floor.

Earle, about fourteen, was holding the axe, looking concerned at our elder brother, Jack, who was sitting on a cord of wood, holding his head in his hands. The headless chicken thrashed about and lay still. Our friend Dan was leaning against the broad boards of the mow.

"Never seen a chicken kilt before, Jack?" asked Earle, incredulous.

Jack shook his head. "No no, it was the... the birthday invitation

— and maybe the blood."

Dan patted Jack on the shoulder. "Never thought asking you to my twenty-second birthday would have this effect!" Dan chuckled. "You sure sat down suddenly!"

I wondered what was going on. I wanted to scramble down the ladder, but decided to stay quiet and watch.

"I guess a soldier I knew came back. After all these years."

You see, when I was young, we Canadians had fought our first war on foreign soil, against the Boers. My eldest brother Jack, still in his twenties, had sailed to South Africa as a Church of England chaplain. So right after he came back, Poppa had given him a piece up on the hill behind our barn, and Jack had built a big house with a wrap-around veranda that he used to circle with his prayer book. Big stone fireplace inside. But he never had much time to come down all the way from Montreal. My sister-in-law, Stella (for Estelle) would bring their three boys, not yet teenagers, down for a month in the summers, but Jack only made it for a couple of weeks. His city parish somewhere in Montreal kept him pretty busy.

"What soldier?" Dan scratched his head. "No soldiers around here nowadays."

"At the Zand River. We'd been ordered to cross after those Boers. But they let fly with such a thunderstorm of bullets — then I heard an unearthly screech." Jack lifted his head and looked like he was about to let out a howl.

The other two looked at him in astonishment.

"You see," Jack mumbled, "when a bullet strikes, you're surprised, you don't... War... You just have no idea."

"The soldier got hit?"

Jack nodded. "I crawled towards him on my elbows. Any second, I felt I'd get mine." He seemed to want to talk about it like never before. "When anything moved, bullets zipped past like flies. But I had to reach him. So hot, Lord! That sun beat down on us. Well, desert, of course. Like most everywhere we fought in South Africa. May, it was." He paused. "You see, just two days before, we'd all celebrated that soldier's twenty-second birthday."

Dan and Earle looked at each other. They understood now. And so did I.

Nobody spoke.

"The bullet was a dum-dum. It entered through his shoulder, came out through his stomach, as he crawled for the river. Guts spilling out. Blood. And flies... I passed him my canteen, and he drank. He kept pleading for me to do something. But what could I do? He was fast heading for the Almighty. I didn't want to tell him. So I just stayed, and held him in my arms... until..."

"He died?" Earle asked.

Jack nodded and straightened. "Every night when I send my prayers heavenward, I ask the good Lord, please, never again send the calamity of war upon the face of the earth again."

In the buggy as Poppa and I trotted on, that rain kept coming down! The gusts beat in on us and above, clouds pressed down as ominously as that war news. The sea on our left was like a battlefield — furious, great menacing whitecaps advancing against our cliffs like waves of Germans. Oh yes, I could just see them as Huns — surging and bashing at our high red rocks. Yessir, I'd make a great soldier, I decided. Nothing would keep me from defending our British Empire.

***

Reaching New Carlisle, we pulled up at St. Andrew's Church, whitewashed walls under a black tarred roof. I jumped out of the buggy and tied Lively to the hitching post. The rain had slackened off. I got the pick, shovel and white cross from under the oilskins, while Poppa went to the graveyard. I'd already carved a little sign, accenting the letters with black tar: James Alford 1777-1863 and his wife, Catherine Garrett 1794-1863.

Poppa'd been talking of doing this trip for ages, on the anniversary of grandfather's death. But this was hay-making month and we had to get feed into that barn. So we had waited.

I walked around behind the church to join Poppa. "Here's where we put him down. July twenty-fifth, two days after he died. Rainy day just like today. Or maybe that was when we buried old Momma. Beside him, same year. October fourth."

"Has this here marker been rotted long?" I dropped the pick and shovel, and laid the cross to one side.

"Dunno, me son. Your brother Jack told me about it. Promised I'd do something."

"Why didn't you put up a marble then?" I could see quite a few around.

"Times was hard. Had to save for what might come." I gestured for him to punch a hole in the turf with his heel where he wanted the cross. I swung the pick to loosen up the ground before digging the hole.

He went on, "When you get that there big job in Montreal, teaching, maybe you'll come and put up a good marble marker."

"What about Jack doing it? He's got that city parish." He had begun as a clergyman on the Canadian Labrador the year I was born.

"Minsters don't make nawthin'; all they got is respect. But that don't buy marble."

I didn't like the idea of teaching, and I didn't like the thought of settling down into some boring life. I wanted to travel. Maybe this war would let me do that.

"So if my grandfather fought, I should too. I'm a terble good shot — with our .32, I can pick off a groundhog two acres away."

"You're not going to no war, me son. You're finishing school." Poppa was a man of few words, but when he said something, he meant it.

"After I finish school in the summer, then I'll go."

"After school, you'll go to university, like Jack."

"Let Earle go." I laid down the pick and picked up the shovel to dig the hole for our cross.

"He don't like books none."

That was true. My older brother was much more a farmer than me. I preferred reading: *Boys Own* annuals, and then G.A. Henty, Kipling of course, and even Ned Buntline, though I thought his westerns a bit corny. My favourite book so far was *Black Beauty*. I wondered if there'd be horses up at the Front.

Even though it was still cold, the rain had finally let up. Poppa was sweating under his wool jersey and waterproofs. "These damn oilskins, hateful rigs." He took them off.

I found them stiff and smelly for sure, all that oil rubbed into the cotton. "Well, at least they kept you dry."

"Are you getting them rocks?"

I walked back and picked up a few good-sized pieces to wedge against the cross. "So why does nobody talk about my grandfather serving under Nelson? That's pretty important."

"He didn't want nobody to know about that, me son."

"Why not?"

"It was told he deserted. You can be shot for that. He jumped ship, they say, in Port Daniel Bay."

That made no sense to me. "What was a British warship doing in Port Daniel Bay, for Pete's sake?" I couldn't make head or tail of that story.

"Well, they say she was chasing American privateers. In them times, Canada and America weren't on the best of terms. They'd just had a revolution below the border a while back and broke away from England. Now let's get on with this, me son."

I knelt and put the rocks in the hole around the cross as a kind of wedge. But I wasn't going to let him get away with that. Here we were putting up a monument to grandfather's memory — didn't I deserve to learn more? "Well, he's the one who built our house, wasn't he?"

"For sure, he built the Old Homestead. But after Jack and the girls was born, before you came along, your mother and I decided to put on that west wing. So that's how it got like it is."

"And we put on that nice new summer kitchen this spring."

Poppa nodded. "I would'a done that sooner, when the railroad gave us the money for the right of way across the farm. But right then, you couldn't hire no one for a decent wage — building that bridge across our hollow put the wages out of sight. So I bided my time, saved what I made — not many others did, o' course. I figured when everyone fell onto hard times, like now, I could get plenty of help."

"You're a canny one, Poppa," I admitted. "That house will never need another addition." But I went on, "I bet your Old Poppa'd be proud if he saw the size of the farm right now, and the house he started."

"I think we better just be putting that sod back, and getting back home afore she starts to rain again."

We filled in the loose earth around and I replaced the sods of grass. Pretty nice job, it looked to me.

Well, I hadn't yet won my right to sail off to England and join the fight for civilization. But I decided: just keep trying.

CHAPTER TWO

Christmas Day 1914

After our big dinner, I snowshoed up the hill behind our house and set off to find Raine. The sun was dropping behind airy clouds that scudded eastward, meaning we'd have clear weather. And only about ten degrees of frost. I had something to tell her, and I had no idea how she'd take it. I was set on going to war, oh yes, and she'd either be so proud of me, or she'd be furious. But anyway, in the canvas bag slung over my shoulder, I'd brought her a present.

By now we'd had a couple of letters from my brother, Jack. He'd joined up as a padre right after Canada entered the conflict and now he was in England, looking after the troops. Even though it was no secret that he hated war, the Empire came first, he told us. Maybe he'd help me twist Poppa's arm and get me to France, too.

I reached the brow of the Hollow: ahead stood the black outline of our new iron railway bridge. I'd worked on it, oh yes. Made me proud. I used to go back with water for the workers. Momma wasn't too taken with me doing that, but Poppa liked the idea of the little money I made. I'd pump three or four pails from our extra deep well in the house, stick them on the wheelbarrow and wheel them back to the crew climbing and hammering away on that great timber falsework holding up the huge trestles and latticed girders. Quite a bridge, all iron like the Eiffel Tower in France, it was said; terble high and maybe four hundred feet long.

I started doing the water as a favour, so they would let me watch. Then the foreman, a tall fellow with a big moustache, he made it into a job. Before school, soon as it was light I'd haul those pails back, and after school I'd pick them up, bring em home to fill and get them back again. Hard work, but although I'm short, I'm well built and I work hard when I get the urge. Five cents a day — that was something for a kid my age, not ten years old. Myself, I would'a just drunk out of the brook below, and some of the men did that, but most loved that fresh water from our deep well.

I looked down. The millpond had already froze, and yesterday a couple of fellas had started to clean off the snow. Manderson's dam, which my brother-in-law Joe Hayes had reinforced to run his sawmill, made a pretty sizeable pond, more like a small lake a couple of hundred feet across. Skating usually started later, in January. We'd strap on our skates by the mill and then we'd sail around, play tag, tease the girls while they did that new-fangled figure-skating out there in the moonlight. Nothing like a silent snow-lit night with the moon reflecting off the glittering landscape for romance, though maybe I was too young to start thinking like that. So pure, everything around us, so untouched, gentle whorls of snow, black trees clutching their precious white bundles with outstretched branches.

I never saw Raine skating even though her shack looked sideways down on the rink. Come to think of it, none of the side-hill children did. I saw she was missing all the fun so had decided to buy her a pair of skates. I saved up and sent away to Eaton's; cost a pretty penny, I'll say: a dollar, just the blades. Then I had to find boots at Mr. Ernie Hayes's store. Almost another two dollars. But worth it, I felt sure.

Now I hadn't really seen Raine since the snow fell to stay. School had kept me busy, and I'd been helping repair stable stalls, doing my homework, and reading a lot, of course. Not much time to go snowshoeing, which was when I used to catch sight of her.

I made my way down the steep Mill Road, and across the Hollow into the trees to where she usually came with her pail. Them side-hill people drank, cooked and washed — if they washed at all — with that brook water. No wells in the shacks, that's for sure. Raine used to get herself clean in the dam, she told me, like all the shack kids. Early morning, I guess. Better than nothing, and our brook sure was clear; the trout loved it.

How could I get her attention if she stayed in that little square wooden house — thrown together, all tilted with unpainted boards and a shaggy roof, one room upstairs, one down. The other two shacks had partitions upstairs, but hers, well, they all just lived like that. I stood far behind a spruce thicket; I had no desire to go bang on her door — they might treat me like we treated them: no trespassing. If she didn't come, maybe her cousin Zotique would. The son of lame François in the third shack, he was a couple of years older than me. Sometimes he worked on farms or got a fill-in job at the mill. Jet black hair, always too long, black eyes, a nice guy but a bit funny.

You see, when the railway had come through, you just can't imagine the crowds o' fellas who filled up our Shigawake — unbelievable! Not all rowdies, no, first came the engineers and the surveyors. My sisters used to get all dressed up and make sure to be seen, playing croquet out in Momma's flower garden in their finery, when them educated fellas come trotting past. But to cut a long story short, they may have come trotting past, they may have stopped for a gossip, they may even have had tea with Old Momma, but when that big bridge over our Hollow got built, off they trotted down the Coast never to be seen again.

They left behind a bunch of ne'er-do-wells. Joe Hayes had told the fellas they could throw up a couple of shacks on his side hill above the millpond — to keep them from bothering us out on the front road. Trouble is, they stayed afterwards. Sundays after church, those side-hill people became a subject of discussion. Their families weren't like us: so poor, all from away. No one knew what they got up to in them shacks, except having children. Raine's poppa, old Tuffield (I guess from Théophile) ended up working for Joe, firing that big kiln where his boards dried: not a bad sort of fellow. His brother, Blind Pierre in the third shack, all he could see to do was make children. And maybe he didn't need eyes to do that, neither. How his poor wife got along, I'll never know.

Hauling water back every day, I got to see this little creature in her threadbare cotton frock, staring at me with big brown eyes. She had short, mousy hair and a skinny frame that never got a square meal. I took to bringing her an apple or two, and sometimes a sandwich of Momma's bread. I'd watch her gulp it down like a starving fox. I found out her name, something like "la reine", which is queen in French, a bit of irony I liked. She was baptised Marie-Reine, but everyone called her Raine. I don't know what her folks did after that huge bridge was built, because the jobs went on down the line with it, and then ended altogether when the rails reached Gaspe.

Later when I'd go back fishing, there she'd be standing watching. So one day I brought back a spare pole and taught her how to thread worms onto the hook. Raine sure got excited at that. You should have seen her when she caught her first trout! She danced round like a fairy. Them trout, I guess they provided her brothers and sisters with a good meal or two.

Sundays me and Raine took to walking back into the woods together, along trails she knew. No stick of work to be done Sundays on our farm, that's for sure. Nor any farm in Shigawake.

I kind of began to rely on those walks, but I sure kept quiet about them, because side-hill folks — well, nice Shigawakers never got along with them. I was the only one. Old Poppa let them use our property to go trapping of a winter, up the east fork over by Mr. Nelson. I trapped up the west fork, which curved past beyond our head field a good ways into the woods. I'd catch a few muskrat and mink over the winter and sell their furs for a bit of cash for the household.

The sun was sinking fast, making it colder. Should I just cross the log bridge and go bang on that door? But what would her family say? Like as not, they wouldn't appreciate a young man who goes banging on doors to meet young ladies. Not that Raine was any young lady, she was just a kid.

Well sir, bang on the door I did. Never trust Tuffield, they said: when drunk, he got kind of wicked. No wonder liquor was never allowed in our house. And I probably subscribe to that. None of us Alfords ever drank.

The door opened and there he stood. Old Tuffield.

I tensed up.

I dunno why we called him "old", he was probably only in his forties, but he rarely shaved, his beard was already white, teeth missing so his mouth made a wide flat line across his grizzled face. Not tall, probably my size, he stood squinting at me with glazed blue eyes.

I found myself blurting out, "I came to say Merry Christmas. Is Raine in?"

Tuffield stood looking at me without saying anything. Then he turned and shut the door.

I turned away, then I heard a commotion inside. The door opened and out came Raine, quickly closing it behind her. She started down the path over the snow with her pail.

I followed. I couldn't take my eyes off her bare, skinny legs under that coat with her mother's worn shoes and thin socks, much too thin and short, for sure. That was no way for a girl to walk in the snow. She didn't even have a tuque. From what I could see, no scarf neither. I felt guilty, with my own scarf knitted by Momma, my warm coat, wool trousers and long socks.

"Raine!" I called.

When she didn't stop, I called again, "Raine!"

She turned.

"Can you get yourself snowshoes?"

She stood and looked, then nodded and ran back to the house. In no time, she came out carrying a ragged pair. I generally used Old Poppa's, also old but well made: gotten from my grandfather who knew Micmacs.

Well, I followed her along the packed path over the snow down the steep hillsides out of sight. Once across the brook, she sat on a stump and struggled to fasten snowshoes on over her indoor shoes.

"Don't you have no moccasins?" High moccasins were soft and warm, and pliable enough for the *babiche,* or rawhide webbing, of the snowshoes.

She shook her head.

I knelt to help. I could see that she had almost nothing on under her mother's coat, just that same cotton dress, and probably a worn undershirt. A plan was forming in my mind. I motioned, and she followed me across the flat Hollow. But when I started up the Mill Road, she stopped. "Where are we going?"

"You'll see." Better not say I was taking her home. I didn't even think about the fuss that might cause. But I was just counting on Old Momma, who had a heart big as an elephant although she was tiny and wizened from years of work. "I can't tell you yet, it's a surprise."

"I don't like surprises."

"Of course you like surprises, Raine. Everyone does."

"I never yet had a surprise that was nice."

"Well, if you trust me, this one might be."

We climbed the Mill Road, tramped along the brow to the level field on the hill behind the house. When we stopped to look down on the Old Homestead, Raine got really balky. "I'm sure not going down there," she said loudly. "You can't make me, and I won't."

Raine had a mind of her own; best go along with it. "All right," I said, "I have to get something; you stay here. I'll go down."

I won't deny that I was even more nervous going into my own house than I had been at Tuffield's door. I knew darn well what Old Poppa thought of those shacks and its colony, and what Earle would say. He'd seen me and Raine once or twice, and he would snigger and make rude remarks — jig-a-jig, and all that stuff, which was the furthest thing from my mind.

I opened the door.

Old Poppa was upstairs having a rest and my sister Lillian was off getting her baby Henry to sleep, three months old and prone to crying. Happily, Earle was out in the barn pulling hay down from the mow to feed the cattle and horses. Now I just had to deal with Old Momma, cleaning up from our big Christmas dinner. In the end, it proved easier than I hoped.

Back out the kitchen door once more, I waved hard. Raine got up, tense as a groundhog when I sight down my .32. I waved again. She shook her head. All right, I started up the hill making as if I was annoyed. Well sir, down she came and we met half way.

"I'm not going into no house."

"Yes you are! I'm telling you, Raine, you're coming in. You're gonna get the surprise o' your life, and you're gonna never regret it, I promise."

"No, I am not going in."

"You mean to tell me you're not hungry? Your stomach is so full from Christmas dinner?"

I could tell by the look in her eyes that no matter what she told me, she needed a good meal. "Please, Raine, let's just you and me go in for a bite."

She hesitated.

"Momma's getting it ready."

In we went, down past our indoor pump and into our new breakfast room, next to the hot kitchen with its big stove and smells of Christmas dinner. The table had been cleared and Momma was setting a place. She straightened and looked closely at Raine.

I went to help Raine off with her coat but she hugged it tight. Then I realized she didn't want to be seen in that old frock on this special day. My heart nearly broke.

"She don't have to take off no coat if she don't want, Eric," Momma said. "You just bring the girl over here and let her eat something. I'll fix her up good."

Raine stood for a moment, bewildered. I guess she wasn't used to people being nice. Whenever them lot from the shacks went to the store, our people kept clear like they was full of meningitis. And here was Old Momma reaching out and putting her hand on her shoulder as if she were her own child.

Well, sir, I never seen anyone eat so much. "Now Raine dear," Old Momma said, "better to take your time and chew slowly. You'll enjoy it more." But still, she wolfed it like a starving puppy.

I sat down and had a glass of milk and some bread and molasses to keep Raine company, while Old Momma disappeared inside. Momma and Lillian baked twice a week I don't know how many loaves. For molasses, I was the one to go down to Mr. Ernest Hayes's store with a gallon jug. So we always had plenty.

Pretty soon Momma came back and said, "Now Raine, you just come upstairs with me. I've got some things for you."

Raine gave me a startled glance and I nodded. I knew Momma never threw anything away, and with my two sisters Winnie and Margaret Jean off in the big city, in the upstairs drawers lay all sorts of warm clothes that couldn't be passed on to me or Earle. So Raine followed Momma.

I was finishing my bread and molasses when in stormed Lillian. She was older than me by a good bit and had been upstairs with her baby, Henry, poor little fella with no father. You see, after Lillian had gone to the Canadian Labrador with my brother Jack in '97, she'd headed west teaching and had fallen in love with a Mr. Wright. But before she could bring him home to meet the family, didn't he up and die of pleurisy in Montreal? So here she was coping with the baby, glad of Old Momma's help. But since she'd arrived, I'd found her acting a bit funny. They say that when you give birth all your emotions change.

Well sir, she stood in the doorway looking as fierce as a badger. "What the blazes do you mean bringing that girl here? You know what Poppa says about them lot back by the bridge."

I got up quickly. "I didn't mean no harm, Lillian, honest. Didn't you see what she's wearing? And listen, it's Christmas Day! She's hungry. I thought you'd not mind if we —"

"Not mind? I didn't see any of them at church this morning. If they're so hungry, why didn't they come and worship with the rest of us? There's plenty of folk would give them a square meal, if only they'd ask."

"What do you mean, come to church, Lillian? What would they wear? And you know what the likes of our churchgoers would say about them coming into our church, no matter what the Reverend Mr. Vibert preaches about loving your fellow man. They're probably Catholic, too."

"Oh. I hadn't thought of that. You're right." I could see her softening.

"Is Henry asleep?"

She nodded and came to snack on the bread and molasses. "Momma's upstairs going through Margaret's and Winifred's clothes. That girl's going to get a bundle."

"Now is that such a bad thing Lillian? Isn't that what Mr. Vibert would have told us to do? And her name is Raine."

Lillian gave me a look. "I hope nawthin's goin' on between you two," she said firmly.

***

When Raine came outside to put on her snowshoes, she was a changed person. What a Christmas Day, she must have thought, all wrapped up with warm wool leggings, Wyn's heavy coat — a bit large but cozy — a nice old wool scarf and tuque, and a good old pair of moccasins: she was one of us. "Right now," she bubbled, "I could snowshoe back past the Second to the Third Range, and way beyond, and just keeping going, far, far away from them shacks and everything." She grinned and my heart almost brimmed over from that look in her eyes.

"Right then, let's go."

It's impossible to describe to someone who's never done it, what it's like to snowshoe across the drifts where no one else has been. The silence is so thick you could almost chew it. You make your way between birch and spruce hung with icicles, or snake around a nice big fir tree capped with tufts of snow, never knowing what to expect: tracks of jackrabbits, and sometimes foxes. I was secretly hoping we'd see a bear track, but they was all bedded down for the winter. Way back, you could sometimes find a cougar's track, or a lynx, but they'd be starving, so best not to run across those fellas.

The only sound was our snowshoes padding over that fluffy surface, everything so muffled. Christmas Day, so no one was cutting wood. Off in the distance I heard barking. "Bet that's some team going out with a brand new dog sled."

Raine grinned. "Sounds travel a good ways in this air." Her spirit was just sailing over the pristine, white, wind-drawn contours.

After our walk over rolling fields and through heavy woods, we reached the forks of the brook. We crossed and I led her up along the east side of the west fork. We soon got to a spruce whose lower branches I'd cut to make a kind of hideaway. In it I'd fashioned a bench for fishing. Raine sat down while I set about breaking twigs for a fire. The brook was mostly frozen, but it still made a nice gurgling background to the crackling fire, once I got it lit by matches from a tin I'd hid. Raine fetched some brush and threw it on and stood watching the tiny sparks flaring out from the pine needles. Then she sat down, too. We'd never sat so close before. I guess now she was beginning to trust me.

We warmed our hands over the flames, saying nothing. Finally I decided I'd better come out with it. "I'm gonna build me a cabin here next autumn," I said. But I stopped myself. First of all, I was not going to stay, and that's not what I came to tell Raine about. I'd better get on with my main purpose. "So Raine, you know there's a war on?"

"Of course. Everyone knows."

Before I could go on, she looked at me sharply. I knew what she was thinking.

Then I remembered the skates. I reached down and handed the package to her. "I had to guess at the size. Could be too big, but I figured maybe you'd be growing..."

She opened the package slowly, bit by bit. Then she looked at the boots with the shiny metal skates attached, turning them over and over. She looked with such big eyes — had she never got any present like that before? Maybe she'd never even got a present.

"I thought maybe ya'd come skating with the rest of us. You know, like anyone."

She leaned over and gave me a kiss.

And then right then and there, she bent down, hauled off her shoe and snowshoe. "You'll have t' learn me how to skate."

"I'll teach you. I'll teach you for sure."

"I see 'em all out there on the ice. I always wanted to go. But I never thought..."

She seemed so happy, trying on the second skate, I thought, well, now's the time to tell her... "Raine," I started.

Something in the tone of my voice made her stop. She looked at me. "The war? Is that what you're going to tell me?" I saw her little form slump, like a bicycle tire with the wind gone out.

"Yes." I paused. "I'm going to join up next summer."

She bent over. I thought she was trying on the other skate, but then I saw, no, she was holding her stomach, trying so hard not to cry.

But I had more say. "My brother, he's a chaplain, he's written us a couple letters from the Front. He says they need every man they can get."

She lifted her head and stared, speechless.

"A bunch of the fellas around here have already gone," I added.

She seemed not to believe what she'd heard. "You don't mean, you'll be leaving here?"

I nodded.

"But Eric..." She looked down into the fire. I think I heard her breathe a word: "Please." So quiet to almost not be heard.

I felt helpless. I reached out and put my arm around her.

That did it. She leaned head against my shoulder and started crying. "You can't, Eric, you just can't." Crying like a little girl.

I didn't know what to do. This sort of thing had never happened to me. Did I mean that much to her? She was just a scrawny kid, probably fifteen maybe sixteen — just looking so young because she was small, never eating enough.

And then I thought, Heavens, am I being selfish? Going off to see the world, and leaving her... Maybe I should think this over again.

We just sat on that log, two helpless souls, kind of young and not really able to say what we felt, while she cried and I held her tight.

Finally, I blurted out, "Well maybe, Raine, maybe I'll think it over some more. I had no idea that you..."

She began to brighten. I hauled out my red handkerchief and handed it to her.

She blew her nose. "I'll be all right, Eric, no matter what, I'll be all right."

But I knew she was just saying that for my benefit. No, I'd better think of her first. The fighting would probably be over by next autumn anyway, they were all saying. So right then and there, I changed my mind. No war. University.

CHAPTER THREE

Spring 1915

"That there Raine, she's so skinny, be like doing jig-a-jig with a lobster." Earle laughed.

That did it. I took a swing at him. He ducked. My punch caught him on the side of the head.

"Well, you little —" Earle lunged at me. He was bigger, taller, twenty pounds heavier. I fell back into the snow and hit my head on a stump.

I felt groggy, but tried to get up anyway. No luck — I just fell over again.

"That'll teach you to take on your brother!" laughed Earle. "Little fellas like you should know their place!"

I wasn't going to let him get away with that! I got to my feet, ready for a real fight when I stopped. That sound!

Earle turned, too. We both looked up the frozen brook.

The spring break-up. Just what we'd been waiting for. Like hundreds of guns going off, cracking and booming with distant thunder. We both grabbed our pickpoles. We had been waiting around since dawn, while Zotique snoozed on a pile of logs we'd roll down into the brook. Poppa had hired him to help. "Zotique!" Earle hollered. "Wake up."

Zotique jumped up, grabbed his axe and stared upstream, all three of us tense, anxious. This was as dangerous as it ever got on the Coast.

For the next few days all over the Gaspe, rivers and streams would be scenes of frenzied activity. The lumber cut during the winter had been hauled by horses and piled up on banks or just dumped on the ice to await the "drive". When the break-up freed the frozen waterways, swirling waters would send this lumber downstream to the sawmills.

Joe's mill in the Hollow was no different. He had sent teams up this east fork of our brook to cut wood for his box factory. Fifteen years ago he had started making these boxes for the Robin's company in Paspébiac to ship its fish abroad, to Europe and the West Indies. Charles Robin, even before my grandfather's time, had started the biggest industry on the Coast: codfish. So Joe became the biggest employer in Shigawake, no doubt.

Joseph Hayes was a tough man, too, as well as a hard worker. Many's the stories told about him, but the one I liked the best was him setting off in a rowboat with one of his men in 1900. They rowed near seventy-five miles through the rough waves to Dalhousie at the upper end of Chaleur Bay. He bought a big wood-planer and rotary saw and the next morning they set off at sunrise — they couldn't swim either, mind you. They rowed back across a bay filled with chunks of spring ice and even arrived at the breakwater by Shigawake Brook before midnight. Some feat, I'll tell you.

The sound was getting closer. Me and Earle stood waiting and watching — pretty scared. From the way Zotique was standing, he looked nervous, too. You see, after he dumped that stack of logs into the water, his job was to blow any jam with the dynamite if we couldn't unblock it with pickpoles.

I'd offered to do that myself, a pretty exciting task. But Joe Hayes had explained that in the spring, sometimes the dynamite froze, so it got harder to blow up. Once it froze and then thawed a bit, watch out! So unpredictable. Dynamite could even freeze at around fifty degrees. And worse, then it could have bits of liquid nitro on the surface, something you'd never see, and this would detonate the whole stick if it took any kind of blow. So I'd have to wait till I'd seen a good few break-ups before he'd let me handle it. In the end, we were all happy to leave the dynamite to Zotique.

"Sure makes you forget all this war stuff, eh Earle?" Of course, we all read about the war every week in the *Family Herald*, but I wouldn't say we paid any mind, except I did feel kinda pressed to go fight for the Empire.

He nodded. "Five more fellas joined up last week: Earl Mackenzie, Stillman Walker and even Will Wylie — I never thought he'd go."

"So you thinking of going?"

"Well, I'd be sure happy to go over and take a slug at them Huns," Earle confessed. "But old Poppa needs me on the farm. If I go, who's gonna help him?"

"Me."

"You?" Earle gave a smile. He started to say something about how bad I was at farm work, but changed his mind: the roar of plunging waters filled with ice and logs was coming closer. "Poppa wants ya to go to university like Jack," he went on. "How you gonna get farm work done when you're off at Bishop's?"

He did have a point.

Zotique turned and looked at us. He seemed anxious. He was a good worker, but of course, we all felt scared.

"She's gonna be big this year," Earle shouted over the noise as it grew second by second.

"Bydam, I sure t'ink so," Zotique replied.

That water, coming closer by the second, you never could count on what it might do next. Tumbling big lumps of ice mixed in with logs that would upend and crash. The flood itself would leap over the top of the ice sometimes and spread all over before it broke through. I took a couple of steps higher up the bank behind some tree-trunks; Earle did, too.

Downstream, two cliffs rose up sheer where the brook had cut through. That's why this was called the Narrows. Who knew what that wall of water would do when it plummeted down that gorge?

But the break-up was always exciting — it marked the beginning of a new season. All up and down the Gaspe, mills would start turning again; their men would get weekly pay; families could send to Eaton's for new spring clothes or go visit Ernie Hayes's general store; in fact, stores up and down the Coast would get their winter accounts paid off.

And not only that. Salmon would start climbing the brooks and rivers, offering tasty meals. And with the salmon came the rich Americans who'd go fishing up the Cascapedia and back Port Daniel River; in fact, all over the Gaspe they'd come by train to drop their bundles of money, and that would flow around, too.

In the fields, iron harrows would smooth the ploughed acres; big seeders drug by teams of horses would plant fresh wheat, oats, and barley. Our farm tipped into the Hollow or heaved back towards the Second in uneven slopes, so our horses had to work extra hard.

By God, she was coming closer. All three of us gripped our poles: about ten feet long with a pick at the end and a solid rig like an iron fish-hook to haul the log if it got stuck. I found myself panting and I hadn't done nothing. Pretty damn dangerous, all this. Three years ago, one fella had got killed on this very fork. Two years before that, two fellas drowned up the Bonaventure River. Nothing more dangerous on the Coast than a log drive, that's for sure.

And this year, it wasn't going to be easy, we could tell by that fast approaching thunder. The next half hour would tell the tale. After that, we'd walk downstream, checking for other logjams. You see, the brook's level never reached this high the whole rest of the year, so we had to get all the logs down as fast as we could.

Well, sir, round the bend she came, three, four, maybe five feet of water, breaking its way over the ice, shattering it, tumbling jagged chunks that smashed everything in their way, never mind the loose logs. Sounded just like a locomotive coming over the Iron Bridge; sometimes we'd dare each other about how close we could stand. But no one got closer than say ten feet — that huge engine pouring steam and hissing defiantly. Pretty scary.

I got behind a big birch that I could hang onto if the waters overflowed and tried to sweep me down. Earle stood his ground; he'd probably done the break-up six or seven times. Zotique too, he never moved, though I knew he was just as scared.

And then, fast — it seemed so fast — didn't she come storming past? Jagged ice-chunks beating against logs that see-sawed back and forth, bouncing up and down, crashing through the ice no matter how thick. What a roar! Who'd think such a little brook — fed, sure, by lots of streams up above — could turn into this ferocious beast? Frightened the life out of me.

Please no logjam, I prayed — that's what caused the trouble. They always jammed at the Narrows. But not yet. The rush of water came barrelling past, sweeping logs, old roots, flotsam and jetsam, all of it thrashing like wild sea monsters struggling to escape.

Zotique knocked out one picket holding his pile of logs. When he came around on the slippery bank to knock out the second he lost his footing, and at the same time a log in the maelstrom lifted up and struck him. Down he went.

Me and Earle ran forward, but Zotique grabbed at a sapling as he swept down. Before we got there, he'd managed to scramble out. He shook himself, and waved. Behind him, his pile of logs fell into the waters and churned off on their frenzied journey to Joe's mill.

Once I got over the fright, that initial shock as the whole break-up came thundering past, I found it could be almost enjoyable. We stood back and watched lumps of ice spinning among the logs, some of which upended when they caught on buried rocks. Darn dangerous if you didn't watch out.

And then it happened. One log jammed between two trees farther down.

Earle and I exchanged looks, and started on the run with our pickpoles. That log caught another two besides, getting them stuck, too. Quick, before it got worse! I'd gotten there first and hauled hard on the log to twist her out, but more logs jammed. I jumped forward.

"Careful Eric! Don't get too close!" hollered Earle. "You gotta watch it. Keep back!"

It felt good when he acted like an older brother, but that jam had to be broke. I worked with my pickpole, but maybe I wasn't careful enough.

"Eric!" Earle hauled me back roughly.

The jam was building and with it the water. Nothing for it but dynamite.

Zotique ran to grab a stick, which he brought forward.

"Better use two!" Earle yelled.

Zotique got the second, stuck it in his pocket, and came to the edge. He stopped, took a second to stare at the jam.

Quite an art to break a logjam. You've got to know where to put that stick of dynamite. You can't just toss it on top. You've gotta get out there in the middle of the brook onto the logs themselves and stick it in somewhere, then run the fuse back so that when it blows, it will shake them all free.

So we watched Zotique, who by now was pretty good at this, grab his shorter peavey as a kind of lever to balance him and begin to leap across the logs. Of course, they ducked under water with his weight, but he stepped lightly over, one after another, with them rolling, and got out onto the jam itself. I was gripping my pickpole so tight my fingers hurt. I tried to relax as I watched him clamber up — you never knew when a log might roll or the whole jam give way and finish you off.

Earle and I couldn't peel our eyes away. I offered up a prayer: "Good Lord, don't let that happen!" His family out at the shacks: they'd starve to death if anything happened to Zotique, his father François being such a lazy bastard.

Holding the wick, Zotique searched for a place to stick his dynamite, found it, turned to check his way back. He waved, bent, shoved the stick into a hole and tried to push it well down into the logs. But then he tapped it with his peavey to drive it in and up she blew! And Zotique with it.

That was some explosion!

The logs lifted into the air, and right then and there Zotique was smashed into the water. He bobbed back up to the surface, still alive, floundering among the tumbling logs. I saw him reach out for the bank, but another bloody great log struck him on the head. That was it.

We turned and ran for the trail past the bluffs of the Narrows.

But we both knew he was finished.

When we got to the other side, no sign of the body. I was real shook up. I mean, I wasn't so close to him, but a fella like him, well, I just hadn't seen anyone killed. Hit me real hard.

Still, we had to hurry downstream a good ways. At another logjam, Earle decided to stay and break that up, but I went on ahead to look for any signs of poor Zotique. I kept praying, even out loud: "Don't let him die... Good Lord, please let me find him, alive and well."

No luck. When I finally got home I alerted everyone, tears in my eyes, darn it, like a baby. The next day, you wouldn't believe it, practically the whole community turned out to search that brook. Never mind he lived in them shacks, he was a young fella and his death certainly got everyone worked up. I was glad to see I wasn't the only one.

Yes, they did find the body, and yes, for his funeral, St. Paul's church was packed. One young fella, his whole life before him, taken up into the arms of Our Lord, well it had such an impact on all of us. Nothing worse.

I wish I could say that afterwards the community rallied around the families in the shacks, but apart from a collection taken up after the funeral, and some folk giving extra food, there was still this invisible line dividing us and them.

Poor Zotique. What would his family do now? And his cousin Raine? No war for me, I could see that. She would need me now more than ever.

CHAPTER FOUR

Autumn 1915

We all bowed our heads as Old Poppa intoned, "God bless us and what's provided for us. Amen."

"And let us remember the soul of the dear lad who was killed in the spring break-up —" Momma added.

"— Zotique," I said.

"Zotique," my mother concluded. "May the Lord cradle his soul in His loving arms forever."

We opened our eyes and started to eat. I was worried that the mention of her cousin might upset Raine, although here we were in September, months afterwards. Old Poppa was at the head of the table, Earle and I sat behind against the partition, with Lillian and Raine across from us and at the end, Old Momma in her usual place by the kitchen. Momma had cooked a special dinner for me because that next day, I was leaving for Bishop's University.

My wanting to invite Raine sure caused some dissension. "Whatever d'you want that child here for?" Momma had asked me last week. She looked at me with those sharp blue eyes that could see through anything. "It's all very well to take her snacks now and then; no harm in giving charity to poor families, no matter what Poppa says. But you two is not gettin' serious, I hope."

"No, Momma, absolutely not. But ya know, it must be a terble hard life back there in them shacks. Now that Zotique is gone, I don't know how they'll manage."

"Doesn't Tuffield work at the mill? And what about that brother of his, the lame one. Surely he could get a job?"

"François is lazy as all get out. But why can't Raine just have one meal with us? It's my last night after all."

Once Momma had agreed, I had the rest of the family to deal with. Earle made jokes, and then asked, "What are ya gonna do now, ask her to marry ya?" I could tell he was kind of scared of that idea. Well, I reassured him, and thankfully, Momma said she would deal with Poppa. Like the rest of Shigawake, he was not so well inclined to a bunch of lazy idlers who kept having children with no means to support them.

Lillian, having had a baby, was another matter. She had been getting warmer towards Raine and the side-hill people. Sometimes when she drove the horses for us during haymaking along the brow of the Hollow, Lillian would look across and say, "Poor folk... Poor Raine." Then she'd mumble, "Mind you, I've heard of some awful goings-on over in them shacks."

"Just gossip, you know how folk are, any chance to spread a bad word." We ate for a while in silence. Momma had made spareribs for us out of a porker we killed the week before. B'ys, it was good. My favourite meal. We only killed pigs in the fall; Will Hayes would come in and butcher them good. And our vegetables! Everyone agreed Momma's flower garden was a sight to behold, but up there on the hill, you should'a seen what we planted for the winter: almost an acre of potatoes and lots of turnips, carrots and beans. I looked across at Raine and could tell she'd never seen so much food: loaves of puffy white bread, jars of molasses, and for dessert, Momma had sent away for two cans of peaches, which cost thirty-eight cents, a huge extravagance. You see, with our own wheat, we never bought a sack of flour, pricey enough at four dollars; our money mainly went on tea, thirty cents a pound.

"Help yourself, Raine, go to it!" Poppa said. "Then when we're finished, maybe Momma will make up a little something fer ya to take back to your family."

That made us all look at Poppa with big eyes — not like him at all. But Raine was now growing up a bit, and though not pretty, she had a certain strength of character he would find attractive. And speaking for myself, I couldn't help liking her.

"Now, Raine, have you managed to find a bit of work?" Lillian asked, passing her the gravy.

"Yes, ma'am. I work a bit at Mr. Hayes's store. But I never been to no school, so they had to teach me figures and all. I think maybe I got him cheated out of a few cents when I started." We all grinned. "But he's taken time to show me, and now he says I'm just as good as anyone else. I only work on weekends though, ma'am."

"Call me Lillian, Raine. I may be older than you, but I'm not as old as Momma!"

"Yes ma'am," Raine blurted again, and then laughed at her own mistake. As we all did. It kind of broke the ice.

***

As we climbed the hill behind the house, Raine allowed as how it was the best supper she'd ever eaten. I felt pleased. High above us, the stars were out in all their brilliance and a nearly full moon poured a solid path of pewter sparkles over the bay. Soon it would sail higher and light our way back. I had told everyone I'd walk Raine home, only the polite thing to do, even though Earle smothered a smile under his napkin.

We got to the brow of a hill and stopped to look down on the Coast road below our large farmhouse. The next house over were my cousins, James and Selina Byers with two children. Next over to that was another cousin, Gavin, grandson of my Uncle John Garrett Alford who'd been given the land by Grandfather James, but who had passed on long before I was born. His wife Phemmie (Euphemia) and three teenage kids worked that farm, too. At the front of their property stood the little Temperance Hall, built by the Women's Christian Temperance Union but now used as a church by the Presbyterians. And to the East off beyond the Hollow, we could see the spire of St. Paul's that Poppa had helped build fifty years ago. We stood for a while, and I put my arm around her waist. Soon she leaned her head on my shoulder.

What a place! I wondered how I could ever leave it. But I knew that schooling, if a fella was lucky enough to get it, was important. Maybe if I got an education, I could sweep her outta those shacks and raise a family. But then, wasn't fighting more honourable? My grandfather, as a sailor, had sure thought so. Jack was over there now, too. The Empire needed every young man in this great fight for civilization. And I had an idea that Poppa expected me to join up, too, if the darned war kept on. Quite a dilemma.

Silence descended. Over beyond cousin Gavin's, a dog began barking. And beyond that, we heard a horse and buggy trotting along. It was still early and the road was busy. As we stood there, the couple passed below and silence fell again like a halo. Overhead, the last seagull cried out, and in the distance I felt sure

I could hear the waves breaking against the red cliffs.

What a place to be born into! What a place to grow up in! What a place to earn a living, farming, or even teaching...

Raine turned to go and I followed her.

As we came to the Mill Road, Raine said, "I've got a surprise for you."

"Me?"

She nodded. "Remember you took me to a place last Christmas back by the cabin you said you was gonna build this autumn?"

"I'll never forget that."

"Well, I got a place now. I got it ready. Just for us. No one knows where it is. I hid it real good."

A place just for us? She was going to show me her secret hideaway. My heart soared.

We got to the bottom of the Mill Road and walked across the open Hollow where the cattle grazed. At one end near the millpond where it was nice and muddy, we had a rail pasture for our old sows.

We crossed the log bridge and she led me along her side of the brook for a good way, wending through the bushes in silence. Because it was night, you couldn't hear no birds, but we passed near an owl that kept up its hooting.

"What's it like, this university of yours?" Raine asked. "What do you do there? I bet there'll be lots of girls."

I hadn't thought about that. "I don't think too many girls go to college," I replied. "But I imagine a good many more than you see here in Shigawake. I don't know much about it, except that my brother Jack went, and said he loved it. He played rugby, he studied, he skated on the St. Francis River, he met all sorts of interesting people. I think I'm going to enjoy myself." I didn't add that, even so, I felt a bit of a wastrel, not going to fight — the pull was still there. I even heard myself admitting: "You know, I still worry that I should maybe join up."

She turned to me. "Don't say that, don't ever say that, Eric." She looked frightened. "I don't want you to get killed. What would I do?"

"Well, you'd still have your family, Raine."

She gave an exclamation of disgust. "You can't use that word for the folks I live with."

I felt really sad for her. We climbed up a bit and then through some of the thickest bushes you could imagine. And then, right where the trees began again, we broke into her little clearing, about six foot across. Around the edge she had planted some wild flowers that I was sure would soon die, with not enough sun. And through the branches of the bushes, she had threaded vines. Very private, and very nice. She sat down. "I picked this place because it's got the softest moss."

She lay back and looked up at the stars.

After a few seconds, I heard her sigh. I wasn't looking at her. "I sure would like to see you off tomorrow," she said.

What a good idea. But then, I realized, it would upset me. And not only me, the family — if they were coming to see me off. It would probably just be Old Poppa — would he like to share me with Raine? And then I had this thought: "You know what? I'll have Old Poppa drive me down to Port Daniel to take the train, instead of from St. Godfrey. And you come by the Iron Bridge. You can stand there on your side of the Hollow close to the tracks and when the train comes, I'll be at the window. And we'll wave to each other."

After a moment, she said, "I like that idea."

I sat listening to the owl for a few moments.

"This moss is sure soft," she murmured.

I wondered if that was an invitation? Or just a statement. And then I became aware of her as a girl. Her and me. Together in this forest bower. What was supposed to happen? I sure wasn't gonna fall on her like the other lads do with their girls. First of all, I was far too shy. And second, I respected her too much.

Anyway, it was real nice, us sitting like this, shafts of moonlight coming down through the bushes, and an owl calling.

I felt a tug at my arm. She put her hand on my shoulder and pulled me down. I lay beside her. Then she nudged closer, and I found my arm going around her. We lay like that for a while.

"Pretty nice place you got here," I said at last.

"I made it just for us," she repeated.

I nodded.

"And now," she said, "I'm going to make sure you won't ever forget me."

She leaned over and kissed me, and then her kisses moved across my cheek and then she pressed her mouth against my own lips. I couldn't stop myself, my arms went round her and I started kissing her, too.

And then her little hands went down to my trousers. She began undoing them and taking them off. It kind of shocked me. Had she done this before? Surely not. But how...

She kept undressing me. It was a warm night, so that was fine. Until she started taking off her own dress.

"Raine," I whispered, "do you know what you're doing?"

"Yes." Nearly naked, she lay beside me. Then she turned her lips to my ear, and she whispered. "I won't if you don't want to."

I knew I did. I loved her so much. But I wanted to understand more about what was going on.

She guessed at my thoughts. "I suppose you want to know how come I know all this?"

"You don't do it with other boys, I know that for sure."

"Of course not." All this was being said very, very quietly, although there was no one to hear us for a long way.

"With you going so far away, I decided to tell you all my secrets. My worst secrets. Shut your eyes." I did. "I'm going to tell you, because I know that if you hear them, you may hate me, but maybe not. Anyway, you'll know everything about me. And there'll be no lies of any kind between us. Only truth."

My heart welled up with feelings for her. "No matter what you tell me, Raine, I'll still always love you."

I couldn't believe the words had come out of my mouth. Imagine me saying that! But when I thought about it, I really meant it. I did love her. So much.

We lay for a long time in silence while I waited for her to tell me these secrets. Finally, she began to whisper. "It was my uncle François first. He made me. I fought hard. But it was no use. He threatened to drown me in the brook if I didn't let him. Even though he's old and had a bad leg, I knew he could. And that no one would ever find out. They'd just see this drowned body. It scared the life out of me. I knew I better not resist or I'd end up in that millpond."

I stayed silent. What story was this I was trying to absorb? It sounded true. My mind went numb. I kept on holding her tight, while she gathered up courage to keep on.

"Over and over again, he'd take me off alone. Every week. Since I was about twelve. And then he made me do it with his other brother. "Poor Blind Pierre," he would say, "he needs it so bad." So I had to do it with him.

"They both saw to it that I got treats — that's the worst of it. Maybe that's what kept me alive and goin'. They wanted me healthy, so they could enjoy themselves."

Finally, it seemed she had finished. I tried my best to absorb it. Did I ever feel for her, poor little girl. Then I started to get angry. So angry, I thought I'd go out right that minute and — "I'm gonna get my .32 and come back and shoot them both."

Anger choked my voice.

She rolled onto me and grabbed me tight. "No no no, don't do that. They'll catch you, and put you away, and hang you for murder. No no no. Anyway, Eric, they've stopped. I swear it. Last year, they stopped. I promise, Eric, they don't do it no more. One of Blind Pierre's daughters, she's thirteen now, I've seen them giving her treats. Maybe they got her to do it. So you don't need to worry."

"I don't need to worry? What you mean!" I got up on one elbow. "Of course I worry. I worry about her."

"You don't even know her. And she..." she grasped for words, "what she told me, she likes it, kind of. She likes the treats. They don't hurt her, she said. Just leave them be. I'm gonna get out of here just as quick as I can. Just as soon as I get more figures into my head, I'm gonna run away and work at some store in New Carlisle, maybe even further away, like Bonaventure, where they won't find me. Don't you worry."

She calmed down a little as she felt me relax. I could see that any wild action on my part might lead to repercussions she didn't need, on top of everything else.

"Eric, now that I've told you, you know everything. But maybe... you don't want me any more?"

I didn't reply right away. I needed time to think. And then, I heard a sound. I turned. She was biting her hand so hard. But it didn't help. She just curled over and cried.

Of course, my heart broke. I couldn't bear the sound of her tiny sobs. I started to kiss her, and to reassure her. I kissed her on the cheeks, and shut her eyes with kisses, and then I found her lips, and I touched them with my own, just softly, and then more and more, and she really responded. I don't know how it all happened, but we were lying together naked, so finally everything built into a kind of wild rushing bonfire, the two of us locked together onto that bed of soft moss in our hidden bower. Like nothing I had ever experienced. And she told me later, neither had she.

Not once, but again. And again. For her, she said, it was a way of sealing our love. And seal it, it sure did.

***

Old Poppa and I drove down to Port Daniel station in silence. Both our hearts were heavy. All we talked about was Poppa coming to meet me at Christmas in New Carlisle, and how I would try to write often.

At the station, four or five other families were saying goodbye, mostly young men, all of them going off to enlist. Lots of tears, let me tell you. I wanted to go with them, and I almost felt like a coward. But I had a new love, Raine, and it would be a long time before I'd forget what happened in that wooded bower with the owl calling.

Well sir, soon I found myself sitting in the window of the train that had only stopped for a couple of minutes to let us on. The whistle blew and so began the mournful journey out of Port Daniel, not only past the Iron Bridge but on to Montreal, where I would transfer to another train for Sherbrooke and then get admitted to Bishop's University.

Thoughts spun through my head as I watched the fields go by. My new life had begun. But Shigawake was still so big inside me, and along with my home, that scared little girl to whom I had given all the love I had.

Before too long, I sat up, because I heard the train blowing for Kruse's crossing. I leaned against the window, and there she was. She had on one of the dresses Old Momma had given her in the spring. All white. Just like a bride. I could see her begin to wave in the distance. Then as the train swept past, much too fast, I was waving frantically and so was she. And trying hard not to cry. Well, maybe she succeeded, I don't know, but for myself, down came the tears. Goodbye Shigawake. Goodbye Raine.

PART TWO

Flanders

CHAPTER FIVE

July 24, 1916

The 35th Howitzer Brigade's march to our Wagon Lines at Zillebeke in Flanders began with great anticipation — at last we were on our way to the Front. In the distance, we could even hear the guns, a muffled roar like when you approach the falls back of Hopetown. Everything was jake; all those months of training in Canada and England were about to pay off. As we swung along through the dusk, me riding Barry, we sang songs: "Mademoiselle from Armentières," "It's a Long Way to Tipperary," changed to "It's the Wrong Way to Tickle Mary," and so on. Farmers were still gathering their cows in for milking while women bent over vegetable gardens. Farm life, so far as I could see, was carrying on and hell, you could even hear birds singing; I saw a couple of hawks, and a kestrel hovering.

But you couldn't help noticing the landscape changing: trees ripped to shreds and the odd shell crater. When I arrived in France ten days ago at Le Havre and took the train eastward, I had pressed my face against the window absorbing all I could. The houses looked different from in Quebec, but the countryside was similar: greener, though, and flowers were blooming. Exciting for me to be at last in a foreign country.

I thought back to my first train ride from Port Daniel when I was saying goodbye to the Old Homestead, and waving to Raine at the Iron Bridge. Sitting, feeling pretty sorry for myself, I heard at the other end of my carriage some fellas from New Carlisle Academy celebrating. They motioned me over and what camaraderie! I hadn't known the like, even at school. We hung onto every story about trench life and the hated Hun. They were off to join up, and I sure felt like going with them. So I let them think I was enlisting too and we had quite a party; I didn't get much sleep.

The next morning I arrived in Montreal, caught the train to Sherbrooke, and then a bus to Lennoxville. It let me off at a crossroads and I saw young men heading out of town. I followed them across railway tracks and started down a slight incline when I saw ahead the red-brick walls and towers of the famous college that my brother Jack had attended some twenty-five years before. I swelled with pride. Soon, I'd be as educated as him. What an experience this would be!

I had decided to take general courses and specialize later, once I had gotten my bearings. But these thoughts were interrupted by a pack of girls, giggling and talking among themselves. One of them, a cute brunette with laughing eyes and a smart hat, came over. Between her finger and thumb, she held a white feather.

She handed it to me and I took it, wondering what it signified — some prize for being good-looking? I hardly thought so, although I had washed my face well on that Sherbrooke train, brushed my hair, and I was wearing a nice new cloth cap. I was conscious of being shorter than her, though. Anyway, I thanked her and stuck it through my shirt buttonhole.

When they saw me do that, they laughed. Real pretty they were, gossiping together. But when they went on ahead, I saw they gave another fella a feather, too, so maybe I wasn't too special.

Wearing my feather, I started up the gravelled roadway towards Bishop's University. Already fellas my age were milling around, gossiping with each other, laughing loudly, generally having a good time, though some looked nervous. Today was admission day for new students.

I passed a desk stuck out alone with three soldiers behind. The officer hailed me with a smile. "Well," he indicated my white feather, "I see you've already been accepted!"

"Pretty nice, eh?" I replied. "Bunch o' girls gave it to me."

"You know what they were saying?"

I almost blushed. Had they singled me out because I was smart or something?

"You're a member of the Cowards' Club."

"Me a coward? No one's ever dared say that!" I felt my hands curl into fists. Not one soul in Shigawake would dare call me coward, no sir.

"I'm sure you have a good reason for not joining up," the officer said, putting his hand on my shoulder, "but they wouldn't know that, of course."

"Oh." I thought a bit. "Well, I'd sure like to go and serve my king and country, but Poppa wants me to go to university first."

The two soldiers looked at each other and smiled. The officer said, "Let's take a walk together." Other girls had gathered about the entrance and were giving out more white feathers.

Well sir, by the end of that walk, he had me convinced. I had to admit that I'd not been able to make up my mind since that day I'd heard war started. And that officer was terble smart, he had an answer to every one of my doubts. Why not take all my courses after we'd won the war? I'd have more money then, and I'd only be putting it off for a year, anyway. He was an officer in the Artillery, a fine branch of the service. So instead of going to university, I joined the Canadian Field Artillery.

Those faraway thoughts of Canada were jolted right out of my mind on this French roadway when the soldiers' singing stopped — well, kind of petered out. I soon saw why. The crossroad had been blasted by some long-range high explosive shell. The huge crater was a shock, but what stunned everyone into silence were the bodies, well, parts of bodies, and chunks of flesh sticking to the bushes. The wounded had been taken off, and a work party now was collecting these remains of the dead.

Men like me, soldiers — torn apart! Some still sat frozen upright, splayed like my sisters' dolls, others blown into the hedge with such force they stuck there, staring with blackened eyes as if alive, but covered in dark, sticky molasses — blood? Some had no mark, killed by the concussion, as we knew from our lectures. Had they been singing like us? Their tunes were gone forever. Not a lot of glory here, more like waste, I'd say.

This poison crept through my veins, numbing every limb and shutting my brain right down. Butchery in the blink of an eye! Barry snorted a couple of times and shied as he passed; I steadied him. So now the jangle of harnesses and clatter of hooves sounded extra loud as our six-horse team pulled a limber (two-wheeled wagon) that towed the 4.5-inch howitzer with another team ahead. Damned heavy gun, for sure. Took five men to fire it. Weighed almost a ton and a half, ten feet from tip of barrel to end of trail. Some gun! We made a long train stretching about a mile and a half, the three other howitzers and their ammunition wagons separated by a hundred feet or more.

Our Sergeant, Quinn McKillop, riding ahead, called back, "Cheer up lads! We'll see a lot more before the week is out!" He coughed hard, then went on. "Jonas, let's have another song." But even Jonas had difficulty starting up.

As I rode on in silence, I knew I was headed into war.

***

After about a month of training in Valcartier north of Quebec City, I had been drawn up with my Battery in a hollow square on the parade ground for the usual service on Sunday morning when who should step up to deliver the sermon but my brother Jack, who'd last written home from the Front. I was so pleased.

Afterwards, I caught up to him as he was walking in surplice and cassock back to change at the officers' mess. Well sir, he looked at me as if he'd seen a ghost. "Eric! What on earth are you doing? I thought you were at Bishop's."

"And you — how come you're here, Jack? We all thought you was in France."

"I was, but my parish insisted I come back. I had to arrange a special leave to sort it out. You see," we walked on together, "I had only signed up for a year, thinking the war would be over soon." He laughed. "Not a hope."

"So you didn't get my letter? I really needed to talk to you." Being in uniform as he was gave me quite a boost.

"No, no letter. Well, here we are, so let's have a bite together."

What a lucky happening! We didn't see each other all that much, even in peace time. "Good sermon you gave, Jack. Very stirring. Made us all want to go and fight them Germans, for sure." Leaving the parade ground, we followed a side track to the officer's mess. The Camp had only been built last year by Sam Hughes, hacked out of the wilderness.

Jack gave me a look. "Well, our cause is just, I'm sure of that." We walked for a moment in silence. "But no matter how just the cause, I'm not sure how I feel about you going." I could see the concern in his eyes. When we arrived, he asked me to wait and joined other officers going in. "Other Ranks" like me were not allowed inside.

"Success!" he beamed, coming out with a hamper. "They fixed me up a picnic! Like the good old days at the cove." We'd swim there next to Shigawake wharf. We headed to some benches in a small park. "So what did you write me about?" He began to lay out the food — and pretty good plates he'd snaffled for us, I must say.

I sure tucked into those cold ham pies, sausages and vegetables, much better than we enlisted men got. "Jack," I said, mouth full, "Old Poppa's gonna be upset I didn't go to college." I explained what had happened in Lennoxville: how I'd come to join up. "So if you think the cause is just and all that, could you talk to him for me?"

"Oh, count on me, Eric. I see you got yourself into the Artillery. Exactly what I joined when I signed on."

"Yes sir, I can hardly wait to get at them big guns. No sign of any new ones around here, though. They say we're going to have to train on old Boer War pieces." I sighed.

"Eric," he sat across from me on the rough table and looked in my eyes, "you know I'm proud to have a brother fighting for civilization. But... it's pretty bloody over there, sometimes." He dropped his eyes and continued eating. "Nothing like my other war in South Africa. Not at all." He shook his head sadly, then went on brightly. "Well, if there's anything I can do within the bounds of decorum, I shall."

I could tell he was moved by what he had seen. After all, he'd been in France for six months before getting this leave. Although he'd been attached to the Divisional Headquarters, he had visited the actual Front on a number of occasions, helping the lads, writing letters, burying the dead, he told me. And now his kid brother was in for all that. No need to spell out how he felt.

So that was my problem with Old Poppa solved. I wished I could feel as easy about Raine.

CHAPTER SIX

July 26, 1916

We arrived at the firing line after midnight. I quickly dismounted and stood ready with my flashlight to direct our lads to our gun-pit. At last, nine months of training was over — I had reached Zillebeke near Ypres, and the real Front. And I'd been made a Corporal.

Sergeant McKillop had already done his reconnoitring. He came over for a hurried consultation, for I was his "Coverer", taking over for him. His hacking cough wasn't getting any better. "Sergeant," I said, "you've got to look after that flu. You leave with the horses, and we'll get things going."

"Corp, it's your first time at the Front —"

"Don't worry, let's get you in shape first. I'll be fine." But to tell the truth, I felt anything but secure. I guess they wouldn't have made me a Corporal if they hadn't figured I could do it, but right now, I felt as if nothing had sunk in.

"All right," he said, "you bring our gun into action, and I'll walk out to the first marker to help you spot it." Quinn McKillop was a fine fellow, though perhaps a bit salty, from down Prince Edward Island way. He'd served in another Battery at the Front so we all respected him. Damn shame he'd come down sick for this first deployment of the 35th. But he'd soon be back.

Two Gunners leapt off the limber and separated it from the gun. "Drive on," I ordered and the Drivers headed our six-horse hitch out of harm's way back to the Wagon Lines. The other three howitzers set off for their own gun-pits, and our second six-horse hitch pulled up to drop its ammunition cart. Its Gunners leapt off and we set about unhooking the cart and manhandling the gun onto its platform as quickly as possible — but we were hardly experts. Sure we'd practised it at Witley and on Salisbury Plane, but what a difference on this churned-up earth in the pitch dark, with Fritz's artillery aiming right at us.

My heavens, getting that howitzer, one and a half tons of metal, turned and backed down into the pit — if the rest of the army was like this, how could we ever win? We were all pretty nervous: our firing lines are normally fifteen hundred yards behind the trenches, so well within range of the Heinie's seventy-seven millimetres. Any minute, one of those flashes on the horizon could be a round coming to blow us to smithereens.

Seeing some sandbags left by the previous detachment, I detailed our Gunners to pile them around the entrance to our gun-pit.

Edward, our Bombardier, murmured, "Corp, don't you think we should unload the ammunition first?" He was the sort of soldier you could always count on; we'd become buddies even though our backgrounds were so different. He hailed from an exclusive part of Montreal called Westmount, and it was rumoured he lived in a great house on top of the mountain. Already, he'd been getting parcels of food from his family that he always generously shared.

"Of course!" Damn. I'd better start shaping up or I'd lose all respect. Oh well, weren't we all new? No one really minded or even noticed as we set about unloading the thirty-five pound shells and brass cartridges.

The only one who didn't help was Harry Oakes. He wasn't very strong, and moreover, he hated this whole dreadful expedition. During our days at the rest camp by Le Havre, he had confided his fears. Quarrelsome little bugger, though, for all his timidity. Got on my nerves, no doubt. Slight, blonde — almost albino — he obviously just made the height and weight limits for enlisting, and they must have waved the chest requirement. Like me, he was the youngest of a large family and only joined up to get a square meal. Well, I sent him first to find the latrines and then see about our sleeping quarters. If none, we'd sleep in the gun-pit.

Our pit had been roofed over with corrugated iron and earth piled on top, all held up by stout timbers. A shelf had been dug into the side wall for storing ammunition, so I set the Gunners to stack it. Next I checked to make sure the gun's sights were directly over the marker placed earlier by the Jumbo, the recce officer. And no, by George, we were six inches off.

Now what? Make a fool of myself again?

"Sorry, boys," I called. "The sights aren't directly over the marker." Muttered grumbling met this announcement, for the boys were as tired as I was: we all wanted to bed down as soon as possible. Also, an unspoken competition existed between us and the other Howitzers to get ours ready the quickest. The four guns had been laid out in a regulation line, twenty paces between. Other Batteries of lighter 18-pounders were positioning closer to the front line, their barrel diameters being three inches as opposed to ours at four and a half inches, which gave ours the name: a 4.5 howitzer.

Well, I ordered "run up" to move the gun forward and "trails left or right" until we hit the mark, and the boys reapplied the brakes. Behind the sights, I looked for the Sergeant. I caught the faint luminous paint on our front aiming post next to his muffled flashlight. Beyond, I saw another fainter gleam on the rear aiming post. Good — we were dead on the zero line.

What now? Oh yes, camouflage our limber. Behind the gun-pit I found a protective covering with a camouflage flap. We hurriedly secured the empty cart under the lean-to. By then the Sarge had returned, and after making sure I felt all right, he set off for the wagon lines with my horse Barry in tow.

Harry Oakes reported where the latrines lay and said the dugout was horrible. "Was it clean?" I asked, and he replied, "Oh yes, clean enough." Nasty piece of work, actually, our Harry. A city boy from the Point (Point St. Charles), he had never slept in the open: his home was probably a crowded shanty down by the Lachine Canal.

So now, two thirty in the morning and damn tired, we headed for our dugout. Whizbangs from those seventy-seven millimetre quick-firing guns kept striking near by; sure made me nervous. But I fell onto the first pallet by the doorway of the dugout. Then instead of dropping off to sleep at once, I lay fearing what might happen once we really engaged the enemy.

***

For some reason, I woke before the cook called, "Breakfast up!" I came out of the dugout to find Edward Whitehead already waiting, having a smoke. I joined him and looked around. The Belgian countryside seemed so peaceful. Our Battery had been placed behind a wood, now mostly destroyed. The skeletons of trees, shorn of leaves by bombardments, pointed their scrawny arms at the sky as if begging for new raiment. When would that come? The war was supposed to have been over in a year. But right now, it seemed as if it would go on forever.

Edward took the pipe out of his mouth, wiped his lips, and murmured, "I wonder if I'll ever see Katie again."

"Who knows. We're in it now, for sure." I had also taken up the pipe during my time in the army. Everyone smoked at the Front; not affordable on the Gaspe Coast. I stuffed my pipe bowl. "You know Edward, I can't get the sight of that awful crossroads out of my mind. Think we'll end up..."

"Maybe."

We smoked in silence. Tall, patrician in manner, Edward had a quiet dignity that usually betokened an officer. He came from a good family but had joined up right out of school. His brother had been in university and so had joined the Officer Corps.

He had often confided his love for his beautiful Katie. So far, I'd kept my mouth shut about Raine. She was about as far as anyone could be from Edward's Katie, who was tall, stylish and stunning, he told me, in those high-waisted long gowns with her dainty little shoes and cunning hats. Raine just had one old cotton frock and bare feet, lovely smooth brown arms, tousled hair. Quite a difference.

We sat for a few moments in silence, and I wondered why Raine had not been more in my thoughts. Driven out, surely, by the incessant drilling in that camp near Sherbrooke, learning how to handle rifles, salute and march and all those instructions on gunnery. So many new faces, too — more than I'd ever met. And then off across the Atlantic. Such a big boat! Getting seasick, just like old Poppa did on the bay. Then arriving in England.

Some of Shigawake did linger: Raine clung to my heart like a shellfish gripping a rock. But then, landing in the Old Country — the home of my own sailor grandfather a century ago — and then training in Witley... where we finally got to fire a proper howitzer. No modern guns in Canada, only old 12 pounders we'd practise hauling with six-horse teams. But in England when I first went to the "Gun Park" expecting a lake, a few birds, maybe an old Boer War cannon like outside barracks in Montreal, I gaped at a line of new guns stretching as far as the eye could see.

I was actually glad those enlisting officers had gotten hold of me. Likely I'd make a better job of my university education when I got back. And this way I met all kinds of fellas: lawyers, bankers, some from farms, though not that many. Recruits came mostly from towns: builders, carpenters and painters, many out of work. Another surprising thing: not too many French fellas. Being as how we trained in Quebec province, you'd think we'd have been flooded. But the French-Canadians were pretty well against this war. The way I heard it, France had done so little for them over the last while, they didn't feel any great compassion to go fight for it. Also, General Hughes insisted on integrating them into English regiments even if they couldn't speak it. And the English? Well, French fellas used to complain we only employed them as maids and woodsmen, and true, I never met a lot behind wickets in banks. So if they didn't want to fight a French war, why the hell would they want to join the British? There was a terrific French Canadian battalion though, the Van Doos, with a great reputation.

This time, Edward pressed me, "You've got this girlfriend back in Shigawake..."

"No 'girlfriend', Edward. Just a friend. I like her, of course." I wasn't about to tell him that once, she meant the world to me.

"Do you write her?"

"Not really." Should I tell him? "Well... you see, Edward, she can't read." There, I had said it.

"The girls up there in Northern Quebec where you come from, do most of them not read or write?"

"Oh no, we all do. It's just ... " How could I explain it? Well, maybe it was time to lay it all out. "You see, she lived with three families back in the woods. They never went to school, that lot."

"You must have seen something in her, Eric?"

"Oh yes sure. She was quite a person. Strong willed, and it wasn't her fault where she was brought up."

"So you've not heard from her?"

"As a matter of fact, one letter. I can't imagine how long it must have taken her to write."

"But I thought you said she couldn't read or write?"

"Well, my older sister Lil was living with us. She used to be a teacher, and kind of took pity on Raine: after I left, she taught her to read and write. In a letter to Jack, she said she found Raine smarter than anyone she ever taught." I lit my pipe.

"I figured she must have something for you to like her, Eric." Edward tapped his pipe on his boot. He then took his penknife and scraped out the bowl.

"Well, right after I got to England, I got this letter from her. She had run off." I don't know why, I felt all emotional when I talked. "Well, it was only a few sentences; a struggle for her, I'm sure. But she told me she was fine. Our storekeeper Ernie Hayes had taught her figures, Lillian had taught her reading and writing, and now she was on her own. She'd got as far as Bonaventure, only thirty miles — but for her pretty damn far. She was trying to go further, because she knew her family would be after her. I bet, Edward, she'll even make it to Montreal."

Just saying that made me feel a lot better. Yes sir, Raine was out of their clutches and like me, onto a new life.

"Seems to me you were a big help in getting her out," Edward remarked with his usual insight.

I thought about that for a bit, and took a draw on my pipe. I gave him a look to show we were on the same track.

Being able to talk about her like that relaxed me. "But still I wonder how I'll find her, to write back, because she left no address."

Edward looked down at his pipe as he folded it into a packet that he stuck in his pocket. "Eric, if she's smart, and in the big city, and seventeen, she won't lack for suitors. If I were you, I'd forget about her. The chances of finding her when — and you know we avoid saying IF — when we get back, are not so good. We all may be getting some pretty big surprises on our return, I'm afraid."

I shook my head. "Oh no, Edward, from what you told me, Katie will be there waiting. I feel sure of it."

He raised his eyes to look into mine, and then back down again. "I sure hope so."

But Raine, I had to agree, was probably gone for good. Into a new and far better life, I was sure of that. With her smart brain and her good sense, she'd get along fine. And I had helped in that, just as Edward said. So Edward was right: just let her go. However sad, that had to be the answer. Better turn my thoughts to what lay ahead — plenty of dangers to watch out for, and my detachment needed all my attention.

CHAPTER SEVEN

July 27, 1916

A bell rang. I reached out to turn off my trusty alarm clock and found my hand touching cold, damp earth. Where was I? "Corp, wake up!" someone shouted. "Battery action! SOS!" Oh my heavens, we're at the Front!

An SOS rocket fired by the Infantry meant a call for help: likely an attack in No Man's Land, on which we kept our guns registered. It was narrow, often only a couple of hundred feet between our trenches and the Germans' — a horrible mess of barbed wire, dead bodies, thickets of rubbish and rats. Why would any soldier try to cross that? Well, that's what our guns were for — to stop any Fritzie fool from trying. I threw on my jacket, shoved my feet into my boots and ran over to the gun in the pitch dark. Our first SOS, two thirty in the morning, the second night after we'd arrived! Our team was in some disarray, to put it mildly. As I neared the gun-pit, Boom! The gun fired. Thank heaven our sentry was awake! "Good for you, Red!" — our nickname for Ralph Rideout, who'd been on sentry duty. He had bright red hair, red eyelashes and flashing brown eyes, and hailed from Sherbrooke, though for some reason never spoke of his family, except that he was the eldest of many children. Fine soldier though, like in one of those enlisting posters.

I dove into the pit and snapped into the drill I had learned, hoping details would not escape me. Harry Oakes, our Number Two stood ready between the breech and the right wheel. Down he levered the barrel and ejected the smoking cartridge. Ralph moved over to the sights, handing me the paper with our SOS data.

"Number one gun," I called out, reading with my flashlight, "azimuth one degree three nul minutes right."

Ralph, our Number Three, checked his sight and nodded.

"HE percussion charge Number Four!" Ed Whitehead, Number Five, tumbled in late, grabbed a high explosive shell from the shelf and handed it to Number Four, Cecil Smith, kneeling beside the ammunition. Ed went on to prepare three more cartridges. You see, the shell itself needed a charge: a separate brass case, about four inches long, containing five cordite packages shaped like doughnuts with holes centred around the brass primer tube. Different charges gave different muzzle velocities chosen by the range to the target and the best trajectory. Right now the Observation Post had called for a range requiring charge four. But Edward was having trouble opening the lid. Finally he managed it and selected the right charge; he chucked the others in a box for destroying later.

Cecil started messing around with the safety pin in the nose of the HE shell. He was rattled, shaking even. Then didn't he drop the shell in the mud? More haste less speed. This SOS had called for rapid bombardment and here we were, dropping rounds in the mud. I just couldn't believe it.

While Harry checked the clinometer for the right elevation, I knelt to help Cecil clean off the mud from the shell so he could withdraw the safety pin. "Now load!" He pushed the shell into the breech.

Damn, where was my rammer? I'd put it down somewhere. I flashed my light around, found it, jumped back to my post and rammed the shell home. Cecil held out the cartridge — I checked its charge and nodded. Although his hands were shaking, he got it into the breech.

At last, Harry slid the breech shut, pushed down the gear lever and reset the barrel back upwards, pretty steep because howitzers shot upwards over high ground and dropped into trenches, whereas the 18-pounders with their smaller charges fired more level.

I double-checked everything. "Number One fire!"

Red yanked back on the firing lever and — BOOM!

The thunder of the charge and the savage recoil shook me, no doubt. I thought for a second that an enemy shell had landed. And I was not alone: everyone's nerves seemed jangled. This live ammunition carried quite a punch, much more than during training in Salisbury where we had never fired from a gun-pit. I recovered my composure as quickly as I could, and found Harry leaning aside, going to be sick; he hadn't even levelled the barrel and opened the breech. I touched him on the shoulder. Embarrassed, he struggled back into action.

Cecil, hands over his ears, crouched and just rocked back and forth. "Up ya get, Gunner Smith!" I reached over to nudge him. He got up, shaking his head, still dazed. But believe it or not, we had been the first of the howitzers to fire. Inexperienced for sure, but could the other three teams have been worse? What a bunch of amateurs!

Keep going! Ed handed the next shell to Cecil who managed to yank its safety pin and place it in the breech. I rammed it home. Harry went to slide the breech shut, but it wouldn't fully close. He turned and looked at me, panic-stricken.

"It's okay, Harry, probably the extractor's got dirt." I got up, pulled out the cartridge, worked the extractor lever, blew in it, and then manoeuvred the cartridge back in. "Try it now."

He shut it with a reassuring click, reset the gun skyward, and I checked everything mentally, and, "Fire!"

BOOM! The second shot got off, striking our ears with tremendous force.

The noise really bothered me. "Come on, Eric," I shouted to myself, "get used to it. You're in the artillery now!" But such a long way from the smooth Battery drill when we'd trained. The deafening explosions unnerved us: all four howitzers blasting away, and the 18-pounders ahead of us going full blast — a dense ocean of noise that, speaking for myself, almost drove me crazy. No wonder we were making mistakes, no wonder we stood like dazed dummies when we should be cracking like lightning.

Well after about ten minutes, didn't we start receiving our own comeuppance? A tremendous explosion struck about fifty yards behind. Another soon ploughed the earth in front, throwing up great chunks and geysers of black smoke in the moonlight. Counter-battery!

Gunner Smith was frozen with fear; Gunner Oakes not much better.

"Atta boy, Cecil, keep her going." I startled him out of his trance, and on he went passing the ammunition. Harry was shivering. "Power of the imagination, Gunner Oakes, forget what's coming in, concentrate on what's going out. We're giving them worse than they're giving us."

"Yes, Corp," he replied and tried to focus.

I had decided that our raspy Sergeant's method of shouting at every mistake hadn't really paid off. This firing drill should have turned out better.

After about fifteen minutes of shelling, each explosion coming closer, one finally came very damned close and caught us all by surprise. No one was hurt, but we were all shaken. Thank heaven, the order came to cease firing.

Before scrambling for the safety of our dugout, we relaid the gun on its SOS target and loaded a round. I made sure the rammer and clinometer were secure; the boys picked up stray brass; Ed and Cecil checked that all ammunition was safe and covered; Red covered the dial sight, put on the muzzle cover, and stayed out on sentry duty.

Later I found that this counter-battery was almost a pattern: when one side opened up, the other fired on too, as if to say: Hey! That's enough, take it easy! And gradually both sides would cease their little exercise.

Little exercise! Even though this was to become a part of my daily existence, I'll never forget how that first night shook us all, how it overwhelmed us. Working in the semi-dark with that cavern of noise around us, the continual din got into our bones and jangled our nerves, especially mine. I couldn't stand the violence. But then, I had joined the artillery and for better or for worse, I was stuck.

As we headed for the dugout, we visited the latrines: one thing for sure, you learned to empty your bladder and intestines before going into the next action, because you couldn't take off in the middle.

When I finally sat on my bunk, I realized I needed to do

something about Cecil, who was nowhere to be seen. He'd gone white at that last blast, and maybe went to hide. I sighed, got up, and found him hunched against the earthen back of the dugout. He had been crying, knees buckled up in front and head bent over.

I stood there for a few moments in the darkness, and pondered: if this one simple barrage had done this, what about heavier enemy barrages sure to come? I sat down next to him. After a time, I said, "Don't worry, Cecil, I'll see what I can do about getting you a transfer. But you have to promise you'll be really good the next few days till I get back to the Wagon Lines." What's worse, his buckteeth gave him a beaver's look, but he was so sensitive about that we never used it against him. He wiped away his tears, and slowly got up.

Later I lay on my bed of chicken wire fastened between boards and reflected on this first experience of being under fire. What could I do to help make our routine go more smoothly? But then, sleep claimed me and I was gone.

***

The problem remained with me the next morning as we set about our regular maintenance. Our gun lines were within range of the German's, but we were still a good way back. In fact, how things worked was this: on our side of No Man's Land (say a hundred yards across, sometimes more) lay our front line trenches, the "firing line", normally with half our infantry battalion. A couple of hundred yards behind that lay a belt of trenches in our "support line" with a quarter of each battalion rotating through the front. The Forward Observers generally worked in and around that. Two hundred yards behind, a reserve line of trenches had been dug as an emergency buffer and the final quarter of each frontline battalion was ready to man them, and often carry supplies forward for the support and firing lines. Our battalion headquarters staff was near the reserve line, with a Gunner Liaison Officer. Other battalions of infantry rested in billets about five thousand yards back, out of range of all but the heavy German guns and ready for anything that might come up. Soldiers exchanged roles from frontline to billets every week or two.

Our gun line, the Field Artillery, lay about 2,500 yards behind the reserve line. In front, our 18-pounders had a range of about 6,200 yards, and then behind them, our howitzers had a maximum range of about 7,200 yards. Within range of the German guns, of course, because our main job was to blast away at them, and also support our infantry and shell the enemy trenches. Further back, our much heavier guns stayed 4,000 to 5,000 yards behind the trenches. They covered us with counter bombardment fire and thickened up the destructive fire on the enemy trenches.

After the maintenance, I took a moment to sit and fill my pipe. Gunner Rideout came up, looking weary. He sat down and pulled out a fag. "What do you think about last night, Eric?"

"Bloody awful. And I don't mean their shelling."

He nodded. "We're going to have to get a lot better, aren't we?"

"Damn right. Any and all ideas welcome." Red was another soldier I relied on, though his demeanour was never quite as warm as others. Quick temper too, tough but solid. I thought he'd soon get recommended for one hook, meaning he'd become a Bombardier, as Lance-Corporals were called in the Artillery; even officer material.

"I kinda liked the way you talked to poor Cecil," he said. "Better that way than our Sergeant — nothing against him, but yelling at us all the time does more harm than good."

I had to agree. "Maybe he won't when he comes back."

"I guess he's like them other regulars — no discussion about methods, for sure." He paused, and then looked at me. "Eric, that Cecil guy, maybe you should get rid of him. And even Oakes..."

I shrugged. I didn't want to discuss it until I'd made up my own mind, which I was in the process of doing. "We're all in it together, Red. It's my job, in fact our job, to make good Gunners out of everyone. No good just sending someone away. We should try to find the best in ourselves. At least that's what my poppa always said about our hired fellas."

"Sorry, Eric, I just don't agree. Where I come from, if you're no good, you're out!" With that, he got up and stumped off. I hoped he'd get over it.

CHAPTER EIGHT

July 31, 1916

ate that afternoon, our Lieutenant came back from his stint at the Observation Post to find me standing in a trance, staring at our beautiful howitzer, wondering how I could make my detachment work better. "Hello there, Alford. How's it going?"

"Well enough, thank you, Mr. Overstreet."

"I knew you'd enjoy the Front." Dick Overstreet was a funny sort of fella. He'd been a mathematics teacher before he'd signed up — had a second degree in mathematics too. Barely thirty, he was almost completely bald, so his head looked like an egg from which two ears protruded. His grey eyes seemed always off on a distant galaxy, or calculating a new formula. He was not much of a people person but pretty smart, which is why I guess they had accepted him into the officer corps.

We started to walk together back to the dugout, glancing up as a single British reconnaissance plane flew over. I'd heard that British pilots were not permitted parachutes, which I found hard to believe. I asked Overstreet, and he confirmed it. "I suppose they think it'll encourage them to save their planes..." He shook his head, and I too felt that was a helluva way to run a war. "And so how did the first night's firing go, Alford?"

"Pretty terrible, sir." I didn't know how much to tell him. "You know, we did have a little problem with one of the Gunners."

"Oakes acting up again? Argumentative little bugger."

"No sir, Cecil Smith."

"Not very bright, I know, but surely had his drill down pat?"

"Oh yes, sir. Down pat..."

"Well then, what's the problem?"

"I think sir, he may have a difficulty... with the noise —"

Overstreet gave a snort and a chuckle. "He'd better get used to it."

"My idea exactly, sir. But I think it goes beyond that." We came to a couple of empty ammunition crates, and sat down. I didn't want to spill the beans, but ended up continuing. "So I think, sir, if we could find another position for him in the Battery, he'd be better off. And then," I added brightly, "I could start getting this team working the way it should. Pretty darned important, I'd say."

"Isn't that more Sergeant McKillop's job?"

"Yes sir, his job." I fell silent.

"Of course, you're his Coverer... You could recommend a course of action."

"Well, there must be other things Cecil could do... and still be useful."

Lieutenant Overstreet paused as he pulled out his pipe and proceeded to fill it. "Well, when Sergeant McKillop comes to relieve you, why don't you ask him if you could raise this with the

BSM yourself, when you go back to the Wagon Lines?"

Now we both knew the Battery Sergeant Major was not an easy fellow. He'd begun in the British Regular Army, and saw no reason why every man couldn't do his duty exactly as the military required.

"Me, sir? You want me to..."

The Lieutenant glanced at me and, as his eyes met mine, we shared an unspoken knowledge of that difficulty.

"Very well, sir," I said. "I'll have a go. That way, if I fail —"

"We don't talk of failure in the 35th." He lit his pipe and then got up. "I'm going to get a bite and some sleep. We were up all night at that damn O-Pip." The Observation Post we called the O-Pip after the signal version of the alphabet. "But you have my best wishes."

"Thank you, Sir." My heart sank as he went off. My spell in the Wagon Lines was not to be as enjoyable as I'd hoped.

***

We reached the Wagon Lines after midnight; half of each detachment alternated every three or four days. I don't need to tell you that, safely out of range of the field guns, I fell asleep in a flash.

The next morning, I woke up shocked to hear reveille. No such thing up in the firing lines, I can tell you. I struggled out to look at our encampment with new eyes. The Wagon Lines were made up of three sections: the limbers, parked in a row, the second area where the horses were stabled and third, the shelters, where we stayed. Here I would find the Battery administration, including our Welsh Battery Sergeant Major, Gwyneth Jones.

For miles around, the whole country was flat. Wagon Lines were often placed near part of a village, or a wood, that would partially hide them, about a mile or two back from the firing line and close enough to resupply it. Because the Front hadn't really changed for a year and a half, some of these establishments had gotten downright comfortable. But still infested with the usual supply of rats — and lice. I had begun scratching in the firing line. We'd all been warned, so we knew what we were up against. Today I'd make my way to the Brigade Medical Post for a supply of creosote, apparently the only thing that chased the little blighters away.

Apart from lice, a more severe problem kept irritating me: getting Cecil into another posting, preferably back at these Wagon Lines. No question of him staying at the Front until he got better accustomed to all the noise and danger, which in the end I believed he would do. Sergeant McKillop had agreed only too happily to let me speak to the BSM. But how to make him understand? With his excessively brisk manner, he'd gotten promoted, not through charm, but because apparently he never let things slip by.

Well, I made an appointment to see him later in the afternoon, and then sat for a pipeful in the sun which had finally come out in force. How on earth would I handle it?

***

I was lining up for my dinner, pretty hungry having missed breakfast, when who should I run into but Gavin from New Carlisle. His father ran a big farm back behind and I saw by his spurs and a whip stuck into the leg guard on his right he was one of the Battery Drivers. Several of our Brigade had gotten sick and he was a replacement.

"Gavin," I said, "good to see you! Just join us?"

"Yep. Couldn't wait to get into action. But I'm beginning to be sorry already. That there BSM Jones, he's sure a stickler."

Oh dear, I thought. What now?

"He makes us shine them harnesses all the damn time, and the horses have to be in top shape, groomed every day. He even checks the limbers. We spend all day polishing, removing the damn limber wheels and greasing axles, and then at night we have to go bring ammunition up to the firing line. No rest for the wicked, I suppose."

"Too bad. You'd think once we're in action, he'd relax that."

Without waiting, he went on. "Water and feed the horses oats before breakfast, fine, but then after breakfast, we polish our own buttons and buckles and right at nine — you missed it today — inspection, and notices. Okay, now for Pete's sake, let's have a bit of rest. No sir. Clean out the manure, more polishing, and at eleven the bugle signals us to proceed to water again, more feeding, hay this time, I dunno, Eric, it's a mad house. No time to yourself."

I'd once thought Drivers had a cushy time back at the Wagon Lines, but no longer. And in the thick of the fighting, their horses came first — the Driver had to hang onto and control both his mount and the horse beside it, so he couldn't dive for the ditch like the rest of us when he heard them whizbangs.

"And which detachment are you with?" he asked.

"Sergeant McKillop's."

"My sister, Nancy, she always had a bit of a shine on you. She keeps writing to ask me about you."

I did remember his sister who was in a grade below: pretty, I remember, with the bluest of eyes, red hair and freckles. I was surprised she still remembered me. "Well, give her all my best.

Tell her if we see this thing through, she'll be the first person I'll ask out." No harm in sounding pleasant.

Gavin nodded. I could see from his expression that he knew she wouldn't be waiting around that long. "I don't think this here war is gonna end any time soon, I'll tell you that much, Eric."

I had to agree with him. "But I'm sure glad you're in the 35th. We're going to make this the best Battery in the whole army."

"Well, with you in it, Eric, I bet we do."

Heavens, had I made that good an impression? I had never seen myself in any leadership role at school, never thought anyone paid me any mind.

"Wait till I tell the folks we're in the same Battery! The Alfords are sure held in high esteem up in New Carlisle, I tell you that much."

Well well, that did my heart good. Who would ever have dreamed?

"Nice to know I've got a fellow Gaspesian in the Battery. We'll have to look out for each other, Gavin."

"Aye, that we will."

But now, having to face down the BSM made me even more apprehensive.

***

Well, time for the dreaded interview! I walked down past the row of tents to the dumpy Belgian farmhouse where the Battery office was located, only partly hidden by what remained of a wood, most of the leaves and branches having been smashed off. The outbuildings were just piles of rubble, but the farmhouse seemed largely intact.

I went in. The BSM had set up his office in what used to be a bedroom behind the kitchen. While waiting, I compared it with Gaspesian farm living: more pictures on these whitewashed plaster walls here, so thick and solid, unlike our own wooden structures. In a great open fireplace, black metal arms hung for kettles and cauldrons. The simple dining table, functional, was hand-made like ours and now served as a desk. The Battery Clerk told me that an old woman lived upstairs, and I saw her open armoire held dishes and a wall shelf contained her religious paraphernalia.

In I went. BSM Jones was reading a letter and looked up, rather surprised. "Corporal Alford! I thought I would be meeting your Sergeant."

"He delegated me to come and see you, sir. His turn on the gun."

"Quite so." He put down the letter. "Well, what seems to be the problem?" His eyes narrowed slightly. A handsome Welshman, no doubt, with broad features, clean shaven and no moustache; I could picture him preaching in the church, or singing in a choir. I could even imagine having a drink with him in a pub.

"Sir, it's my desire to have the best howitzer detachment, not only in the 35th Battery, but anywhere."

"A laudable aim, Corporal. Perhaps a bit elevated for someone in your position."

"Well sir, whether it befits a Corporal or not, that's what I want. And in order to achieve this, the Sergeant and I would like to have one of our men temporarily assigned to other duties and replaced with someone better suited. I could spend time with the new man, helping him fit into our team."

"Out of the question, Corporal."

I looked straight at him. "You see, sir, we have a soldier who, while not exactly 'foolish' is not perhaps up to our standards." Foolish is how we referred to simpletons on the Gaspe.

"Hmm. And you hadn't noticed that previously?"

"We've been helping him along, sir, because he's so very keen, he's strong, and he did learn the drill."

"Corporal, I fail to see where this is leading."

"Sir, I don't want to be forced to say some things I might feel bad about later. But could you take it on my say so, and that of our Sergeant, that Gunner Smith would be better off back at the Wagon Lines, just for a while. At least until we get him accustomed to those, er, difficulties up at the Front?"

"You don't mean to tell me the man's afraid, Corporal?" He looked right back at me. "We're all of us afraid. He'd better just get used to it."

"Sir — "

He cut me off. "A fool's errand, Corporal. The less said the better. Request denied."

He must have seen the disappointment because then he went on to ask, "Corporal, have you ever been to an eisteddfod?"

I was in no mood for a gossip. "No sir. What is that?"

"It's a competitive song festival. And verse. You know, my family comes from Glan Conway, a local farming community near Llandudno, which is, as you might have heard, one of the great seaside resorts in North Wales."

I could see he was trying to soften the blow. I tried to look appreciative.

"Some of my family are still there; they didn't immigrate into Canada when I did with my brother, who is a chaplain by the way. I see here," he waved the letter, beaming, "that my sister has just won harping at the last eisteddfod in our area."

"Well done, sir. You must be proud of her."

"I am that. Well, Corporal, that will be all."

I turned, and left the farmhouse. What would happen with poor Cecil now?

CHAPTER NINE

August 4, 1916

Well, being pretty depressed, I went over to where the horses were stabled: I wanted to check if my mount Barry had been well looked after. Men from our gun did that when I was forward, but I made sure to groom him myself while here. I'd brought him from England, where we had gotten used to each other.

"Here, Barry, munch on this." I fed him some oats. The names of horses in our Battery all began with B. Amazing when you think of the number of horses we had here, almost a couple of hundred in the 35th Battery alone.

I grabbed a curry comb and proceeded to give Barry a good brush; soothing for me to work at his fine brown hide. Why did I insist on carrying the cares of our gun all the darn time? Why not just sit and relax. But then, with the quiet munching of the horses around me, just as in our own barn, my thoughts began to wander, and I hit on another idea.

Guns each had two teams of three Gunners and a Bombardier working in rotation, in addition to the Corporal and Sergeant. Maybe another gun had someone they would trade to us?

So after giving Barry a going over for half an hour, which I think he enjoyed, I wandered around until I found the Sergeant of another howitzer in our section, whose Coverer was up at the line. I explained about Gunner Smith, though maybe not being fully honest.

He recommended a tough soldier nicknamed Finn, whose real name was Arto Heiskanen. I gathered that the Sergeant would be happy to get the fellow off his gun, not because he was a jellyfish, quite the reverse, a bit too abrasive, perhaps. Each Battery has "Remounts," spare Gunners to replace the injured; men were moved around a good bit.

I girded my loins and went off to find Finn's tent. I found him lying on his blanket, writing a letter. A small wiry fellow with a high forehead, whose small black eyes gave me warning he'd not be easy.

I sat on the ground opposite and, without too many preliminaries, told him my mission. "We need a new gun number on our howitzer, Finn, and we'd be honoured if you would volunteer to join us."

"Now why would I do that?"

"Your Sergeant recommends it."

"Let him go, then."

"Now Finn, if I tell you he'd be most pleased for you to do it — and I've heard about your Sergeant... (I was actually lying, assuming he'd be like the others). If you don't want to volunteer..."

"If I don't...?"

I shook my head. "Finn, I thought you Finnish fellows were noted for your imaginations. (I had no idea if this were true, by the way.) Has yours become temporarily misplaced?"

Finn nodded wearily. "I get your meaning." He paused and looked at me. "But why me?"

"We need someone who is not afraid. The Sarge tells me — "

"He's right." He snorted. "I'm not afraid of nothin'!"

I beamed. "Well then! You'll be a great favourite on our gun! Most of us are terrified of everything." I thought overdoing it was justified.

Did I see a faint hint of a smile? "Whatever you say, Corp." He went back to his writing, not that well pleased.

"You'll enjoy our detachment, Finn. Fine bunch of lads, they'd sure welcome you. With your help, we'll become the best Sub-Division in the Battery."

Another grin appeared and then as quickly disappeared. "Good for you, Corp." He went back to his writing.

I left his tent with some misgivings, but at least this might hand us some respite until a better solution could be found.

And his letter writing had prodded me. As you might guess, our family was not great at corresponding. Any mail to the Front came mainly to Jack, who usually responded. So I returned to my tent and proceeded to get a letter off home.

Dear Poppa,

All is well here on the firing line. Since I last wrote, when I was made a Corporal in England, we've come across the English Channel and I've been seeing a bit of France. Right now we're in Flanders, Belgium, near a town called Ypres, which we call Wipers. We have a good gun team, though we could do better. That will soon come, for we are firing fairly often now and the more we fire the better we get.

I shall have lots to tell when I get home. I hope Earle is working hard and young Henry is not yelling his head off any more. Please remember me to Lillian and Momma and tell them all is well over here.

I hope to see Jack one of these days. As a chaplain he can

get around, whereas I am pretty tied up close to my Battery,
especially while we're in action here.

    Your loving son,

    Eric

I finished the letter, and while I was dozing off, I actually found
myself wanting to get back into action on the firing line.

***

I'd been working most of the night, bringing ammunition from
the Wagon Lines and unloading it, but still when I heard the call
"Breakfast up" I swung out fast, ready for my second stint at the
Front. (Up here, you always slept in your clothes.) Luckily, no
firing until after breakfast — an unspoken convention that kept
us and the Fritzies from stirring up trouble. Convenient, I must
say. Allowed us time for a little talking and visiting the latrines.
But what would the day bring?

As we were eating by the gun-pit, I wondered how Cecil had
managed under the Sergeant's eye while I was gone. In the night,
we had fired fifteen rounds of High Explosive requested by the
infantry. Ralph Rideout was having breakfast; I sat down to join
him and brought up the subject.

"That new Finnish fella you sent up yesterday from the Wagon
lines? Seems all right." He was finishing his porridge and bread
fried in fat, our usual fare, and even bacon this morning, though
we didn't often get that. Dinner, which we ate at twelve, could
have been more generous: a potato boiled in its jacket, a little
piece of meat, half a slice of bread, and some pudding. "I seen ya
took my advice after all." I noticed a new hint of admiration in
his look.

"Yes, Red, I sure did. Not easy though." I took a gulp of what they called "tea," tasting as usual of petrol. "So Cecil stayed then? They didn't send him back? How did he do?"

"Got McKillop real mad. The Sarge yelled at him but o' course that only got Cecil worse. He started falling around, dropping shells, and even throwing up." His voice dropped. "I heard him moaning for his mommy. Don't say nothing eh?" I nodded. "Finally, Sarge put Finn in Cecil's place. Dunno what else he could do."

Just as I suspected.

Then Red voiced my own thoughts. "You get court-martialled for that stuff."

I sighed. That's the last thing we wanted. Poor Cecil shot.

I headed over to Edward. Apparently, he told me, while enemy planes were overhead and the rest of us took cover, Cecil hadn't grasped the danger — perhaps because they hadn't dropped explosives. Only the noise of our guns threw him into a fit, and also those big explosions when we got shelled. Distant rifle fire and aeroplanes overhead had little effect.

Then I had an idea: why not propose him as a Brigade Signaller and Runner. He had a basic simpleton's intuition about direction, I had noticed. Like an animal, he always knew it. So maybe I should try that out on the Lieutenant? I still dreaded having Cecil as our Number Four, especially if we were ordered to achieve rapid fire.

Edward agreed, then added, "You know our Lieutenant is getting all worked up about his new formula for aiming the guns."

"No!" I imagined he might, with his mathematical turn of mind. "So he's all excited then?"

"Sure is".

I soon found out, because after breakfast Lieutenant. Overstreet put us into action, registering the gun afresh. That meant deciding on a target somewhere behind the Heinie lines, and then checking to see if our gun actually hit the target, and what was our error. He kept a little chart and when he'd got reports back from the O-Pip, he'd shake his head and try over. Finally, I thought we'd gotten pretty damn good, but he still wasn't satisfied. "I've got to work on this some more," he said as he dismissed us. We headed off for our dinners.

After dinner, I saw the Lieutenant sitting down for a smoke, and wandered over. After a few pleasantries, I broached my idea.

"Well, Alford, that's not too likely," he replied. "I doubt that our CO would accept anyone less than a stellar soldier as one of only twenty-eight men in his HQ. We're more likely to get him transferred to the Division Ammunition Column. Lots of fellows are needed to resupply the ammunition, and I've often seen less good soldiers transferred there. We can see how he does, and if he works out, who knows, they might upgrade him to Runner afterwards."

I nodded. Anything was better than what we had.

"You know," he went on, "I did spend the last couple of nights at the O-Pip with our Major. Fine fellow, right kind of chap to command a Battery, I'll tell you. When I talked to him, he allowed as how we should get some more practice, due to our new replacement. That's how I got that extra time this morning." I saw a slight smile cross his face, and then he added enigmatically. "I did get time to bring up some other matters, too..."

He had been scanning a definite rise behind the enemy lines, when suddenly he shouted, "Number one gun, action!" He handed me the binoculars for a look, and I saw two Germans sauntering along, right where we had been registered.

Everyone jumped to it. I raced back at top speed, leapt into the pit and called out the orders as the Lieutenant hollered them to me.

Edward quickly passed a shell up to Cecil, who stood dumbly looking at it. Oh hell! I grabbed the shell and put it in the breech. I rammed it home, by which time Edward had gotten out the cartridge, set the charge, and passed it on. Harry thrust it in, shut the breech, and returned the gun to the set elevation for firing.

BOOM!

"That's it!" Overstreet hollered.

Only one round? And only us? I wondered what was up.

I trotted back to our Lieutenant, listening closely to his O-Pip.

"We got them!"

He handed me the binocs, and I saw a crater where they had been walking. Two men, oh yes, strolling along without a care. And now, nothing.

So two dead Germans, for sure.

We congratulated each other, delighted, as we headed to the gun. Mr. Overstreet called for quiet and I caught a little gleam in his eye. "Where is Gunner Smith?"

I scurried behind the gun-pit where Cecil had gone again to hide, and brought him forward. "Well men, we have all seen now that Gunner Smith has exceptional qualities." Oh-oh I wondered, what was coming? "These mark him as ideal for our Division Ammunition Column." Overstreet and I traded looks. "I know we shall be sorry to lose him from our detachment." Cecil frowned, trying to absorb it all. "But you see, Gunner Smith, I'm afraid the Division comes before the needs of one of its Batteries. So, tonight you will go back to the Wagon Lines and report to Brigade Headquarters. From there, you will be sent for training and your place taken by Gunner Heiskanen. He's already had a taste of our detachment and I know he'll be welcomed by all of us."

Good old Dick! I didn't know whether this should be greeted with applause, but surely, no one would court-martial me for starting it. So I clapped, and everyone joined in. "Bravo Cecil," we called. Overstreet winked and walked away.

Cecil beamed with pleasure, but I don't think he knew what was going on. After being dismissed and putting the gun to sleep, I went over and, with my arm round his shoulder, took him for a short walk. "Cecil, this is great news. The Division needs you! You'll do great in the Ammunition Column." I prayed that would be so, and then he could get promoted to Runner.

"I don't know if mother is gonna let me stay. I'd better write her again. I told her I wanted to go home."

"Well, in the meantime, you'll get some good training, and you'll have a whole new job, far away from the guns."

"What do you mean?"

"Well, that's what the Lieutenant said. You don't have to worry, you'll be a hero in no time." I hoped I made it sound good.

He seemed to absorb that, and then looked pleased. "No more noise?"

"Well, a bit of noise Cecil, but not like before. And I know you'll get used to that. Certainly, no noise like you've been having."

I went back to the gun rejoicing.

That night, as I lay back covered in my greatcoat, I thought about the day's happening. We had actually killed two Germans all by ourselves. The other targets were so generalized, you never saw results. But this time, we had definitely killed two. Two enemies, yes, but still, two living men.

Back I went, back to Zotique. All Shigawake had mourned. Was there some little farming community up in Prussia who would get a telegram? Would they attend a memorial service? Would they mourn? What about the sisters and brothers of the two men? And maybe they even had children?

All right, a million men had died in 1914 and that many again in 1915. Enormous, oh yes, but just figures, to me, so big they overloaded the imagination. Not like those two Boches

I'd seen just walking down a road, probably talking about their sweethearts, who would hear from them no more. Tonight some work party would collect their remains, their arms and legs, and bury them, maybe in that same shell hole beside the road.

Well, that's what we came to do: kill Germans. Do our job, oh yes. I felt the need to talk about it, but then I realized it would just put doubts in others: better keep it to myself. I rolled over and tried to get some sleep. We would have another day of firing tomorrow and perhaps an SOS tonight. I must stay alert. But it was a good while before those phantoms let me slide off into an uneasy sleep.

CHAPTER TEN

After knocking out those two soldiers with one shell, we saw action around Ypres all through August and September, hitting the Hun with bombardments night and day and, when we had time, maintaining and cleaning our gun, unloading ammunition, stacking salvage and generally wearing ourselves out, but of course getting ourselves into shape as a proper fighting unit.

During this period, not being overly distraught by counter-batteries and enemy incursions, I found myself remembering my time in England, when I had met my brother Jack and met a couple of young ladies. Jack, now an Honorary Colonel, had been appointed Assistant to the Head of the Chaplaincy Service and posted to Headquarters in France. During my training at Witley he had rarely come to England, so in May when he did, I got leave and caught a train up to London. Wouldn't you know he picked me up with this darned great automobile?

Volunteer drivers took officers around and, as a Colonel, he had been given an occasional car. Him and me rode in the back. And in the front seat, one driving, another along for the ride, sat two of the prettiest girls you ever did see. Not a lot of women around those tents on Salisbury plain. Though I did get to a pub, sometimes. Women you saw there were older, likely wives or widows in little knots of two and three, looking a bit worn down. Imagine, women smoking and drinking in public! I don't know what Old Momma would have said about that. None of us Alfords did any drinking, of course. But now, I enjoyed a nice pint of bitter.

But those two in the front seat! From Brentwood, Essex, a county, they explained, northeast of London on the Thames. Their Daimler, German made(!) was the only car in their town. Pretty sure of themselves, them two girls, I mean *those* two girls. I decided I'd better get my way of talking adjusted, I can tell you, after their giggles.

The prettier one was named Rene — short for Irene, a name she didn't like. She pronounced it "Ree-nee." Kind of close to Raine, I had to admit. Was that some kind of fate? The other was called Leo, though that's a fella's name in Shigawake. But no matter how they were named, they were sure a lot of fun.

I sat back and tried to have a serious conversation with my brother but they kept turning around and giving us the eye. Leo was driving, so Rene would lean her chin on her elbow on the back of the seat and look at me with them brown eyes — by god, my heart sure did flutter. But she was so far out of my reach — that front seat seemed a million miles away. When I was tempted to think about her at night, I'd put the thought right out of my mind. She'd never be interested in the likes of me. So I guess I kind of idealised her.

Over lunch Jack told me that he usually asked for them. He thought his kid brother would enjoy being driven by two pretty English girls. Well sir, he was right.

We ate lunch in a Corner House restaurant: sure must have cost Jack something. But no, he told me, there were far nicer places.

He even apologized because most of the brass ate at the Savoy, the Strand Palace, or any number of grander places, all out of a chaplain's reach, even an Honorary Colonel.

"Well, Jack, you don't need to worry about this here hotel," I said to him. "I never seen the like."

"You have never seen anything like it!" he corrected. "You'll have to change that way of talking if you want to interest English girls — no more "this here" automobile and "that there" building." He must have noticed how much fun they'd made of my way of talking — rough edges that needed planing, like boards in Joe's mill.

As I mentioned, my brother was now assistant to Richard Steacy, head of the Chaplaincy Service which included Church of England of course, but also Presbyterians, Baptists, and oh yes, them — I mean *those* — Catholics! Every group wanted its own clergymen at the Front. And Jack's boss, well, he'd been put in charge of all that. So Jack had his hands full.

But mainly we talked about the Old Homestead and he gave me any up-to-date news. Poppa never wrote me; I guess he thought that Jack would pass it all on.

"And when do you think you'll get to the Front, Eric?" he had asked, frowning. I could see he had become uneasy about my going.

"Not long now. Some say next autumn, but maybe sooner. I can't wait to get my hands on them bloodthirsty Germans and wring their necks. We'll push em right back to Berlin, you watch!" I stopped because of the look on his face.

He'd already been to the Front, and didn't like the idea of his kid brother going off. "Eric, you know the front line hasn't changed since 1914?"

I frowned. "I've heard that, but..."

He leaned forward. "When war broke out, Germany pushed

through Belgium. You see, they hoped to curve down from the north to Paris. That way, they could avoid those fortifications the French had built in preparation for war."

"You think them French fellas knew war was on its way?"

He nodded. "Everyone was aware that the Central Powers had been preparing for some time. Too much to explain now, but once the Boches hit Paris, that would have meant the end of France. At Mons, those monsters sure gave us a terrible beating."

My eyes widened. I'd heard nothing about a beating.

"Yes, but then at Marne, the British piled in and we Allies stopped them." He leaned back. "After that, the lines stiffened, everyone dug in, and Eric, there's been no movement since then. Nowhere on that whole Front, which as you know stretches from the English Channel down to neutral Switzerland, around four hundred and fifty miles." He shook his head sadly. "Not what we expected when we started out."

Well, I hadn't actually gotten the picture that clearly. "So what we're facing is war in trenches that don't move?"

He nodded. "And you know, Eric, a million men were killed in 1914 and a million more last year. They don't put that out, but I talk to the generals from time to time." No doubt, I could see he was beginning to have his own thoughts about the war and its effect on men.

"I bet you do, Jack." I was full of admiration for him. But two million dead. Was this the sort of thing I'd planned? I was glad we had talked. I could see what I might be in for.

***

On my second (and last) leave in England, Jack again picked me up at the station in that splendid automobile, driven by the two sisters, Leo and Rene, just as I had hoped. But I was so shy that I just kept talking to Jack about home and my latest training.

"I wondered if you'd mind waiting, Eric?" We had arrived on Horse Guards Parade. "I have someone to see, but it shouldn't take too long."

Of course I didn't mind. But when he got out, I found myself alone with the girls. Leo did her best to make conversation about the weather, which was happily warm, although London always seemed covered in clouds. None of those sunny days we got in the Gaspe.

"Eric," Rene suggested, "why don't we go have a look at the Thames; it's just down there."

I accepted quickly.

"I'd better stay with the car," Leo said. "Some bobby will come by and I'll have to explain we're on military business."

As we strolled down towards the river, Rene said, "I gather from your conversation that you and Father John come from the province of Quebec." I had soon found out everyone referred to him that way.

Talking about the Old Homestead made me feel safer, and I told her about my sisters and Earle working back there and even how I intended to go to Bishop's University. In no time at all, we reached Victoria Embankment and crossed the wide street to lean at the railings. She pointed out Hungerford Bridge to our left, and then Westminster Bridge and the Houses of Parliament — what a sight!

"I hope Big Ben sounds while we're here," she remarked. "Ever heard it?"

"Never. In fact, all this is so new. Just what I hoped for when I joined up. To come and see London." I didn't add, and then France. Being shown London by a beautiful English girl, well, I don't think anything could get better. I said as much, trying not to blush.

She smiled. "Well, it is our job to look after our soldiers fighting for the Empire, and for civilization itself."

I wondered if that meant I wasn't so special after all. Stop thinking so much, I told myself, and just enjoy it all. We stayed leaning there, and I asked her a bit about herself.

"My oldest brother, George, he's been declared unfit, so he's clerking somewhere. My older sister, Hilda, she joined the Scottish Women's Regiment. She's going off with an ambulance brigade."

That shook me. "You mean she is going to the Front?"

"Probably Greece. She's the adventurous one. I'm going to be a dancer." She paused. "That will drive my mother crazy..."

"What kind of a dancer?"

"I'm studying classical Greek dancing. I love it."

That sounded pretty strange to me. I allowed myself to look at her. Was she ever attractive: her lovely round face made a perfect setting for flawless features under that smart hat. "Leo wants to stay at home. She doesn't have any ambition, I don't know why. A bit like George." She turned. "You must be adventurous yourself, leaving a little farm in Quebec to join up and come over to London?"

"It's not a little farm," I replied stoutly. "We have a couple of hundred acres, and we do very well."

"Oh, I'm sorry," she dropped her eyes, "I only meant that you seem quite adventurous, like Hilda."

No one had told me that before. It gave me a warm feeling. She was full of surprises.

"You know, Eric, your brother... No one from a farm in England would get to be what amounts to being a bishop! When we drive him, he talks of meetings with generals, and with the highest levels of our government. He's doing a wonderful job. Leo and I both think the world of him."

Amazing to see your brother through someone else's eyes. I never got no great sense of his warmth. Sure he liked me, as I liked him, but we didn't fraternize much. After all, twenty years or more separated us.

"Volunteering must mean you meet lots of other military men," I said as innocently as I could, trying not to be obvious.

She didn't look at me. "Yes lots... Well, I suppose we should get back. We don't want to keep someone as important as your brother waiting. I believe he has a reservation for lunch for you two. Leo and I will have a snack at a nearby café while we wait."

We turned to walk back. "Hasn't he invited you to eat with him?"

"Oh no; we're just volunteers." She pointed. "Number 10 Downing Street is just around the corner. The residence of our Prime Minister, Herbert Asquith."

I did know that; I'd read it in the papers. But I never thought I'd be within a toad's spit like now.

"We meet a lot of officers, but we prefer Canadians. Or Australians. Our own officers are... well, they think too much of themselves."

Which confirmed my own beliefs. But she did like Canadians. Good! Another point in my favour. Just as well, because I'd not see her again before leaving.

PART THREE

The Somme, Vimy Ridge, Hill 70, and Passchendaele

CHAPTER ELEVEN

The Somme, October 7th 1916: The Brigade completed a March of 43 miles in 26 hours and arrived in time to take part in the operations at 4:40 a.m. on the 8th.

WAR DIARIES: 8TH BRIGADE CFA

Pitch black. Cold rain soaking us, harnesses jingling, I rode with my Battery as it pressed on, guns nose to tail. The stench filling our nostrils would soon become visible as the rotting flesh of men and horses. Ypres had stunk too, but this smelled of more recent death. Back there, the worst had been latrines, especially when the wind was up. But our Sanitary Detail (we called them the "shit wallahs") did a pretty good job, covering the pits with chloride of lime every chance they got, burning the refuse and digging new latrines. But now, what were we entering? Some strange subterranean hell? No, just the Somme salient.

Less than a week ago after some pretty harsh action, we'd been resting at Kemmel when the rain started pouring down. The very next day, didn't we get orders to move south? We marched and rode continuously in a downpour for four days with only woollen greatcoats to protect us: drenched. Being October, the nights were getting cold and the days not much better; I felt chilled through and through.

No doubt about it, with Harry Oakes overcoming his initial fears and Finn replacing Cecil, our gun crew had developed a speed and accuracy that might well be the envy of other Batteries. So it was a pretty self-satisfied bunch that came to reinforce the Front here at the Somme — a battle that had been going on since July.

Self-satisfied, yes, when we started out, but after four rain-soaked days — more like worn out, depressed, exhausted, caring only for a warm bed, a wash and a good meal, though none of those would be ours for a long time.

I don't know who was more tired, Barry or me. Poor horse, he'd carried me faithfully, head down, following the gun. I don't know how the walking men did it, though most rode on limbers. But coming to any slight rise, BSM Jones made them get off. I wondered why; surely our energy was more important than our horses, much as we admired our animals. Anyway, on we went hoping that the coming dawn would hold off long enough to get us to our gun-pit safely.

The British had pushed Fritz back so we were slithering over mush in the former No Man's Land, the actual Front being a couple of miles further, though less to our gun lines. I wanted to hurry — with Heinie binoculars beaming in our direction, their 5.9s might shatter our somnolence at any second, automatons that we were, unable to respond. I was half asleep myself.

As Barry carried me into this cratered land of horrors, I found myself propelled into a new awareness — that my preoccupation with making us the best howitzer team anywhere had been overly simple, like wanting a fine haymaking team. As our strung-out caravan of death-dealing guns moved into an awakening day, another awakening was shaking me inside. A new battleground, one of the spirit as well as muck and flesh, would somehow lift me onto another profound level. Forced into this offensive stew of death and decay — the lost and dying breaths of thousands of souls and spirits created an almost palpable desolation of spirit to match the devastation of body and mind.

In my half-waking state after twenty-six hours of continuous travel, I grappled with new concepts. Was this horrible slaughter a contest where one side won and one side lost? No, we were being swept into a kind of ultimate cataclysm — no victors and no vanquished — only an entwining of so many fine souls, ground into one great grave of the spirit.

The horse bobbed forward, my body throbbing in rhythm — just as we were all, every one of us, in rhythm with each other. How many human beings would we kill, released from their earthly bondage into a heaven that would surely embrace each and every one of us: German, French, Australian and Canadian, too. How many would return home? Would I myself join this legion of souls drifting forever the forlorn landscape? The thought made me sit up and take notice of my surroundings, no matter how fearful. Day was coming fast. And with it, danger.

Surely this long caterpillar of men, limbers and guns, would soon be seen by the enemy. Any devastation we had up our sleeve would be returned upon us, as we persevered, squelching our way over the awful Somme clay. Get there fast, I prayed.

Before sunrise, still happily hidden by ground mist and light rain, we were directed to a new position, previously fortified for a Hun machine-gun nest or trench mortar. A broken barn wall on one side gave us protection and the gun-pit, cement at the bottom, made a secure footing. The Germans had been dug in on the Somme front for two years and had built their positions well, another reason for the enormous British losses on that first day of the Somme battle, July 1st.

After we stopped, the Drivers went off with their horses while the rest of us ached for a sleep. But we had to get our ton-and-a-half howitzer properly placed — the barrage had been called for at 4:40 a.m., hard to believe. Of course the pit faced in the opposite direction so I set two men to shovel a ramp down. Others laboured to right the gun so it would roll into position. The Somme clay was so wet and clingy, even the Sergeant lost one of his boots: he was peering around to see where it had disappeared into the ooze.

And believe me, moving a heavy howitzer after no sleep for two long days was almost impossible for even the best of us. Any minute, a shrapnel burst could take us all out of the war forever. But with a pile of grunting and complaining, we got the gun into position and the ammunition unloaded for the pre-dawn barrage.

And then right away, we had to begin registration. Hard in the mist to even set a proper zero line: we did it, as they say, by guess and by God. In the meantime, the Sergeant found his boot and Harry had located an old German dugout for us; his slight frame and skinny body had been no use moving the gun. Finally, McKillop broke us off and told us to get our heads down for a few minutes while he headed for the telephone pit to confirm the barrage orders. We had done it!

Twenty-six hours on the march and straight into action — and now time to spare. I was due to head back to the Wagon Lines, but was far too tired to struggle in daylight back over that mud. Besides, extra hands were always welcome during a barrage.

Now we'd all been warned about dugouts being booby-trapped. But this one, with its corrugated iron thrown against the entrance, looked as though it hadn't been touched since Heinie left. I figured as Corporal I had to lead the way and check for anything that might trigger an explosion and send us all to kingdom come.

Cautiously, pointing my flashlight, I slowly clambered down, all of fifteen feet. Vile water covered the mud floor and even the duckboards, bath-mats as we called them.

So far so good. Long, roomy, and well built: the corrugated iron ceiling had been reinforced with stout beams, so it looked safe. The enemy had been here for two years with nothing much else to do but fix it up, apparently, having taken a decidedly defensive posture. I moved forward, and then stopped.

There at my feet lay a dead German in his grey uniform (ours being khaki), and beyond, another on his back. What a stench! How long had they been here? Long enough, obviously!

Well sir, no use calling for a burial party.

"Whitehead! Rideout!" I knelt and checked closely around the body with my flashlight. No sign of wires, so safe. I guessed he'd been shot while coming towards the ladder.

Red came down with his flashlight and took in the grisly scene. Then he grabbed the corpse by one arm and dragged it to the ladder.

"Wait, Red!" I remembered a cow that had broken out of her pasture one spring and died near the brook. When I tried to pull her to one side, the leg had come off.

Well sir, Red, always impulsive, didn't listen — he wanted the stench out fast. Up the stairs he climbed, hauling the dead German by one arm. But half way up, didn't the arm pull out? So the corpse flopped back down on the slats with a loud pouf! The stomach bust open and maggots squirmed over the duckboard slats. Gas got released and when it hit me, I had to lean back against the wall and, I'm sorry to report, threw up.

Just great, I thought, now we have the stink of my vomit added to the dead German.

Red threw the arm to Edward, who chucked it to one side, pulling back quickly as the odour hit him. Red came down again. "Sorry. Never handled a dead body before... So what now?"

How should we gather up these remains of flesh and maggots? And my vomit: it was all just so disgusting.

"Is there something we could ladle him into?" I was still gasping.

Red called up, "Ed, throw down a shovel."

Not often you shovel a dead body onto something. I cast my flashlight around and saw a greatcoat. I grabbed it and threw it beside the body while Edward handed down the shovel. Red shovelled on it the severed head and what remained of the body, heavy enough, though eaten by rats. I picked up the booted legs and threw them up over the edge of the pit.

We climbed the ladder, each holding the greatcoat: him the collar and me gripping two coattails. We got about six feet up when didn't one of my ends drop? The remains fell out with another ghastly splattering thud.

In spite of myself, I began to laugh. So did Red.

Down we climbed and this time only shovelled half the remains onto the greatcoat. Then Red, holding both ends in one hand, climbed up himself and handed the bundle to Edward, who made such a face, I had to laugh again. He and Finn grabbed the greatcoat, threw the remains off to one side, and handed back the filthy coat.

While I held the flashlight, Ralph shovelled the rest of the remains onto it and also scraped up my vomit. He wiped the shovel on the greatcoat, and looked at me.

I sighed. "Okay, Red, my turn."

Hardly able to breathe in the dreadful stench, I gave him the light and grabbed the ends of the greatcoat and collar and managed to climb the steep ladder with one hand. Carefully, I handed up the remains so Edward could throw them aside, too.

"Corp," Red called, "There's another one."

"Oh no! Edward, you'll have to come down."

"Do I have to?" he asked plaintively.

"Afraid so." Then we both grinned. Back down I went, and Edward followed.

"Okay," I said, "let's not mess this one up. Edward, you take hold of the two legs and I'll grab the coat around the shoulders. You go first with the legs, but step-by-step, and gently. Let's keep him intact."

Edward climbed with the two legs under one arm while I kept saying, "Slowly Edward, slowly!"

Well, Edward got halfway up the ladder, me hefting the corpse's shoulders, until Edward got the legs up and Finn took them. "Take it easy!" I said.

Finn started to pull it all up while I lifted the shoulders, one arm hooked around the ladder. Well, didn't the face come past, six inches away, skin pulled tight over the bones, all ghastly, and then flopping to one side, it looked straight at me. And I swear to God, out of the nose crawled a maggot.

I let out a screech and heaved on the corpse. With the other lads, we threw it out of the dugout for disposal later.

I got out quick and sat on a bunk, holding my head. Not an experience I wanted to repeat. Then didn't the familiar cry of "Battery Action" rouse us, and we all had to sprint back to the gun? Only the dead get any rest in this war, I thought, as our barrage lit the grey light of dawn.

CHAPTER TWELVE

The Somme, Oct 10th 1916: The Brigade had a successful day shooting, so the Infantry supported were able to carry out their operation to good effect.

Oct 11th: The Brigade carried out a normal bombardment of the enemy's trenches. The 30th Battery, while moving ammunition, had four men wounded and four horses killed.

WAR DIARIES: 8TH BRIGADE CFA

The night after that everlasting march and our barrage at 4:50 a.m., we still got almost no sleep. All day we answered calls for fire so that finally, I was so tired I could hardly work the gun, but our drills stayed pretty sharp. Over the next two days firing away, the already god-awful weather got colder and foggier. But at least we'd made headway with our dugout, all of us pitching in to clean the place up. Fritz had left behind a table, some chairs, and even cots. The smell made us sick, so Red got quicklime from the sanitary fellas and sprinkled that. Someone else had the bright idea of a can of creoline, a trade name for creosote, which came in large drums and is doled out liberally to kill lice. It smelt bad, but better than vomit and corpses.

Yesterday, our 30th Battery had the bad luck to be struggling up from the Wagon Lines through all that mud, Drivers hauling away on the wheels to move their limbers up to our firing line with ammunition, when flares revealed them and Heinie shrapnel wounded four Drivers and killed four horses. We knew everyone in the Brigade pretty well so it came as a big shock. That mud was just so restricting, if you went out you were a sitting duck. We took extra care, but what can you do when a shell has your name on it?

But this morning, Jonas, a renowned scavenger, had managed to find eggs, so Jason, our cook, and his assistant, served them up with our bacon. I tell you, that raised our spirits!

The rain let up a bit, so after maintenance on our precious gun we were having a quiet smoke by the pit when who did we see through the mist but Battery Sergeant Major Jones. A surprise inspection! We jumped up.

At his command of "Stand easy men," we relaxed. He offered us all a decent cigarette that we accepted gratefully. "Well, Corporal Alford, I hear you got the team you wanted. How is it going?"

"Very well, sir, thank you." The others nodded agreement.

"As it turns out, you were right about Gunner Smith. Apparently, he's doing fine in the D.A.C. Just so long as he steers clear of the guns."

"So we've heard, sir," Edward responded. "A fine chap. Just not quite right on our gun, but good he's a help elsewhere."

Jones nodded. We lapsed into silence as the BSM looked around our gun-pit. As the Major's senior adviser on gunnery and discipline, the BSM checked us out fairly often, but now, he came to relax against sandbags we'd rebuilt and we saw that this was to be a casual chat — most unusual. "Corporal Alford, I have noted there is a Colonel Alford in the Chaplaincy Service. Any relation?"

"My brother, sir."

"Is he now? You see him much?"

"Not really, he's quite busy, and the chaplaincy headquarters are up at Neue Chappelle."

"Oh? I think now they've moved down near Albert, not too far. He does visit, I gather, the Front from time to time."

I wondered if Jack would make an effort to find me. "One thing I know about my brother, sir, is that he is a hard worker. Our father drilled that into both of us."

Jones nodded again. "You know, my brother is a chaplain."

Aha! I thought, maybe I'll get a few points.

"So there are two Joneses serving on the Front?" Ed asked. "I have a brother too, but he's an officer in the Infantry."

"Three, actually — one with HQ," Jones went on. "Yes, my younger brother went to Sandhurst, stayed in England and now, being on the General Staff, he seems to get the skinny on what's going on." He smiled. I guess he felt he could relax with us, which made me think that maybe we were, after all, his ace howitzer.

"So tell us, sir," Harry spoke up, "are those reports of horrendous casualties on this Somme front true?" The little bastard, I could see he was going to get us all into hot water.

"Well, yes, they have been pretty bad."

Harry went on, "They say a hundred thousand men since July."

Jones nodded. "I'm afraid those figures probably do approach the truth, Gunner Oakes."

I thought I'd step in: "Don't listen to Harry Oakes, sir. He thinks he's a bit of a military historian, but we all take him with a grain of salt."

Harry gave me a dirty look, but I could see I had not deterred him.

"Well then," continued the BSM, "he should know that General

Haig attacked in July against his better judgment." We all believed, though, that every time Haig ordered a new battle across the Western Front, the tears of widows and daughters would fill a bucket.

"Are you just trying to excuse that disaster, sir?" Such a cheeky response, I thought.

"You know, Gunner Oakes, we must give him his due. He's a fine general, but from what I hear, he'd had his feet put to the fire by the French. They'd been under tremendous pressure at Verdun. The Empire was forced to come to the rescue, and did so by opening a new offensive on another front. That's why we're here on the Somme."

"Sir," Red butted in, "Harry here told me this 'Somme' is actually Picardy. I've heard of "Roses Are Blooming in Picardy" and all that, but is he right? No roses I can see hereabouts!"

We laughed, but Harry let out an exasperated snort.

"Gunner Oakes is in fact quite right," Jones said. "Lots of battles fought over this Somme, it's a Department, like a province."

"Created a hundred years ago?" chimed in Harry.

"Well well, a real historian!" How easygoing of our BSM, I thought; by now I'd have had the little rascal's guts for garters. "Yes, around 1790. You'd know, then, that Julius Caesar fought here; in the fourteenth century, Edward III took on the French, then Henry V engaged them again on his way to Agincourt."

"Don't forget the Franco-Prussian War —" Harry added.

"— when the Germans and French went at it again, only forty years ago." Jones sighed and shook his head. "We never learn, it seems."

"So you mean to say, sir," Harry pressed, "because of some pressure from those French buggers, Haig went and threw away thousands of British lives?"

Aha! I thought, now he'll get it for sure. "I wouldn't put it quite that way." Jones's demeanour darkened. "The French are our allies. He's a smart general."

Harry soldiered on, regardless. "I've heard that on the first day, we had over fifty thousand casualties, and Haig still kept on throwing more troops across No Man's Land to get killed, day after day, week after week. I don't call that very smart myself." Now he'd get his real comeuppance, I thought

"You are talking about General Sir Douglas Haig, our Commander-in-chief, Gunner. Shouldn't you be a bit more respectful?"

"All very well, sir, pull his rank on us if you want." Harry was turning red, becoming pretty agitated. "But that's no way to conduct a war, in my view."

Jones took up his challenge, rather too calmly, I thought. "Listen, Gunner Oakes, if Verdun had fallen, as it was bound to the way things were going, the Germans would have marched right into Paris!" He paused for emphasis, then said slowly, "The end of France. We'd have had to turn tail and run for the Channel. So although the Somme might have been a bit of a disaster in terms of achieving any real breakthrough — "

"And in terms of lives lost!" Harry interrupted.

"On the other hand," Jones pressed on, "my brother at HQ tells me that, in fact, we did give the Boche a beating: we made him pull men and supplies from Verdun so that the French could hold on satisfactorily." He stared off into the mist, as the rain began to sprinkle. "The tactics of war, of this war especially, won't really be known until it is all over and we've beaten the Boche properly."

BSM Jones did have a few points, I'll admit. He went on, "You do have to give our generals some credit, Gunner. Not always possessed of the best judgments, but just think of the pressures they are under. The war cabinet in England — they also give General Haig instructions. He has a lot to consider."

"Maybe it's about time he considered the thousands of lives — "

I saw Red and Edward stunned by Harry's vehemence, but Jones changed the subject. "Well, Gunner Oakes, history will tell us both the truth — if we live to see that day." He gave a perfunctory smile and turning, took me aside. "Alford," he dropped his voice, "I didn't really come up to the firing line to debate strategy with Oakes... I rather wanted to find out if you'd be agreeable to putting in a word with your brother?"

Aha, so that's why he was so calm with Oakes: he wanted to corner me. But it did take me back a bit. "Of course, sir. But in what way?"

"You see, my brother, Chaplain Llewellyn Jones, wants to be with the Welsh Fusiliers. But because he signed up in Canada, he's been put with some Saskatchewan Regiment." I let him go on. "Well, that Chaplain Steacy — not that I want to say anything against a man of the cloth — but as your brother's immediate superior, he's known as rather a miserable so-and-so, not well suited for the job. Now," he glanced behind him, "this is all just between you and me, Alford, right?

I nodded. He went on louder to include the others as if we had been discussing this appointment: "From all accounts, Corporal Alford, your brother would be a much better head of that Service himself."

I was pleased. No one had told me how well he was doing. "Well, if I ever get a moment I'll write to him and of course I'll put in a word. We are all, in fact, part of the 35th!" And here I went perhaps beyond decorum, "As the best Battery in our Brigade, can we not ask a few favours from those in charge of spiritual matters?" I grinned. I thought I had said that rather well.

Our usually strict BSM smiled, and nodded. Then, he waved to the others. "As you were, men. It's been a fine conversation. One I'd like to continue, Gunner Oakes, when we next have time."

And off he went into the slowly thickening mist.

***

The Infantry stayed on the attack, and we supported them with firepower, though the weather itself defeated any decent counter-battery. It depressed us, for we liked to maintain our accuracy, something we were especially proud of. To make matters worse, on the third night as we were eating supper, Harry Oakes came steaming up out of the dugout. "Cats!"

I frowned. "What do you mean, Harry?"

The others put down their mess tins and got up. "Really?" Red asked. "Kitties?"

"No, I mean great big cats, scampering around; I just caught sight of a couple."

We ambled over to investigate as Red pronounced, "I'd love to adopt a cat. We have three at home. You know, the Infantry often have pet dogs, to carry messages. A cat might be fun."

Well sir, no cats at all. These were RATS— the biggest bloody rats I've ever seen. And from then on, when we were trying to go to sleep, we heard them rustling around, even jumping on our beds and waking us with their cold noses. Harry cried out in his sleep: he was scared, but as we'd been told the next morning, they don't usually take a bite out of you — far too many dead bodies lying around to feed on. With all this rain and muck, they preferred a warm deep dugout, I guess. But you had to watch your food, or any parcel from home, because they'd soon tear into it, even in daylight.

Rats, rain, damage, and death: not such an enjoyable adventure, I decided. I rolled over, tried to ignore the situation, and grab some sleep.

CHAPTER THIRTEEN

Regina Trench

The Somme, Oct 21st 1916: Zero time fixed for barrage at 12:06 p.m., with Batteries registered on new zones.

22-23rd The Brigade moved forward to new positions during the night. The whole move was carried out in good order in spite of the very difficult conditions of the routes available.

WAR DIARIES: 8TH BRIGADE CFA

Six minutes past noon. Another tremendous explosion and recoil joined the opening roar of the barrage. Acrid white smoke drifted around us as we began the sequence, firing again in less than a minute. The battle had begun.

We went through the motions like automatons. Well, I tell a lie. Although the rain of the past few days had stopped, today was the coldest so far — that wind must have blasted down from Siberia; even the ground was frozen. Our fingers felt like ice and the ammunition was wet. After our first four days here, we had been back at the Wagon Lines on rotation but right now we were tired, hungry and cold. Had we not developed into a smooth firing machine, chaos would have reigned.

The day before yesterday, we had registered our gun on new zones to support another attack on what we now knew was Regina Trench. Another big Allied push was on and we felt a growing excitement. This was not just one of your counter-batteries, no simple SOS called for by Infantry; this was another wide frontal bombardment, and we were part of it.

This barrage had been called for yesterday but incessant rain and poor visibility caused High Command to postpone the attack. So here we were, cramming shell after shell into the breech — unbelievable noise! Not only us four howitzers, but all the 18-pounders in our Brigade and some six hundred other guns, all joined in a general mayhem.

I blessed our automatic reflexes and training because that kept us all from going crazy with the noise. Two shells from our gun every minute and from every gun in our Battery, and remember, each shell weighed thirty-five pounds — handled three times: once to unload it from the limber, once to prepare and stack it, and once again into the breech. In the continuous roar, nothing could be heard. We were all going deaf, I was sure. I had to write new gun data down, no amount of yelling even close to an ear would be heard. The cacophony was getting to all of us — not often have we joined in such a massive barrage and overhead, shells from our heavier guns kept whistling past. Who'd want to be a German this afternoon?

As shell after shell screamed towards Fritz, all I could think about was Old Momma's beef stew. Visions of my Old Homestead flashed across my mind until I put them aside. Never think of home here or you'll go crazy.

I checked the others: Finn, working cheerfully, seemed the least concerned, for he hated the Germans. Edward was not enjoying himself but moving his tall elegant body well, stopping every few seconds to blow on his fingers. Harry Oakes worried me: no fat on his bones to shield him from the cold; shuddering hard, the brave little fella kept at it, elevating and lowering the gun, slamming the breech shut, doing everything he had to do. And of course Red, so strong, continued as a bastion of strength.

Forty minutes past zero hour we stopped, which allowed the gun to cool, but only for a while. The left portion of bloody Regina Trench had been taken. The cook's helper, who seldom got any thanks, handed hot tea around while we waited in silence for that dreaded call back into action. Our infantry would need continued support if they were to hold the ground.

I don't know how we did it, but we kept going for hours, punishing the Boche as they pushed hard to take back their Trench. Thank heaven we had been stockpiling rounds and, God knows how, another ammunition limber arrived before dawn — we were going through ammunition like blazes.

With all the rain, our dugout had begun to fill with water, maybe a foot deep. Rubbish under the slats rose to the surface; no fun slogging through it to get to your cot, happily still above water. And by gosh, when we copped our chance for sleep, we just forgot food and clambered down the ladder to stretch out — blink! Fast asleep.

***

The next day, Heinie started a counter-battery. After trying different ranges, he found us. No calls for firing so we huddled together in our dugout, listening to 5.9s exploding all around. I tell you it was enough to break anyone's nerve. We just sat and listened. And wondered. No hope of our cook crossing the open ground to bring us food. But in one corner of the dugout, the Germans had made a little grill for a fire. So we brewed up a pot of tea to pass around. But not without wondering what second a shell might arrive with our name on it. I was definitely scared.

They didn't let up all morning, and then a messenger dashed in between bursts of artillery and scrambled down the stairs. And who do you think it was? Cecil!

We were so pleased to see him! We crowded round to ask what he'd been doing.

"I been transferred back to the Brigade Signals Section," he explained. "See, I was in an ammunition column. It was okay. Got a bit used to noise. But this is better. Much better. It's fun." He beamed, his teeth sticking out even more.

"So how come you're here now, Cecil?" I asked.

"I had to bring orders up to your Major." He grinned. "So I grabbed me a few minutes to run over here."

We clustered around, congratulating him. But of course, he couldn't stay long: duty called, and he was sure proud of his new responsibilities. He scrambled back up the ladder, waited a moment, then dashed off, brave as all get out.

Our orders now had us moving another half a mile ahead, to keep the retreating Germans in range. With Heinie targeting us here, none of us were unhappy with that. But how on earth would we ever move that damn gun half a mile through the viscous clay of the Somme? The challenge put a real damper on our excitement at seeing old Cecil. Oh yes, all he'd needed was some understanding. Not a lot of that around these days. Rumours spoke of the British taking any man who shirked his duty and shooting them, I suppose to set an example. But who needed that to do his duty?

***

By God it was cold. The rain had lessened and the ice melted somewhat so now at dusk we faced a quagmire. I wanted to get started: it might take all night to go that half mile towards the Front. But we had to wait for the horses from the Wagon Lines. As I stood beside Edward, waiting, I noticed he seemed strangely downcast. He kept swearing about Drivers who were late, a lack of understanding unusual for him.

An hour after dark they made it, and we hitched a team onto our howitzer. In the pitch dark we set off, rain falling, slimy mud, no footing for us or the horses, the six of them sliding around. We hitched on the second team from the other limber and with us hauling on the spokes and drag ropes, the twelve horses got the howitzer up out of the pit. As we grunted along, I mumbled, "Edward, did something happen today?"

He shook his head. Well, he'd tell me later.

As we rolled the gun across the terrain pitted with craters, I slipped into a shell hole. I tried to clamber out, but Somme mud gripped my feet like a crocodile. I'd push one foot down to lift the other and it just sunk deeper. Now what? I heard the others moving on ahead.

"Ed," I called. "Edward, come back!" He didn't hear. I yelled again as loud as I could. Marching behind, Red turned, ran over and grabbed my arm. We managed to wrestle my legs bit by bit up out of the mud, and finally I got free.

I made some joke as I joined Edward in pulling on the ropes, and finally, he admitted he was in a bad mood.

"We all get like that, sometimes."

"Maybe." He seemed to want to talk. "You know, sometimes it's better not to get any letters."

"How so? Surely you like letters from Katie?"

"She stopped writing two months ago."

"Maybe she's written and you just haven't got them. Sometimes letters don't get through." We were slipping along in the mud and falling, the horses themselves with their good instincts avoiding most of the holes. Lieutenant Overstreet kept in front, trying to guide us along a route he'd found earlier. No road for sure.

"No, my family've written..." A shout came that a plank road was just up ahead. "I even got one last week from Katie's friend. She always talks about how Katie misses me. This time, she made not one mention..."

Not good. "Look Edward, don't read too much into all this."

"I can read as much as I like," came his abrupt reply.

So that was it, then. Katie had probably gone her own way. Poor Edward. And here we were, mired in mud. But we hit the plank road laid by the British, and manhandled the gun onto it, no easy job. As our going proved easier, I decided to unhitch one horse team. Those Drivers went back for our other limber, but they'd find it hard going with their thin rims and heavy with shells,

"In her last letter maybe three months ago she said, 'Edward, you don't know how hard it is for me. Everyone wanting me to go out with them, my friends, having such a good time. I don't know what to do.'"

"I gotta say Edward, it's damned hard for girls left behind. Remember, you were the one to tell me to forget that Shigawake girl. And I did, you know; it sure helped. I put her out of my mind."

"Are you saying I should put Katie out of my mind?" Edward eyed me angrily.

"No no no, Edward, I was just remembering. I thought it would help."

We grabbed the wheels and heaved the gun off the end of the plank road. After an hour more, staggering like a bunch of drunken sailors, falling and getting up, covered in slimy mud, we managed to get the gun into its new position, I would say by around four in the morning.

When we got the gun set, Edward came over to me. "Eric," he said, "I know what you were saying. And I know you're right. It's just... it's just the hardest thing to do. Katie, she's... she's so important to me. She fills my whole brain. I don't know what I'll do." Unusual to see the noble Edward down in the dumps. I felt badly.

I had to agree it was not a good predicament, with us facing our own horrible challenges just to stay alive. "Edward, let's just wait and see what happens. Don't get your hopes up, but don't get them down either. Let's just wait."

What a time, unloading the ammunition, stacking it, lying down and getting up again. At dawn the cook brewed up some tea and bacon. We got a rough registration going, with more rain and mist hugging the ground like a wool blanket. So now, how long before Heinie located us here in these new positions? Would those flashes from our muzzles give us away? Were we here at last, only to meet our end? Edward might have even welcomed that, but I sure didn't. I just longed for the Old Homestead and for all this slaughter to end, once and for all.

CHAPTER FOURTEEN:

Regina Trench

The Somme, Nov 3rd, 1916: This morning the 35th Battery had two men wounded by a premature from a 4.5 Howitzer Battery in rear of them. One man had to be evacuated, the other returned to duty.

Nov 4th: A cartridge exploded in the breech of No 2 gun of 31st Battery; ammunition started to explode; two men killed, two slightly wounded.

During the afternoon some shelling by 4.2"s [German 105mm howitzers] around the 35th Battery. Its Lieutenant, slightly wounded, returned to duty.

WAR DIARIES: 8TH BRIGADE CFA

I woke up with a feeling of foreboding that dragged me down. I'd slept well enough but couldn't get out of my mind what happened yesterday. When that HE round exploded right over our heads, Finn's back was pretty well shattered, lots of skin and flesh torn off; Edward got hurt, too. I later heard that due to the rushed nature of ammunition production, over ten percent of the rounds we fired might be duds or prematures. Dangerous.

Well of course, it cast a pall over the rest of us. Finn was taken behind to base hospital quickly, but that journey itself was dangerous. They got him out on a horse — that plucky Driver had made it in full daylight, slipping and sliding over the cratered clay. Must have hurt Finn like hell. As for Edward, they bandaged his shoulder and his head where a fragment had skimmed off a bit of scalp, but he said he felt fine: he was just not about to leave us. In fact, he said he'd felt worse when he got that letter from Katie's best friend. I had to sympathize with him. Bad luck all around.

When I got to breakfast today, Jason had managed to cook hot porridge on his portable stove. "Just like home, eh Jason?"

"Hard to get supplies up. None last night. Don't know what we'll do for suppers. Maybe they'll try in daylight."

"No food last night with the ammunition?"

He shook his head. "No ammunition neither. Just that new replacement for Finn. He came on foot."

And then I saw the new man: one of our alternate spare Gunners, young Jimmy Heath was tall, well over six feet, angular, with a bleak, scholarly face and scrawny arms and legs, like a giant spider. Quite different from Finn, for sure. An intellectual, I suspected, later proved by his incessant arguing with Harry.

I thanked Jason and was moving on with my tin plate and mug when I noticed a Gunner and Sergeant from the 31st Battery, the 18-pounders, eating with us. They had gotten lost before dawn.

Howard Williams was a bold-faced, handsome soldier, blond with blue eyes, who hailed from the prairies. We had compared notes on the odd occasion and now found ourselves sitting next to each other. "Just coming up from the Wagon Lines?"

Howard nodded. "Decent sleep back there. Almost as good as a real bed of hay."

"Oh, please don't mention that. Reminds me I never slept better than naps on fresh hay. I even miss that nice smell of manure."

"I know what you mean," Howard replied. "But no cows on our farm. Just horses, o' course, but we farmed mainly wheat, acres and acres of wheat."

"Yeah?" I thought I could visualize that; I'd heard about the prairies. "Ours is a mixed farm: cows, sheep, even goats. We make butter, then feed the skimmed butter-milk to a pig we slaughter every autumn. Nothing better than a roast porker!"

Howard grinned. "I bet. Don't eat much pork where I come from. Mostly beef. Lot of beef cattle out there on the prairies, I'll tell you."

We talked some more about our respective farms and looked at pictures of our families, then got onto the subject of the weather — the worst autumn anyone could remember in Europe.

Sergeant Harris came to join us; his family were farmers, too. He looked tough: black-haired, gaunt, with dark eyes. He interrupted our moaning about the conditions: "But we're giving them Heinies hell. You fellas heard of this here new tank we put into action?"

I had heard rumours of tanks being used hereabouts, certainly something new, but I didn't know much about them. Neither Howard nor I had seen one. "Bloody great lumbering monsters, a dozen feet wide, triangular looking, bullet-proof too," Sergeant Harris explained. "Got these here treads on the outside, climbs over anything. Two six-pounders it has, and four machine guns. They say it scares Fritz out of his wits."

"Well, let's hope something scares him," I said. "We're not doing a great job of that ourselves, or beating the daylights out of them, which is why I joined up." There was a chorus of agreement.

"Come on now, Corporal, we've moved them back three miles since summer. And we keep backing them up. Didn't you notice we moved up half a mile just last week? We'll keep doing that till we get to Berlin."

The Sergeant seemed a bit optimistic, but I said nothing; I had finished my breakfast and gulped the last of my tea. They said they'd better get back to the war, and soon disappeared into the fresh rain. I found a relatively clean shell hole and washed my mug and tin plate.

***

Well, sir, didn't my foreboding persist? I just couldn't get those ominous thoughts out of my mind as we began to register on a new target. But mist and rain rendered our visibility negligible.

"Oh no no no, Harry," Jimmy Heath, our new Number Four, was arguing as he passed the shells over. "France was dying to get back Alsace-Lorraine. That's why the French were so bloody pleased when this damn war started."

"Jim, you're the one who's wrong," Oakes scolded. "That Kaiser, he's so military, even with his withered arm, he kept wanting to prove himself. Saw Germany getting surrounded by the Imperial power-sharing, so *he* started the war —"

A darned great explosion cut him short. I thought one of the big naval guns had struck just ahead. We stopped in our tracks and looked at each other. That's where the 31st Battery was positioned! Then we heard a series of rapid detonations, like machine guns.

"A raiding party!" cried Red. "Where's our rifles?"

I didn't think Fritz could have made it this far. "No!" I ordered. "Stay here and look after things." But then I found myself unaccountably running forward. As I came closer, I slowed down, horrified.

One gun was in ruins: its ammunition had exploded and torn a Gunner to pieces. Two other fellas were staggering away, one holding his stomach that had been bust open, another on the ground missing a leg. Then I saw Sergeant Harris, holding someone's arm in both hands. The hand was on a level with his face, and he kept repeating, "George... George," as though talking to a real person, and walking in circles, dazed.

Immediately, one of their Lieutenants tore open a First Aid pack and used a tourniquet to staunch the blood on the other Gunner's stump. A couple of others leaned against sandbags, dazed and immobile. One soldier charged off to summon the Brigade Medical Officer, while another headed to get rum, our only ready anaesthetic.

I went forward and stumbled over something. I looked down. There at my feet was a torso. Just a torso, head attached, no legs. Howard!

It took me a while to absorb this. I'd just been talking to him. What was going on? Then I came to my senses. What had I been doing, leaving my post? I turned from the gruesome carnage and hurried back. Heavens, not often I lose my head like that.

When I got to our gun, I told the boys that our own ammunition had been at fault. And indeed, as we found out later, a round had exploded in the breech. Yes, but what about our own breech? Their tragedy could just as easily been ours. This faulty ammo was nerve-wracking, but what could we do? We had to keep firing.

So that's why I'd been in the doldrums: some kind of premonition. And again, that sight of the torso at my feet sprang up. I don't think I'll ever forget it.

After dinner, another fierce battering from Fritz's 5.9s. Myself, I thought our position had now become untenable. But only the Major could decide to move us. Overstreet hurried over: "That ammunition going off must have alerted the enemy. Gave them a better fix for counter-battery. I'm going up to our O-Pip and see if we can't hit back."

As he was crossing open ground, an HE round with a time fuze exploded above him. Black, expanding smoke enveloped him and when it lifted, he lay crumpled on the ground.

Two signallers ran over and dragged him under cover. I wanted to tear across, but we were firing. As soon as the shelling stopped, I ran over too and found that, fortunately, the fragments had only grazed his leg. Still, he should get right back to the Wagon Lines and see the MO.

"Thanks, Corp," Overstreet said. "I'm all right. Hurts like hell but I have a job to do here. I'm not leaving my boys."

It did my heart good to hear him. We all liked him so much. After being bandaged, he stayed up till after dark when his relief came. We were all proud of the guts he'd shown.

No doubt about it, that night as we tumbled into our blankets beside the gun, exhausted, the day's events got a going over. Two mishaps in our own brigade! As if the enemy's bombardments weren't bad enough — we had done this to ourselves. What next?

How on earth could I sleep? What about Howard's family? Again I saw the pictures of his mother and father, and his little sister. What would happen when they got that telegram? And every time I saw that torso at my feet, I asked the same question: how long before I'd meet the same fate?

CHAPTER FIFTEEN

Regina Trench

The Somme, November 11th 1916: After the taking of Regina Trench during early morning, bombardment carried out as per orders.

12th: One OR (other rank) killed in action during the night at the 40th Battery.

13th: We were shelled heavily with 5.9s during the day at Martinpuich. Direct hit on a gun-pit destroyed 450 rounds of ammunition and put the gun out of action. The Lieutenant wounded but returned to duty.

[COL. THE REV. JOHN M. ALMOND MENTIONED IN DISPATCHES.]

WAR DIARIES: 8TH BRIGADE CFA

We started our barrage at midnight last night, the 11th. Must have been tens of thousands of shells loosed over the last while. Now, in the small hours of Sunday, we hoped this would be our final assault on the rest of that bloody Regina Trench. The recent events, the accidents and the wounds and killings and everlasting din, had gotten to all of us. Ralph Rideout had lapsed into a morose silence; Edward would sing tunelessly to himself; Harry couldn't stop talking, cursing everything and everyone, including me; and lanky Jim, well, he wore an odd expression and his face started twitching.

But we fired with precision and regularity until around 3 a.m. and then slept beside the gun, ready for instant action in case of another SOS. Before breakfast we were roused again to throw more shells Fritz's way. Tough work, but not nearly as tough as those Infantry fellows, slogging through mud and slime till the word came: our barrage had been perfect; Regina Trench was ours. Right after our dinners, such as they were, we worked on our dugouts to make them more secure for the ever imminent counter-battery.

Monday I awoke to find it unseasonably sunny and bright. With breakfast finished, we cleaned and serviced our trusty gun and then most of the boys went back to the shelter. Myself, I preferred to remain in the gun-pit in case of an SOS, when I saw two figures approaching.

"I've got a bit of a surprise for you, Corporal Alford." BSM Jones was leading another officer. "Father John and I have been having a fine chat about my brother, Llewellyn."

And indeed what a surprise! My brother Jack.

I grabbed his hand and we both looked into each other's eyes, happy to see each other. "So what are you doing here?" I asked. It was more of a thrill than ever, seeing him here, under fire.

"I came to see you, of course." He beamed. "And find out how our 8th Brigade is getting on. Since I got back, I've been on a tour of the firing line. I was given three weeks in England, supposedly on 'leave', but I spent most of the time on chaplaincy matters, of course."

Well well, he'd been on leave. And of course my next question followed. "Did you see Rene?"

I saw his face become a mask as he reached in his pocket and handed me a letter from her. "Not only did I see her, but she wrote you a note. Read it later."

Yes, later, especially with this rare visit from my brother. "All well at the Old Homestead?"

"Big news there is that Jean is getting married to Bert Finnie, he's in my congregation at Trinity. Fine young man, got a bit of money, it seems. Going to be married in December. On the winter solstice, I believe."

Good news indeed, and I said so. More explosions made us flinch, so Jack volunteered: "I hear we've been giving them even worse. The BSM here told me of our new creeping bombardments. I got an earlier lowdown from General Currie, and it sounds interesting."

"The creeping barrage?" I knew we had fired on different coordinates every few minutes in the recent barrages, but we "Other Ranks" were the last to know the real details. I was sure pleased to hear my brother talked to our great Canadian General, from Vancouver so I'd heard. Made me proud, for sure. I was taking quite a liking to Jack, which may sound odd, but war was erasing the years that separated us.

"Currie worked out," Jones amplified, "that we should lay down an 18-pounder barrage just ahead of our Infantry's advance using tighter lifts, meaning we shell closer to their line of attack."

"Don't we hit our own men?" I asked.

"Sometimes," the BSM admitted. "But better a few men than great numbers mown down with those deadly machine guns."

"So you mean our tighter bombardments don't give the enemy much time to get out of his dugouts and man his guns?"

Jones nodded. "It's like a steel rake, our 18-pounder shrapnel shells, dragging through No Man's Land. First the enemy outposts, then the front lines, and finally we strike with HE at the rear areas to stop reserve troops from rushing up to fill the gap."

"General Currie put it this way," Jack said, "the Infantry should follow the Artillery barrage as closely as a horse follows a nosebag filled with corn." They both smiled.

Our conversation was interrupted by a terrific explosion about a hundred yards away, followed by another, and another. Oh no! What a time to be targeted. "Come on!" I yelled. Jack followed me as we tore for the shelter of our deep pits, while the BSM went to the next gun.

We dived down the rough steps with explosions going off behind. Harry and skinny Jim were already there, wrangling about military matters so I introduced my brother.

Seeing his Colonel's insignia, they gave a salute, though the low dugout prevented Jim's awkward frame from standing straight.

"At ease, men." Jack nodded. "I always feel uncomfortable when men salute me. Never got used to it." He grinned cheerfully. "But of course, when in Rome, do as the Romans do, I suppose."

He wasn't in Rome, so I didn't know what on earth he was talking about.

"And how are you getting on here in the 8th?" he asked brightly.

"Very well, sir," replied Jim, still with his twitch.

"Your chaplains taking good care of you?"

"Well, sir," interjected Harry "yesterday was Sunday — no hint of a church service." Oh boy, not another altercation! Trust Oakes.

"I am sorry. I suppose our Brigade chaplain was up at the Front with the Infantry lads, who face death every minute. Their needs are often seen to be greater. I'll see what I can do to get him back here every so often."

"My brother is assistant to the head of the Chaplaincy Corps at our Canadian Headquarters," I said proudly.

"If they're not conducting church services, I don't see what use your chaplains are anyway," said Harry, forever the cheeky bugger.

"You told me you never go to church, Harry," broke in Jim, his stick-like arms folded across his chest, "so what's the odds?"

A bloody great explosion shook the ground nearby, and some of the earthen covering fell on us. "Maybe there's got to be chaplains," Jim went on as he brushed it off, "but what good do they do apart from Sunday preaching?" Rather too much of a challenge, I thought.

"Well, Gunner, you may think it wasteful. I first served in the Boer War, and we had the same criticisms then, too. But since I've been accorded some influence here, I have managed to institute a few practices which, I am told, do make the soldiers' lives better."

"Such as?" Harry interrupted insolently.

"Well, the British forbade chaplains at the front line, but I got that changed for Canadians. We go out into No Man's Land and help medical officers and stretcher bearers. We hold services in dressing station dugouts and ruined cellars." Jack looked up anxiously as another shell exploded quite close by.

"Holding services..." Harry said. "What about those who don't care about services?"

"Well, as I said, they help get the wounded out. Already two of my chaplains have been wounded while doing so." I saw Jack could give as good as he got. "Another couple have won Military Crosses risking their lives in this manner. I would call that helping soldiers, wouldn't you, Gunner?"

"I didn't know any of that," mumbled Harry. "Yes Sir, that certainly is helping soldiers." First time I'd seen him bested.

Good for you, Jack, I thought, and ducked as the loud whine of a shell came to land behind us.

"And then," pressed Jack, "I set up a department to serve coffee. The Aussies gave us one of their old coffee machines at Suicide Corner. Night and day, our chaplains dole out coffee in cups made of cigarette tins. Wherever trench routes meet the roads, and also at Casualty Clearing Stations, we serve coffee, tea, biscuits, and even distribute cigarettes. Canon Scott was instrumental in advising me, you know. You should be seeing him one of these days."

Well, that certainly opened my eyes, and impressed Harry and Jim huddling there. The conversation made me almost forget the awful battering our emplacements were getting. No good worrying about a direct hit; I had long since decided that if I were going to go, it would probably be instantaneous, like those two fellows blown apart over in the 31st with not a second to feel what happened.

And then, bless my soul, didn't it all stop at dinner time? Jack seemed relieved.

"You see, Heinie enjoys his snack, like us." I grinned. "When we eat breakfast, too, both of us lay off the other fellow."

Jack sighed. "I see. Well, this barrage is one of the heaviest I've been in. Last week, I toured the front lines several times, encouraging our men. Something," he muttered, "our worthy DCS doesn't often do."

"DCS?" Jim asked.

"Director of Chaplaincy Services."

Jim nodded. "Mmm. I hear you have problems..."

"And how would you know about that?" asked Harry, hoping for another argument.

Jim twisted his scrawny body to look at him. "A little birdie." I led the way as we scrambled up and crossed the blasted earth to the cook's area.

"You should be eating with our officers, Jack."

"No, after witnessing what happened in that last war, my place is with the men. I'll be eating with you, Eric — if there's enough."

After we collected our mess tins, I led Jack over to one side of the gun-pit where we sat on a couple of boxes.

"So you've got problems with your boss?" I asked, tucking in. As always, I was starving.

Jack shrugged. He didn't want to go on, so I pressed. "Jack, if you can't talk to your brother, who else is there? Me, a lowly Corporal, I talk to no one. It won't go any further."

"Well," he heaved a sigh, "for starters, the DCS tried to get some of my best men — his friends of course — reassigned back to England out of harm's way, in spite of our being understaffed here." He sighed and shook his head. "Made me furious. He's back there now, preoccupied with trivialities when he should be up here at the Front." He paused, then went on, "You see, Eric, the Catholics are in a state, they want more chaplains, and the DCS being from Ontario, he doesn't care about them. The Methodists and the Presbyterians, they all want chaplains of their own, so there's all this infighting." He shook his head. "Like trying to keep peace in a cellar of feral tomcats."

I could see he had his work cut out for him, though I had no idea what a feral cat was. "And he won't listen to you?"

Jack shook his head. "I've given up trying. I get things done on my own, and possibly he'll be replaced. That's all I can hope for. Getting some good fellow to head us up." He paused to eat. "And how are you doing, Eric? The family is worried."

"Tell them not to; I feel just fine. I wish we got bigger meals and more sleep, but we're pounding away at Fritz, as I'm sure you've heard from BSM Jones."

He nodded and scooped up the last of his bedraggled corned

beef.

"I should write more letters, Jack, but there just isn't time. We've been building the best howitzer team in the Battery, maybe in the Brigade. We've got a great Lieutenant, too. He got wounded the other day, and he's still with us."

"And I hear you had a man killed last night in the 40th. I'm going to stay and conduct the burial tonight."

"You do that a lot, Jack? Burials?"

"Usually at night, poor fellows. You wouldn't believe the numbers I have committed to the arms of the Almighty in the last year. So many. As Dante says, I had not thought death had undone so many."

Well, this Dante fellow sure spoke the truth. So many dead.

"Now look, Eric," Jack motioned to the letter in my breast pocket, "don't get any ideas about Rene. You may not have much of a chance with her."

"Then why did she write to me?" I wasn't going to take this lying down, though I now understood why he'd avoided any emotion when he gave it to me.

"Oh, I agree, she might be a bit smitten. She did talk about you a lot when she and Leo drove me around these last three weeks. She asked me about our farm, and I confirmed what I gather you had told her. But Eric, this is England. She's wealthy, well connected, and you, well, you're like me, from a farm..."

"Yeah, and look what a poor farm boy turned cleric has achieved! You get to talk to generals and almost run a whole huge Chaplaincy service!"

"True. I was only saying what I did to save you disappointment."

"Maybe so. But Jack, I'm going to University when I go back." He looked sad. I knew what he was thinking: *IF you go back.*

"That's a laudable aim," he said. "I know Old Momma and Old Poppa would be pleased. And of course, if you get a degree, that would give you more chances in life..."

"What's so wrong with having hope?"

"Nothing." He paused. "How many lads have I buried with letters still in their pockets to loved ones? I end up sending them on. Must be just as hard on those at home as for their fellows who've gone marching into heaven, even with all the honours they've accumulated. I pity those young wives and sweethearts almost more than I do our boys at the Front. This time when I was in England, I made a point of visiting several families who'd lost loved ones."

I shook my head. "Amazing. A padre's work never ends?"

Later that night, in the mist and freezing cold, Jack stood in his cassock and surplice and read the service beside a muddy hole filled with water into which they carefully laid the body of our Gunner from the 40th Battery. They shovelled clay over him while the bugler blew that mournful Last Post. His buddies had scrounged a white cross to erect.

I was reminded of the cross Old Poppa and me had stuck up on my grandfather's grave in New Carlisle. There, under green lawns shaded by trees, my grandparents slept. But here, this Gunner would lie in bare, blasted earth under deafening bombardments while, as in the poem we all sort of knew by heart: "During the day the larks are still bravely singing, when they fly."

Back sipping an extra cup of coffee, Jack had managed to get from the Cook, he corrected me: "*And in the sky, the larks still bravely singing, fly,* yes. Major John McCrae is a fine doctor and a fine soldier. You know, he served with me in the Boer War? This time, we came over on the boat together."

"Did you now? You mean this summer?"

"When I enlisted in the autumn of 1914. He and I both joined up right away, and we've been in touch ever since. A good godly man, no doubt about it." Jack shook his head. "He's out there in the thick of it, at a field hospital. I just hope he survives.

"Oh, I see. Anyway, I think he's one terble poet," I said, our way of agreeing he was mighty fine.

Well, as soon as I was alone, I did read Rene's letter.

Dear Eric,

We have been driving Father John around and he suggested I write now so that he could bring the letter when he saw you, which he intends as soon as possible when he gets back to France.

Leo and I think of you often, Leo of course teasing me dreadfully.

Father John has told me all about your beautiful farm in Gaspe. I fancy it is rather like the great estates up in Scotland that we read about. He described the valley that you own, called The Hollow. Father John told me of the house he built that looks down into it, and your brother-in-law Joe's sawmill. It must be very beautiful.

I don't think any of us can imagine how hard it must be for you over there on the firing line. One day, when you get back home, you must tell me all about it. I think it is just as well that I don't know now, because I would worry far too much.

The news in The Times *seems good, but we do get the other side of it from some of the more indiscreet officers whom we drive, the best way to get news of the Front. What you are going through must be dreadful for even the bravest, which I know you are.*

I don't expect you to write back, because I know you will be occupied every minute of the day, fighting that dreadful Hun. Thank heaven you are ridding our civilised world of this menace. I'm so proud of you, doing your bit for the Empire.

Affectionately yours,
Rene

I wanted to grab a pen right away. But I remembered Jack's warning; he's older and smarter in things like this. As he said, what hope would there be? To really think about it, had I not better let things lie? He'd tell her I was okay when next he saw her. I shouldn't let myself get involved in dreams, false hopes, wild yearnings. And anyway, stay focussed on this everlasting fight, I decided. But not for much longer. Finally Haig called a halt to the offensive and on November the 24th, at long last, we marched away from the Somme, its scars now covered with the first snows.

CHAPTER SIXTEEN

Vimy Ridge

Berthonval Farm, March 25/26, 1917: Sections of the Batteries moved into their new positions behind the Third Canadian Division. The group now consists of the 30th, 31st, 35th, 40th Batteries, all of which have been made six- gun batteries.

April 1st: Batteries of the group continued heavy fire on enemy front and support line. There was considerable hostile fire in the neighbourhood of our Battery positions.

War Diaries: 8th Brigade CFA

"There's a big attack coming. I just know it."

We were sure preparing for a big assault, no question about

that. Vimy Ridge. We could see it ahead just north of Arras, a long, low slope up, stretching across five miles on a northwest southeast axis. Like a whale some said, not much of an escarpment compared to our Canadian mountains, but high enough, about two hundred feet above the surrounding plains, making it tough for our Infantry. Pretty impregnable. Harry argued with Jim last week that the French here had lost 150,000 men by March 1916 when the British took over. But Harry countered that the British had also tried to take it themselves, and failed. "Not too optimistic," I mumbled.

Edward glanced at me. "For sure. But I wish they'd tell us when!"

"Why are you guys so jumpy?" Now that dusk had settled, Sergeant McKillop was leaning against our dugout ladder, watching Edward and me going over the seams in our shirts, picking out lice. Earlier, Edward had received a great bundle of goodies from home that he had shared with his gun, as usual. McKillop, hoping to find some left-overs, had dropped in and was indeed finishing the only apple Edward had saved for himself.

I felt my temper rise. "I'm not jumpy! Like Edward, I just want to know when it's going to happen."

"Actually, who cares when?" Edward grumbled. " Just more of the same." We all three glanced up as another explosion shook the ground. The Sergeant was going back to the Wagon Lines tonight, having passed command of the gun over to me. I think everyone was relieved.

This big salient-wide barrage had begun almost two weeks ago and it just drove us crazy, firing shell after shell without stopping, such a head-splitting thunder with the five other howitzers now in line, and all the 18-pounders, three batteries of six guns in each. And that was just our 8th Brigade. Almost two weeks we'd gone at it. Yesterday was Palm Sunday and no one even noticed. No clergyman, just me remembering how we used to decorate our St. Paul's Church with spruce boughs down the aisle, because of course, no palms in Shigawake. Mind you, I said to myself, as a team we were pretty darned good, all awkwardness smoothed out. Same with the others. So I should feel satisfied.

"Seems like they got some of their bigger guns aimed at us." Edward was nervous, too. There is always an air of apprehension when you know something big is on the way.

"You've both been back at the Wagon Lines. That should put you in shape," McKillop said.

Indeed we had, but getting back here through that mud and rain last night had been hell. Dark and rainy, ammunition carried on mules. Lorries, limbers, transports, horses and men were crowding along that plank road in the dark — so many guns to resupply — no flashlights of course, though those muzzle flashes lighting the night sky made quite a spectacle. So often traffic blocked; you just waited in the cold rain. Hard to avoid being run over, because if you stepped off the boards, you sank right up to your knees in mud.

I felt my ears redden. "We are in shape. But I've never seen so many guns lined up this way before." By now, I was pretty experienced: nine months since I'd arrived, and another four months since I'd been in the firing line at the Somme. But the last thing I'd admit was that now again, I was darn scared.

"Look, Sarge," Edward said, "you never know what's going to happen with a big attack. Look at that first day of the Somme."

"You fellows weren't there," baited McKillop.

"Thank God!" I exclaimed. I looked down: another seam loaded with lice — or "chats" as we called them. Like most soldiers, we were chatting as often as we could. I scraped out the little grey devils with my fingernails, dipped my fingers into the can of creoline and flicked some along the seams. Such hell to wear a shirt after creoline before it dries. But then, we were going to sleep soon.

"No matter what happens in the assault, I never worry." McKillop finished his last gulp of that dreadful tea. He'd apparently gone through a tot of rum before he'd arrived, which made him gossipy.

"Just think how many got wiped out back then." Edward flicked a couple of grey-backed critters into the creoline can. "If the Hun does it again, no telling, he could just come sweeping down and finish us all off."

"You wouldn't believe the numbers of Canadian troops I've seen coming up to the Front." McKillop sounded impressed. "Have to be a pretty big Hun counter attack to get through that many."

"You can't be sure," I said. "Fritz can get up to some powerful tricks."

"It's the first time all four Canadian divisions are massed together on one front, isn't it?" Edward asked. "First time we're fighting as a complete corps."

McKillop nodded.

"But then," Ed went on, "how many of us might get wiped out by Boche machine guns, like at the Somme?"

"Surely the brass have learned something since then?" My little devils were really leaping away from that creoline, fleeing for their lives. Would I soon be doing the same?

"Don't be too sure of that," said McKillop. "Damned British generals, you can't tell them nothin'. Bunch of stiff-assed bastards if you ask me."

Edward looked up from his shirt. "But this time we're led by Canadians."

"You think General Sir Julian Byng is a Canadian?" the Sarge asked.

"Well no. But he's near enough like us. Regular fella," Edward affirmed. "Breaks the mould. And that General Arthur Currie, I'd stand by him any day."

"He's not hidebound, like those British," I agreed. "He's a real Canadian. But he's over running the First Division. Under Byng. Nothing to do with us right now."

"Oh God," McKillop said suddenly, "when the bloody hell are they going to get me to England. I've been a Sergeant far too long. It gets to a man, it really does. Why can't they put me up to Lieutenant?"

I wondered if Edward would have the courage to tell him he'd never make an officer. I certainly didn't.

He did, without thinking. "You'll never make it." I saw McKillop stiffen and turn to the ladder. Edward never noticed, focussed on his chats. Just in time, he said, "Though you never know... If you were British I'd say impossible. Tommies never get promoted — but sometimes we Canadians do."

"Well, my turn will come." With that, McKillop mounted a few steps, then turned. "Oh, I forgot to ask. How's your precious Katie doing?"

Had he heard Edward's dream love had fled?

Edward got up and I thought he'd smash the Sergeant in the face. Tall enough to do damage — and get himself court-martialled! I grabbed him by the hand and pulled him back down.

McKillop grinned smugly and disappeared up the dozen stairs.

"One thing I will say, Edward," I blurted out fast to change the subject, "this clay and chalk at Vimy Ridge sure makes for good bivouacs. You seen them tunnels up near the front?"

"No, I've not been."

"They're just everywhere, and big, too. Great rooms for hundreds of men. And damn long tunnels, right up to the front."

"What amazes me," Edward went on, absently, "are those

bloody long railways I've heard they built over the ground, for the ammunition!"

I agreed. "The amount of planning here, it's unbelievable."

Edward nodded, his mind far away.

I could see he was thinking about McKillop's remark. I thought it might do him good to talk about it again, so I gave him an opening. "Myself, I gave up long ago thinking about Raine. She's gonna be fine back there. I just made myself put her out of my mind."

He looked at the floor without saying anything, and then he picked up his shirt, got a couple more lice out and shook on some creoline before hanging it up.

We soon turned in. After I'd blown out the lantern, we lay on our bunks and I thought about the lights mounted in tunnels up front. If you looked out from your gun position here across the plain to Vimy Ridge two miles away, you couldn't see a soul — all underground: men, command posts, very deep. Just as well, with this harsh spring weather, still biting cold.

Well, no wonder I was a bit cheerless. We'd been at it since the Somme. Actually, we'd had some rest over Christmas and January, trucking up to Vandelicourt briefly, then stopping at Acq. But then, lots of action at Comblain l'Abbé (or Complain Abbey as we called it), more moving about at Bully Grenay in February, and finally plenty here, softening up the Ridge — in such nasty weather, coldest winter in a long time. Not so cold as Gaspe, of course, but there you had your snug house and winter woollies.

"I guess, Edward, I'd have to say, we're lucky to be alive. Damn lucky not to be missing a leg, or an arm."

"I know." He sighed. "I've got to stop thinking about Katie. I guess being in the biggest Canadian offensive ever should make me forget. Should even make me proud."

I yawned. "I just can't take that constant din, those everlasting blasts from all our guns."

"Someone said there are practically a thousand of our guns, all lined up. Think of the tons of shells we must be sending over."

We both lapsed into our own thoughts, and I started to drift off. But I couldn't get rid of a dark feeling about the coming assault. So much had been talked about all those waves of British troops slaughtered on the Somme. I mean, sixty thousand casualties the first day. Would that happen to us?

CHAPTER SEVENTEEN

Vimy Ridge

Berthonval Farm, April 5th, 1917: At 7:25 a.m. Vimy received the general bombardments ordered. At 8 a.m., a feint bombardment in accordance with Operation Order #9.

WAR DIARIES: 8TH BRIGADE CFA

We were sitting around finishing our suppers in our gun-pit out of the wind. Dazed, of course, after yet another long day of firing. So many batteries both near and far had rendered me deaf from the noise and unable to think. So far our own gun had fired several tons. The continual battering, the unholy din piercing our brains made them, like the omnipresent mud, into a mush of Momma's porridge, no sharp or clear ideas. I prayed for a bit of respite.

Perhaps that's why I looked up and saw riding towards us an officer on a horse. When he got to our Battery, Lieutenant Overstreet went forward to greet him, and I saw them point in our direction. The officer dismounted and came over. Who it could be?

"Is Corporal Alford anywhere about?" The nose of the tall, gaunt man forged forward like the prow of a ship, grey hair indicating he should be nowhere near all this activity. Was he one of our generals?

I leapt up and saluted. "Corporal Alford, at your service, sir."

The clergyman, for now I saw his collar and insignia of the Chaplaincy Corps, returned the salute and then came to join us. "Your brother told me you were in the 35th and asked me to look in on you." He held out his hand. "Canon Scott."

I had heard him spoken of before. In fact, we all had: a senior chaplain and bit of a legend, for he never shirked a battle. "Oh yes sir, it's an honour to meet you. I've heard about you visiting the Front."

"Yes sir," Harry added — trust him to add his two cents, "when most others stay back in Wagon Lines, or in the dressing stations and base hospitals, nowhere near any real danger."

Canon Scott looked pleased, offered some rather good cigarettes around and sat down. We exchanged news of my brother. "You know, he's now been appointed Head of the Chaplaincy Service? In February, finally. Pleased us all. Doing a good job of reorganization, too."

Well, that was news indeed! "Thank you sir!" I replied. "Old Poppa taught us to work hard."

"You know, Father John and I met in Quebec City before the Boer War. Kept in touch ever since. Our views may diverge from time to time, but we are united in devotion to Our Lord's commandments. Did you know that your brother's been mentioned in dispatches three times?"

"News to me, sir. But from what I hear, you've been doing terrific work, too." I hoped I was not being too impertinent.

"Well, in 1899 I preached to the First Canadian Contingent as they were leaving for South Africa. But I never got there. So now I'm doing my best to make up for that. Oh, have you heard the great good news?" I shook my head. "A couple of days ago, President Wilson spoke to a joint session of Congress, and the expectation is that America will declare war on Germany tomorrow, the sixth!" His bright blue eyes gleamed with delight.

"That is news indeed, sir!" He seemed to have an underlying warmth, but not enough to encourage me to unburden my soul to him. What I mainly saw was a resolute soldier, a patriotic preacher, here to do his duty no matter what.

"Here we are in Holy Week. I presume you had no Palm Sunday service here on the gun line?"

"No sir. In fact, I don't think any of us really had time. We just feed those shells into the gun, fire them off and reload, till we're dizzy."

He shook his head, not well pleased, and rose. "Well, Corporal, I'm glad to see you're still doing well. If I talk to your brother, I'll tell him I saw you, but of course he's back in England now, at Headquarters: Cavendish House I believe, in Mayfair." So that's why we hadn't seen him. I frowned, I couldn't keep up with his goings and comings. "Well, I trust you'll carry on this great fight for civilization with the requisite bravery you have displayed up to now."

I wonder how he knew what bravery I had displayed.

He must have seen my puzzled look, and went on, "In the Somme, where Father John told me you served, the Germans have withdrawn, just last month I believe." I raised my eyebrows.

"Oh yes, they fell back some distance and established another bulwark, the Hindenberg line. Thanks to the glorious courage and bravery of our troops."

"That's tremendously good, sir."

"I expect it has something to do with Asquith getting booted out. That Lloyd George, the new British prime minister, he's a real fighter. You know he's brought in conscription?"

"No, I didn't." Funny, usually Harry and Jim kept up on that sort of news. But then, neither of them seemed keen on Brits, or their officers.

"It'll be coming to Canada soon, I have no doubt. Too many shirkers back there, not stepping up to do their duty."

I hoped that wasn't true. But I wondered how the notion of conscription would sit with my province of Quebec.

"No shirkers around here, that's for sure," Red said.

"And if there are," Scott added, "a terrifying justice is speedily meted out!"

"How do you mean, sir?" I asked. "Executions?"

"Sure," Harry burst out. "Like Reynolds and Laliberté, last year?

"You'd think they'd want to keep that stuff secret," Jim blurted, "but they paraded the whole battalion to watch. Disgusting."

"Yeah, they want us all to know," Harry went on. "I heard some other fellow from Prince Edward Island was executed for desertion just last December."

"And what about Private Henry Kerr," Jim added, "shot on November 21, even after having actually braved the Somme. Can you imagine?"

Scott sighed, and sat down. "You know, boys, nothing brings home so forcefully the iron discipline of war as does the execution of men who desert. It was my painful duty on one occasion to watch a death sentence carried out."

We were all surprised. I leaned forward. Why didn't our

Canadian Parliament veto all that?

"I was asked to visit him. Poor fellow was sitting back in his chair with a dazed expression. He rose and shook hands and we began to talk. He was steeling himself, trying to fortify his mind at the great injustice."

"I bet he was!" Jim folded his long body into a protective corner.

"Well of course, I tried to get his sentence commuted. You see, the poor lad mentioned that on both sides of his family, there had been cases of mental weakness. I spent the whole of that night galloping hither and yon, even got to wake up the Commanding Officer at Divisional Headquarters, but to no avail." He shook his head.

"Well, when I got back with the dismal news," he continued, "I urged him to go out and meet death bravely."

I shook my head. "I'm shocked, sir."

"So am I," Harry added forcefully. "The Aussies don't execute fellows. Why can't we follow their example?"

"I sure agree," said Jim.

Scott shrugged. "But the failure of one man to do his duty might spoil the morale of his Platoon, and spread the contagion of fear from the Platoon to the Company and from the Company to the Battalion, endangering the fate of the whole line."

We listened, but not a man among us agreed. "Look what happened to Cecil," I burst out. "We had a man here, Canon, who was terrified. He refused to pass the ammunition. He refused orders. But we found him another position. He turned out to be fine."

"I agree," Edward sounded shocked himself. "He didn't 'spread contagion', poor Cecil. And no one else would, either!"

"No," Jim agreed. "That's just balderdash, sir, if you'll excuse my saying so."

Canon Scott looked uncomfortable.

"But do go on, Canon," I urged. "Did you stay with the man?"

"I did. When we finally went together, he was blindfolded and led to a box behind which a post had been driven into the ground. A drizzling rain was falling, so chilly and drear. He sat, hands handcuffed behind the post. A target was pinned to his shirt. And then... the firing squad did its work."

An awful silence fell on us. How we hated that whole idea! Especially as the poor fellow obviously needed care and attention, not execution. And so I said.

Scott shook his head. "Well, when we marched back and drew up in the courtyard, I saw how deeply all ranks felt the occasion. Nothing but the dire necessity of guarding the lives of the men in the front line from the panic and rout that might result through one individual's failure would compel such measures of punishment."

"Panic and rout," Harry snorted. "What rot!"

"I agree," Jim chimed in. "Begging your pardon, sir."

"And indeed you should, Gunner. For I myself felt the whole episode keenly. I have often seen what men suffer here at the Front, but nothing brought it home to me so deeply as did that lonely death on that hillside in the early morning."

I confess it sure made me wonder, how does the Good Lord countenance the killing of our own men? Lots going on here that made no sense, for sure.

"But I believe that among all the men found guilty of desertion from the Front, only a small percentage were executed." And then he got up, changing the subject. "You know the beastly Hun declared unrestricted submarine warfare in February. Already they've gone and sunk hospital ships in the Med. Hospital ships! The world needs be rid of such a people, and you fine soldiers are contributing." He paused before going off. "Shall I pronounce a blessing on you?"

"I'd be most grateful, sir. I'm sure we all would."

He stood and pronounced a short blessing and made the sign of the cross over our bowed heads.

He saluted again as we leapt to our feet, and off he went on his horse. A big weekend ahead for him, with Good Friday, Easter Sunday. But he had opened the debate. Debate? No one I knew took his side. We all agreed that shooting your own soldier just because the horrors of trench warfare proved too much — well, it was a travesty just too dreadful and not suited to our nation of pioneers.

CHAPTER EIGHTEEN

Vimy Ridge

April 9th. [Easter Monday, 1917]: At 5:30 a.m. our attack on Vimy Ridge commenced.

5:57 a.m. L.O. [Liaison Officer] 8th C.I.B. reports our Infantry passed Flapper Trench. Barrage very good. Their barrage very weak.

6:12 a.m. One of our planes seen. Weather conditions very bad for flying. Snowstorms and heavy weather soon turning into rain [and driving sleet].

6:21 a.m. 38th Battery reports 5.9s falling close to Battery position.

6:35 a.m. 35th Battery reports all okay now. No shrapnel close to Battery.

6:44 a.m. L.O. reports all Infantry into Swischen Stellung [trench]. 100 prisoners taken.

6:55 a.m. 30th Battery reports 100 prisoners coming over crater with their hands up.

7:04 a.m. O.C. 40th Battery reports situation good on our front. Our Infantry pass Swischen Stellung. It can be seen on the skyline.

7:22 a.m. 30th, 31st, 35th, 38th and 40th Batteries report all guns okay.

7:29 a.m. 1,000 prisoners going down in batches of 10 and 20.

7:55 a.m. About 45 prisoners passed.

8:08 a.m. 35th Battery has telephone line going forward with Lieutenant.

8:40 a.m. L.O. 8th C.I.B. report Infantry have stopped at Red Line.

9:10 a.m. 35th Battery report that their Lieutenant has a phone at the head of Frinz Arnodf Graben trench. He reports situation good. Enemy shelling fairly heavy with 77mms.

10:40 a.m. All of our Infantry have reached final objective and are digging in. As far as can be told the battalions are in touch with each other.

April 10th: Action on Petit Vimy. Ammo dumps set on fire

April 13th: Heavy Snowstorm. Batteries did very little firing owing to our Infantry patrols being out.

WAR DIARIES: 8TH BRIGADE CFA

It all began with a chance remark. Lieutenant Overstreet had come over to watch us cleaning the gun, which it sorely needed after all the firing these last three weeks. Even though it was snowing, we were doing a full workout. "Well, boys, we did it. We took the Ridge. Everyone else tried, but we did it. Four days later and I still can't get over it."

"Single-handedly," Edward remarked wryly.

"Well, not single-handedly. A thousand guns."

Jim straightened from his task of removing the safety from the breech. "You don't think maybe the Infantry had something to do with it?"

The boys were oiling or greasing all the moving gears and teeth. We had wrapped oily rags round our brush and punched it through the bore, pitch black from all the firing. Back and forth we pushed it until the rag came out clean — about thirty pull-throughs and twenty rags before the bore was nice and shiny again. Jim got busy disassembling and cleaning the breech. I enjoyed periods like this, when we got working together like normal human beings.

"Well, of course the Infantry did, but they sure as hell tried lots of times before." Overstreet was fairly bursting with excitement. "The French and then the British. What do you think made the difference? The accuracy of our guns!" The heavy snowstorm had not dampened his enthusiasm. He was sailing, as the metaphor goes, on clouds.

"You don't think the British or the French Artillery were accurate too?" asked Ed.

"Nowhere near as us," said Harry.

"You honestly think that rig that they made us fire our gun through, whatever you call it —" I started to say. I was prepared to believe him, but I wanted to challenge it. And I liked the snowfall. Reminded me of home.

"The Boulangé electromechanical chronograph?" asked Harry. Trust him to know the correct name.

"I remember," echoed Jim, gesticulating with his stick-like fingers. "We had to fire through two electrically charged wire screens, and somehow they could tell how far the shell would go."

"That measures muzzle velocity," explained Harry. "They never did that before."

"No sir," Overstreet said. "Vimy was the most accurate barrage ever. Having every gun's actual muzzle velocity, not just estimated from a bunch of tables, meant we could fire a barrage so accurately that our infantry could really hug it. That paved their way up the Ridge. And Andy even insisted on correcting for weather conditions. He also brought in the chronograph, along with some other great ideas."

"Oh so now Colonel McNaughton is Andy?" Red snorted.

"Well, he went to my old school: he was known as Andy then."

"What school was that?" I asked.

"Bishop's."

"Oh, that's where I was heading when they got me to enlist. My brother Jack went there."

"No no, not Bishop's University," Overstreet said, "I'm talking about Bishop's College School. After that, he took engineering at McGill. Studied under Rutherford, too."

Now who was Rutherford, I wondered. Obviously someone important.

"Just a minute," Jim said. "I have an elder brother in the Infantry. He got shot up three days ago in that assault. He's going to be okay, but I don't like anyone saying that the Artillery did more than the Infantry."

"I agree," echoed Ed. "One of my brothers was an officer in the assault, too. He got through it, thank God."

"A lot of them got through it," said Harry, "thanks to us. Thanks to the accuracy of our guns, don't you understand?"

I remembered that early in the mornings we had seen parties of German prisoners being brought back. Not warlike, for sure, them fellas, really beaten down, usually half a dozen or even more, guarded by only a couple of Infantrymen. I waved occasionally as they passed — well, why not? Poor buggers, they seemed just like us, only on the wrong side. Wish I could speak German, but no one on our gun knew how, though Jim claimed a smattering. But he hated them and wouldn't even lift his eyes as they straggled past.

"Just because you stick up some screening to measure our muzzle velocity," interrupted Jim again, "I agree no one's done it before, but you mean to tell me —"

"Hold on," Overstreet said, "That was just a small part of it. First of all, 'Lieutenant-Colonel Andrew McNaughton' brought a bunch of scientists turned soldiers here and they set up a flash-spotting unit."

"A what?" I asked.

"Flash-spotters: they used transits like surveyors," he gestured to illustrate, "so they could get good bearings on the flashes of enemy guns."

"So geometry helped us find enemy guns?"

"Yes indeed. See, when you observe a particular gun flash —"

"A lot of guns, you can't see the flash," Harry objected.

"Well, I'm not talking about poor light conditions!" Overstreet hated being interrupted. He went on quickly, "One observer will see a flash and take a bearing. He reports it to his command post by phone, because that by itself is no use."

"Why not?"

"You need at least two angles, right?" Harry asked.

"Right. Three is best," the Lieutenant affirmed. "So the command post tells the others roughly where the flash should be visible. They all push a button on the next flash, and that actually makes lights go on in the command post. When all lights go up at the same time, the officer knows the posts are seeing the same flash. Then he plots it on a map, and where the lines meet is exactly where that gun is!"

"And you phone that back to HQ?" Red asked.

"No no, not HQ, that's the whole point — they have this new counter-battery section that Andy set up. They do the calculating, and stick the enemy's positions on a map."

"And then we smash 'em?" I asked.

"Yep. They send the coordinates to the heavy guns, too."

"Yeah, but you just wait for the next battle," Jim said. "The Germans'll catch on and he'll move his guns every night."

"Okay, if he figures out his batteries are being hit with amazing accuracy," Overstreet went on, "but don't forget those gun-pits, dug deep for sure, with sandbags and roofing, they'll not be jumping for joy to move them." We could see that. "So BAM! We keep hitting them, and wipe them out."

"You'd wonder why the British never did that before," Harry said. "Seems obvious."

"So you think that a few surveying instruments allowed us to take the Ridge?" Edward was getting angry, working his steel wool at any corrosion and oiling the area afterwards. "No sir! It was our Infantry slogging through that mud, rolling up that hill..."

"Wait, Ed," Dick protested, "don't forget sound waves got measured, too. With delicate oscillographs and microphones..."

We all looked at each other "What oscillographs?" I asked.

"When a forward listening post hears an enemy gun, a button is pushed." Dick was in his element explaining all this. "And then behind the lines, microphones are activated and they print the stuff out on graphs. The first proper sound ranging section in the whole Imperial army — all thanks to Andy."

"I hear the British officers laughed him to scorn," Harry said.

"Damn right they should," said Jim. "Think you can win a battle with a bunch of microphones?"

"Listen, Andy's scientists can calculate a position within

twenty-five yards of any gun. With our HE, that's close enough. We were firing right on target."

"So that's how we shut down so many batteries?" I asked.

"Don't you think those thousand guns blasting away made the difference?" threw in Jim. "We figured our one gun alone sent over fifty tons of shells."

"We had lots of guns blasting away at the Somme, but it didn't seem to help," argued Harry. "Give up Jim, it was our accuracy that won the day."

"And this time," Dick's patience was running out, "we silenced around eighty percent of the German guns facing us. The best estimate for the Somme was around a third — the reason why this time our infantry didn't suffer nearly as much."

That all made sense, for sure.

"Plus, our new 106 fuzes could cut those wire entanglements that often stop our Infantry."

"Yes, but our Infantry took the Ridge," snapped Edward, still annoyed. "Maybe we helped, maybe we didn't, but they're the ones who slogged up that hill, through the driving sleet —"

"Edward's right. Think of all the planning they got beforehand." I could see Jim was getting convinced. "I heard General Byng made all units practise on fields with marked positions using different coloured ribbons and flags. They trained and trained."

"Aye, that they did," added Edward. "And you know what else my brother told me? In the British Army, only officers got maps so Other Ranks often got lost. But Byng ordered tons of maps so that every soldier knew exactly what he was doing and where he was headed. Never happened before, my brother told me. He thinks Byng is a genius — flying in the face of the High Command, he got it done, with his commanders of course. And the result? We took the Ridge."

"Well, it just feels good to me," I said, "being in a major assault that we won."

"Amen to that," said Dick Overstreet, as he saw Edward re-assembling the breech. "Well, boys, looks like you got your gun back in shape."

"Shouldn't we be rolling up ahead?" Jim asked. "Now that we've taken the Ridge."

Overstreet nodded. "Headquarters would like that. But the ground is just impassable."

"Doesn't bother me being stuck here," Red commented. "No nicer dugout; that chalk makes good walls. Once we get the water pumped out."

Dick left and I checked the gun. Yes, good shape for the next barrage. Well, time for a well-deserved rest, even if only for half an hour. I led the way, and we trooped off to our hole in the ground. Home sweet home!

CHAPTER NINETEEN

Hill 70

July 25th, 1917. 10 p.m. Brigade headquarters and batteries withdrew from fighting positions [at Petit Vimy] and proceeded to Wagon Lines near Berthonval Farm and the next day on to Noeuz les Mines [facing Hill 70].
Aug 8th: We are expecting operations to come off any day. We do a little night firing, principally with the 35th Battery. At night the enemy shells our roads and approaches to our positions.
Aug 10th: A few more shells than usual falling near our batteries. A goodly lot of gas shells sprinkled in tonight, giving us quite a test. Every precaution taken by all concerned.

WAR DIARIES: 10TH BRIGADE CFA

Dawn was just breaking and I found myself already awake, even though being back at the Wagon Lines I could sleep as long as I wanted. I heard a commotion in the distance. What was it?

Screaming and shouting? Men in pain? From what? I swung out of my cot. Another Coverer, Corporal Phil Hayes who'd become a friend, was fast asleep, mouth open, lean cheekbones smooth like an Indian's, tuft of jet black hair protruding over his greatcoat.

I tugged on my boots, wound my puttees, put on my tunic and belt and crawled out. In the light rain, I listened again. That noise, like men in pain, came from the direction of the gun line. I headed over to the roadway. Would they need help? Had there been some special heavy bombardment? The batteries had been ordered not to do much firing, and I thought that Heinie had not found our positions. So what could it be?

I waited anxiously as the noise approached. We had been fighting for weeks around Petit Vimy when our orders had come to move. After Vimy Ridge in May, my 35th Battery had been switched from the 8th to the 10th Brigade. We had marched out in a loop westward around the big mining town of Lens (which the British were poised to attack) and on to the north to face Hill 70.

The Canadian Corps had been ordered to attack Lens — as the Germans obviously anticipated. But our new Corps commander, General Currie, had decided instead to try for Hill 70 (about two hundred feet high) overlooking the town, a harder obstacle to conquer, but one that could give the element of surprise. Once we took Hill 70, the enemy would counter attack again and again, and that would allow us to wage a battle of attrition from above, wearing Fritz down, so that Lens could more easily be taken by the British later.

The sorry procession grew louder and then hove into sight: some men draped over empty ammunition limbers, three Drivers leading their horses and others pushing the stretcher carts with large wheels to traverse such dreadfully pitted ground. As I ran across, one lad was screaming, "Shoot me, shoot me, please, I can't stand it."

Where the hell was the Brigade MO? We hurried the soldier to the Aid Post and helped others from the limbers: some blinded. I guided another to the empty cots. The Drivers were jumpy, having listened to the moaning and crying all the way from the firing line, a mile or two.

One of these I knew, Frederick, who looked at me and shook his head. A grizzled older soldier about forty, he had been a farmer. "I never seen anything like it," he said. "Gas attack."

So, that was what had happened! I knew the dirty Boche had used gas in Ypres a couple of years ago. These attacks had become more and more frequent, and in fact we ourselves used gas now, too. But I hadn't seen the horrifying consequences up close.

The Medical Sergeant took charge immediately and told us he'd sent for ambulances. The plank road was often subject to shelling, being easily seen by aircraft and balloons, so our Wagon Lines had been situated a couple of hundred yards away.

Before long, the Brigade Medical Officer arrived and went right to work. I wasn't used to hearing screams. Back at the firing line, apart from when we had misfires or deaths from high explosives, we weren't subjected to that continual mutilation suffered by the Infantry every time they went into, or repulsed, an attack.

I felt helpless. I didn't know what to do. The blinded fellow I'd helped bore his pain stoically but now he started to mumble. "We didn't know it was a gas attack. Our orders were to keep firing and keep firing we did. Somebody smelled garlic but we never thought much about it, so we kept going. It was dark, so you didn't see gas clouds or anything. But then, one fellow started to sneeze and cough, and the cry went up: "Gas gas gas!" By then, the damage was done. I got out my gas mask and kept loading, but I'd taken out my eye pieces — you know they steam up, and you can't set a damn fuze or anything. So on I went handing up the shells, but my eyes started to hurt something terrible."

Oh my Lord, I thought, this poor guy did his duty and now he's blind.

"Corporal," the MO cried, "over here, please."

I left the blinded Gunner as another soldier came round to dole out tots of rum, our only painkiller at the moment. I went over to the MO who was working on the lad crying out in pain. "I've got to cut his clothes off. Hold his legs, please, he keeps kicking."

He was horribly burned on his face and over the rest of his skin. The MO was trying to remove clothing stuck to his flesh. "Mustard gas," he murmured. "Terrible stuff."

The kid kept screaming and crying and then, mercifully, passed out. I released his legs.

Some twenty minutes later, another soldier ran in from the direction of the plank road. "We've got two ambulances — take everyone over."

At once we began to shift the wounded. I went first to the young lad who'd passed out on his cot, but the MO stopped me. "No point. Dead by nightfall." When he saw the look on my face, he went on, "Two ambulances, only room for the ones they can save. These two here, we'll leave and try to make them comfortable."

I stood for a moment, dazed. So that was it for those two. No hope?

The next soldier had burns on his face and throat and was gasping horribly. "I can't breathe, I can't breathe." He kept choking and vomiting. I gestured towards him but the MO shook his head. Leave him, too.

So I went to the blinded fellow, got him up, and led another by the hand. With the dawn lifting, we stumbled a good way across to the plank road. What a journey! How brave was my companion! In the end, we got everyone safely into the ambulances for the bumpy drive back to the Main Dressing Station, four miles at least. But good care there, I presumed, before they'd be sent on to the Base Hospital.

With a couple of others I walked back to the Wagon Lines where that poor burned fellow was screaming again. Wouldn't it be kinder to put him out of his misery, as he begged?

I said as much to the MO and he nodded. "But it's not allowed. We can only make him comfortable till he goes. He and the other chap. I don't know how they let themselves get so burned."

Well, I knew. Doing their duty.

Phil Hayes came over. "I was talking to a couple of them, sir. You see, it was so hot out there, they'd taken their shirts off. When the shout came: gas! They put on their masks but not their shirts until too late."

The MO nodded. "That's what's so beastly about this new mustard gas. You can't see it. Then it kills your nerve cells so you don't feel what's happening until too late. Imagine what their lungs look like! No wonder they vomit up their burned insides."

Oh my God! What on earth had we humans devised? I couldn't believe my ears.

***

Later the bugler announced lunch, and Phil and me lined up. I saw a new face coming past to eat, so I motioned to Phil and we followed; I like being neighbourly and it's always good to make new fellows welcome. Short and squat, with a square black moustache, his name turned out to be Charles, Sergeant Peter Charles.

"Well, Sergeant," I asked, "are you going to join us in the Howitzers?"

He shook his head. "I'm not with any Battery. I'm with Brigade."

"So what are you doing here?"

He looked at us with wary eyes.

What is it with some fellas? Don't they trust you?

"I've been assigned the 10th Brigade," he said.

"Don't tell me you're taking over from one of our Sergeants, like Quinn McKillop?"

"I'm not taking over from anybody."

Snooty sort, I decided. And not very forthcoming. So we ate in silence, me and Phil exchanging a couple of looks, until I guess Sergeant Charles felt more comfortable. "I've just attended the new Canadian gas training in an old mining building in northern France," he said. "Their first course, beginning of August."

"A gas school?" I frowned. "What are they teaching, for heaven's sake?"

"Yeah, we all know how to avoid the damn stuff," Phil chimed in.

The Sergeant looked askance at Phil. "Chlorine? Phosgene, diphosgene, mustard? And that lacrimatory stuff so you sneeze and cry? You know it all, do you?" Phil readily backed down.

I thought a bit. "That General Currie, he sure must be smart. They're using gas, we're using gas, he must think we should know something about it."

Phil sighed. "Don't we have enough to do just firing shells?"

"I didn't ask to go to the school: I was sent. But let me tell you, Corporal, I'm damned glad. Though to my way of thinking, I got handed the worst job in the Brigade, even though it'll help save lives." He shook his head. "When any bombardment starts, we're the fellas to stay in the open because we're trained to know which shells are gas."

"We can always tell a gas shell," Phil insisted. "The way it lands. You hear a sort of a phut, instead of a bloody great explosion."

The Sergeant shrugged. "But now they're sending gas in with

the high explosives. Bloody hard to tell. Phosgene usually comes that way, so it sounds no different when it lands. But our casualties should lessen once us graduates are out working."

Oh my God, I thought. "And what's the difference between phosgene and mustard?"

"Phosgene attacks the ability of your blood to carry oxygen. Mainly colourless, and often takes up to forty-eight hours to show symptoms. Then..." he paused, "you suffocate and die."

How awful! I shook my head. "So how can we tell?"

He shrugged. "Smells like new mown hay, that's the problem... not unpleasant, like mustard or chlorine. That's why we've been trained," the Sarge explained. "Shout: "Gas, gas, gas," and ring a bell or bang away on some cartridge case, to let everyone know."

"Didn't they try chlorine first at Wipers Two?" Phil wondered.

Charles nodded. "But that damn Fritz keeps getting better and better ideas." He snorted. "Invention of the devil, if you ask me. Couldn't believe my ears when I heard it all."

Well, at least he's opening up, which is all to the good. "They don't use chlorine any more?"

"Not so much. We do. But they use mainly mustard, and we use mainly phosgene."

"Worse and worse," muttered Phil.

"You don't know how much worse," the Sergeant went on. "They mix 'em up. And that's what we're doing, too. Listen to this! They send over lacrimatory gas to make you cry, so when your eyes hurt like hell and you can't see, you vomit. When you vomit in your gas mask, you tear it off, and then comes the phosgene. That kills you."

"My God, don't take off your gas mask, even if you're sick in it?" I asked

"Well, you can of course," he said. "If you want to end up dead."

A nice set of alternatives, I thought to myself. Phil blanched and mumbled, "I'm not too sure I want to go back to the gun line tonight." Well, gas had been used before, but this brought it home all the more.

The Sergeant eyed him. "Well, you can always face a court-martial, I suppose. They don't execute everyone, I've heard. Better think up some damned good excuse, though. Your chances of getting away with it are almost nil."

"Look Phil," I added quickly, "we may be okay; they haven't found our position yet. They may not send over any gas shells. If they do, we'll just put on our masks. So don't worry." But in fact, myself, I wasn't looking forward to going up there tonight. I just prayed there'd be no more gas.

***

We set off that night for the firing line with our ammunition strapped to mules, the road being impassable for limbers. The Sergeant walked; we had lost quite a few horses, but I was riding my horse, Barry. The track curved a lot to throw Heinie off target. But before long, didn't they start a counter-battery? I could tell by where the shells were striking, none of them too close, that this wasn't directed at the plank road but formed a general harassment to make sure we weren't bringing up ammunition.

We were still a good way from the firing lines when we heard the terrible words shouted: "Gas, gas, gas!"

In a flash, we all put on our respirators and closed up our shirt buttons; I even put on gloves. But Barry... I dismounted and tried to rig up some sort of nosebag. Quickly I peed into a cloth and put it around — not much good, I knew, but what else to do? Turn and run? Out of the question.

Soon, though I kept stroking Barry, he started kicking his heels and I couldn't hold him. He broke away, galloping on ahead with a terrified whinny. The others started screaming and rolling their heads, snorting, such a frightful noise as ever I've heard. The other Drivers kept pulling at them to get the ammunition forward. A couple of mules went galloping ahead only to fall over sideways, foaming — their agonies were just awful to hear. I tried to run after Barry, but there wasn't enough oxygen coming in through the mask to let me go fast enough. I lost him in the darkness.

All dozen animals ended up dying in terrible contortions, kicking legs in the air and emitting those awful cries, heaving, screaming. By the time I reached Barry in a crater, mercifully he was already gone. My flashlight revealed the mud around him chewed up by his thrashing. I stood there, absolutely broken. How could we do this to our horses? Why had I ridden him up this time? Mightn't I have known there'd be another instance of gas? No good chastising myself, though, I had a job, up ahead. But being from a farm, I hated all this. I just never wanted to go through it again. Couldn't they just find some way to protect our animals?

And as I found out later, no. Eventually, they did try nosebag masks, but then, of course, the horses and mules wouldn't travel with these because it made it so hard to breathe. Effective way to shut down all transport, I'll tell you. What a day to go through! When I got to the firing line, I felt a changed man.

CHAPTER TWENTY

Hill 70

August 13th, 1917: 35th Battery fired harassing fire during morning and late afternoon.

14th: Busy day preparing for attack tomorrow.

WAR DIARIES, 10TH BRIGADE CFA

Today, I got up well before the cook's breakfast call and Zero Hour. My sleep, although long enough, had been uneasy. I walked over to the gun using my flashlight. I felt both excited and anxious. This was our first big battle since Vimy Ridge four months ago. Yes, we had taken the Ridge, and yes, our Battery had been exceptional and so remarked on by all levels of command. But still, in war, you just never know.

Maybe I felt jittery because the incessant noise of a major assault wreaked havoc on us all. This was General Currie's first big fight as our new Corps Commander. But more likely, the experience of seeing all that horrible pain from enemy gas — well, that too had unsettled me. Taking time in peace and quiet to go over our great gun might steady my nerves. I stepped down into the pit, rested against the sandbags, and breathed deeply as I stared at our magnificent weapon, and smelled the grease and oil. Was there anything we had forgotten?

Yesterday, our preparations had been extra careful. In a way, I was pleased that I would be running the gun. Our Sergeant had been seconded to another howitzer whose NCO had come down with one of the many diseases affecting everyone — germs from the rotting corpses, the filth everywhere, and the rats that never left us alone. You just could not get used to the little bastards, squeaking and scrambling, attacking every food parcel, even diving in coat pockets hung on pegs; you'd think they'd have enough to eat with all the corpses around. But no, they were into everything.

What a mighty gun! No wonder it took five of us to operate it. How many tons of explosive had this one gun thrown at the Germans! I suppose I should be proud of that. Well, I'd been on the front line for over a year, and in spite of the noise, explosions, danger, I never stopped marvelling at its power.

I moved off the sandbags to check the ammunition stacked on shelves at the rear. As I shone my flashlight, I stopped.

Gas shells.

Our very own phosgene rounds. Now, we had fired gas shells before, no doubt about it, but I hadn't really absorbed the idea. After that experience back at the Wagon Lines, and then, watching what happened to Barry, this really hit home. I was going to fire a gun that was going to do to the enemy what I had seen done to us.

Well, it was only right in one way. But for some reason now, and I don't know what possessed me, I just couldn't stomach it. In the distance, I heard the call for breakfast. But I didn't go — I just stood looking at all the gas shells. Oh yes, lots of high explosive, some shrapnel, but those gas shells... did I really want to blast them off towards the enemy lines?

From what I'd seen, these devilish Boche, as the preachers call them, these hounds from Hell, these debauched monsters — well, I'd looked in their faces, especially at Vimy, as they trudged past us. No different than us — just doing their jobs. I know we're not supposed to think that way, but your eyes don't lie. These young kids were no different. Confused as hell, most of them. Terrified. "Kamarad! Kamarad!" they'd call. They'd offer us watches, anything to save their lives. Wouldn't I have done the same? I bet some of them even came from farms, though how could you tell?

Then for us to scorch their human bodies with the searing white hot pain of gas? Have them die a slow choking death over days, unable to breathe? My thoughts were whirling. What was my mind doing to me? I could see that in my excitement for the coming attack, another voice was saying, No! You cannot do this. You've got to draw the line somewhere. You've got to stop.

I shook my head. What was I doing? Refusing to fight? Shirking my command? Just step up out of the gun-pit and start walking towards the Wagon Lines?

Without prompting from my brain, I did just that — step out. In the distance, I heard our boys chatting as they lined up for breakfast. Was I heading for them? No. My body seemed to be taking me back — away from the firing line. I rounded the gun-pit, but before heading off, I paused. Something allowed me to sink down. With my back to the sandbags, I had to think this over.

The one thing sure in my mind: I'd be a deserter, likely lined up and shot. But, I told myself, surely some stuff I should not bring myself to do? Wasn't it about time to make my own statement? I pressed my head down on bent knees, huddled up as I remembered Cecil had been. I didn't know what was happening to my brain: revolt! Be a man, say No More To This War! And just walk out of here.

On the other hand, another voice said, my team needs me, so stand by them.

I stayed that way without moving for what seemed an age, though maybe only a few minutes, until I heard the men coming back, talking and laughing among themselves, pretty excited on this morning before the big attack on Hill 70. And then they went kind of quiet. Because they couldn't see me? Where was their Corporal? What had happened?

I heard footsteps and a beam of flashlight caught me. I looked up. Edward.

He stood looking at me for a time, and then came and sat. We said nothing for the longest while. Then he spoke. "Zero hour in about eight minutes, Eric." Kindly, as a simple reminder.

"I can't. I can't do it. I just can't send over gas shells." I shook my head dumbly.

To no one else would I have admitted that. I rejected the impulse to jump up and run. I liked Edward: he had a warmth, a steadiness, that I needed.

"You saw those fellows wounded by chlorine a couple of days ago?"

I nodded.

"Pretty terrible," he agreed.

We didn't have to do a lot of talking. What could he say? Good going, Eric, just leave and we'll follow. That wouldn't happen, I knew. Or would he say, More power to you, Eric, we're not following, but you do what you have to do?

But he said neither.

"Eric, you must have seen fellows with their stomachs ripped out?"

I nodded.

"You must have seen fellows with an arm hanging by a tendon. Or fellows bleeding from stumps of legs?"

"Of course."

"Now, are you trying to tell me that although we're doing that every day, yes, tearing Germans to pieces with our HE, that's okay? But putting over gas is completely different?"

Well, no, I had to agree, there wasn't a lot of difference. For the first time, I lifted my head and turned to look at him.

"Eric, I know what you're going through. I went through it myself after Vimy. I wanted to quit this whole business. Get shot as a deserter, who knows? I had seen too many guys on both sides, ordinary people like you and me, their lives ruined, even if they did stay alive. Imagine surviving with half a face shot away, or no right arm or one leg. Eric, this is a war that we've got to win."

I nodded.

"And you've got to help us. We're a team. If we start thinking about the effects of our barrages, we'll never do anything. We've got to keep going, all of us, until this war finally ends." He paused, then added, "Think how many of our own infantry will get slaughtered if we don't cover them, if we don't silence those Fritz machine guns. Up ahead, our Canadian boys need us. And we have to stick by them."

He stayed beside me as the seconds ticked on to Zero hour. Slowly his words sunk in.

I got up. "Thanks, Edward." We both went around the gun-pit. The men were standing, looking at me, uncertain.

"Well, two minutes to Zero," I said brightly. They looked at me. "Number Two gun, Battery action, take posts!" Funny, giving that familiar order made me feel a lot better. Their muted cheer greeted my remark. We sprung into position for the great attack.

Aug 15th, 1917: 4:25 a.m. the attack on Hill 70 was begun. We are covering the 15th Brigade on the extreme left of the attack. Lieutenant Youell F.O.O. [Forward Observation Officer] of the 35th Battery goes forward with the attack.

6 a.m. F.O.O. of the 35th Battery telephones in that he is sitting in the final objective. The Boche lose no time in beginning counter attacks which go on all day until 11 p.m. From Zero hour our batteries fired without cessation for 12 hours 7 minutes, when there was a lull. Ammunition began to run short in the afternoon so it was brought up on the trot in full view of the enemy, who diverted some fire to stop them without success.

Aug 16th: The enemy made repeated counter attacks on our new front line. Over 30,000 rounds of ammunition have been spent these last two days.

WAR DIARIES: 10TH BATTALION

What long days! The first chance to catch our breath was when we lined up to grab a bite of supper. I couldn't believe the number of shells we poured over the enemy: high explosive, shrapnel, even phosgene, we threw the works at them. But we'd achieved another success. Just like Vimy Ridge. Quicker, this time, getting to the objectives. But afterwards, an awful lot of counter attacks had battered away at us. And of course, in our Battery by now we were all completely deaf.

Being deafened after a day's shooting was nothing new, but this was the worst yet. I feared this time we would just not recover. We spoke to each other only in sign language. Over the months we had become pretty good at expressing our ideas through our hands. You weren't allowed to plug your ears. And you know? It was also against military law to cover your ears with your hands! Supposedly, you wouldn't hear commands if you did. Anyway, such a useless regulation because you had no time, shot following shot. And all the other howitzers and 18-pounders around were blasting, too. It was just an absolutely thunderously thick din, no matter what you did.

And then, before we got to our supper rations, back we went for another SOS and twenty minutes more of hard firing. But we knew we were helping our boys hold Hill 70.

Late in the day, I thought surely to God we'd get time for tea with a bit of bread and jam; I'd gotten to like one called "Ticklers". We were all so exhausted, we could hardly move. I don't know how we did it, lifting those 35-pound shells all day long. We changed positions to share the work; I even loaded for a while. Sure over the last year we'd gotten used to it but all the same, eighteen hours hard at it? Enough to break even the hardest man.

I wiped the blood from my nose, bleeding from the constant concussion. My head was spinning, I was completely deaf, utterly worn out, and I just sat staring off in the distance towards Hill 70, our target. Just a bald tuft, hardly a hill by Canadian standards. And now that I looked, I could see smashed cottages sprawled up the hillside: those half-cellars and broken stone walkways had given lots of cover to the Germans counter attacking, for sure.

Everything was so muffled, even in this enforced silence. I sipped my tea and absently studied the clouds of gas hovering above the hill like the mist that used to drift about the wharf or back in the Hollow early in the morning. My God, how far away was all that? But where was I now? Everything seemed so unreal, in this world without sound.

And then, like a wind-stripped spruce, Jim bent and tapped me. I glanced up. He wore an odd look, and motioned. I turned back to the hill. Then I got up.

The setting sun had illuminated and coloured some weird configurations of gas or cloud, so that they seemed to glow. Was that a cross I saw? I felt another tap. Jim held out his diary. We all communicated by written words in times like this. I looked at the diary. "Angel" it said. I looked back again at the hill. Some of us had previously heard talk of another vision, the Angel of Mons.

Yes, there did seem to be a white eminence. Was it not standing tall? And was that a cross I saw? In the right hand of what looked like a man, or rather, as he said, an angel? Some sort of being...

A couple of other Gunners had stopped and stood, holding mugs of tea, also peering hard. Had they seen it, too? Edward came over and held out his diary. I looked down. "St. George" was written plainly. I looked back. Yes, that's what I saw. And the more we all looked, the clearer it seemed: the patron saint of England. Riding on a charger? No, too fanciful. A heavenly figure astride the hill, cross in one hand, and what was that? A sword in the other? We all stood staring for several long minutes. Then, slowly, the wind wafted it away.

I looked down. In this dense, thudding silence, I knew that we had all been given some sort of gift. Perhaps a vision of victory? For the time being, no one would ever know. I had seen something, I was sure. Victory in this war, oh yes. But would I live to see that?

CHAPTER TWENTY-ONE

Gauchin-Legal, Oct 10-12: In rest billets.

WAR DIARIES: 10TH BRIGADE CFA

"Your brother? When did you hear, Edward?"

"BSM Jones called me into his office this afternoon. He'd just heard it himself. During an attack, he said. Wounded. And then, last week..." Edward sat, slumped on his cot. "Poor Mum. She begged us both not to go. And now..."

"I'm awfully sorry, Edward." What else could I say? His only brother. He had often spoken of him with such affection, and even, yes, admiration. I didn't know his mother, but now, she only had one son alive.

"I feel like going out and getting drunk!"

I didn't blame him in the least. Luckily we were in billets well back of the lines, outside a small town called Gauchin-Legal, awaiting the next fight.

Those soldiers who survived, every year and a half or so, got a longer leave to go to Paris or London, but the officers got more. During our respite behind the lines, with discipline somewhat relaxed, we got to bathe, sleep in, draw new kit or mend our old, see properly to the horses and mules, play some sports, and try to rid our minds of the horrible images, before being thrown back to face them once more. In the summer, there'd even been a Divisional Sports Day, in which Edward had distinguished himself. And now...

"Look, I heard some fellows went to an *estaminet* in the little farming village a mile away," I suggested. "Pretty awful, they said, but lots of beer and wine. Want to try it?" I thought I should support him in his expressed desire, even though I wasn't much on getting drunk myself.

Edward looked up at me and nodded. "Let's have a celebration. My treat." That's how Edward was: wanting everyone to be happy. Warmed my heart.

Well, I got permission and before dark, off went our gun, all five of us, down a track into the village to seek out this *estaminet*. In a small village square surrounded by ruined houses, a sign: "Beer and Wine, *Bière et Vin*" beckoned us towards a nondescript farmhouse. We went in.

More or less what I'd been led to expect: a fairly forlorn room, four long wooden tables and benches with clusters of Gunners and Other Ranks. The largely barren walls boasted shelves containing glasses and a couple of pasted-up pictures.

Once inside the door we were pounced on by the robust French owner who looked capable of controlling any drunken altercation that arose, a frequent happening in these establishments. With what might be interpreted as a smile, she ushered us to a table near the open fireplace. In it burned the smallest logs I've ever seen, not near enough to liven up the place. Harry and Jim ordered beer, but Red and Edward and I split a bottle of wine at two francs a bottle. A solemn toast was offered to his brother, who gave his life for our cause.

I had been worried about Harry and Jim coming along —

would their squabbling ruin the party? — but no worries. Jim took a big long slug and rose. "Here's to your brother, Ed," he said soulfully. "I've asked myself over and over, what kind of God or Providence would stand idly by and allow all this to happen? How in the name of heaven could all this be part of a grander scheme, like the preachers say? How does good ever come from all this senseless and violent destruction?"

Who could not agree with that, but it took us in a philosophical direction that precluded any jolly celebration.

"Let's not dwell on my brother," Edward said.

"Yes," I begged, "we're supposed to be here having a bit of a party tonight. Let Edward forget his troubles. We don't get to party often!" In the back of my mind, I still harboured inhibitions from Momma and the family, and indeed from most of us in Shigawake who didn't hold with going to bars. English pubs, though, with their cheerfulness and conviviality, I did like. But this just looked like a place to get drunk in — which was, of course, Edward's avowed aim.

We fell to discussing the concert we'd seen soon after we had arrived at our rest stop. A British regiment was putting on a show, and our Commanding Officer had arranged for us to be ferried over to watch it. We plunged into a more cheerful discussion on the good points of that fairly professional review with its many and varied offerings, and soon finished our beer and wine, so Ed ordered more.

"That there men's chorus was pretty damn good, I thought," spluttered Red. "They sang the best." Red, stalwart, afraid of nothing, was a soldier we all respected. He looked the part too, square jaw, handsome profile, every inch a hero, though his red hair and eyebrows were pretty distinctive.

"That female impersonator — by golly, I thought she was just something!" Harry chirped up. "What about you, Jim?"

"I dunno, Harry, I never was much taken with fake women," mumbled Jim, eyeing the waitress who had brought us our drinks — well, I say waitress, but really a harassed French housewife whose husband had probably been killed. Her wild auburn hair disguised a lot, but when she turned around even the masses of red lipstick could not conceal her tight lips and dead eyes.

"Well, you've got some real women here." Edward smothered a grin. That tough-looking owner and her beat-up waitress were hardly specimens to admire. But I imagined that was what this war drove them to.

"Why are ya looking in the direction of that waitress, Jim?" teased Red. "She's sure nothing to write home about."

"I don't think any of us are going to write home about this evening, do you?" I quipped, but noticed that my words were getting slurred.

Before long, the owner came over and whispered to Edward, who was by far the best looking among us, with Red not far behind. I noticed Jim twist his scrawny body round to look, and then saw Edward shake his head.

"What did she want?" Red asked.

"What do you think?" Edward said, and nudged me.

We all looked at each other. Harry alone grinned. "She wanted to know if any of us wanted to go upstairs with her. Right Ed?"

We looked at each other in astonishment.

Ed nodded. "But I couldn't figure out how to say we'd never be caught dead with the likes of her."

A bit harsh, I felt, but then, war hardens the best of us.

Right then, down the stairs came a skinny girl, maybe fifteen or sixteen, and undernourished. Red hair, like Ralph Rideout, and a small mousy face like a chipmunk. But no mistaking her likeness to the owner. Behind, a few seconds later, came a sergeant who rejoined his table, to applause.

I wondered how that made her feel.

Ed looked at Jim. "Now there is someone more appetizing."

Hardly, I thought. We fell to discussing girls back home, and Jim took the chance while we were engrossed to wave the owner over.

I saw Ralph staring at the daughter, leaning against a sideboard and brushing back her long red hair. She picked up a tankard of ale and downed a good slug to buck herself up.

Ralph stood, swaying slightly. "What's up?" I asked him.

"She looks just like my sister."

And yes, now he mentioned it, we could also see a likeness there, her tall forehead and red hair especially.

The owner, having spoken to Jim, crossed to her daughter, and jerking her head at Jim, motioned her up the stairs.

Jim unfolded his scrawny body, hoping we wouldn't notice, but of course we all did.

Red tore around the table. "No, Jim, you're not going nowhere with that girl!"

Jim looked mortified. Red was certainly much stronger, not someone to disobey, let alone by a bean-pole like Jim.

"I just want to go up for ten minutes," said young Jim. "I just want to."

Oh-oh, I could see an altercation developing.

"Not a chance," insisted Red, his hands curling into fists. "No one here is going to get their hands on that young lady." See, he'd downed several glasses of wine by now and I think he was pretty drunk. "You're going to leave my sister alone."

"That's not your sister, Red," exploded Harry. "Just let him be."

Red could barely see straight, let alone see reason. What should I do? Up to now, we had all enjoyed the evening, and I wasn't going to have a fight in a tavern break down this tight gun's relationship.

Fortunately, Ed spoke up. "Listen, we've all had a nice drink, and we've all celebrated. Why not leave together and try out some other place? I've heard there's more than one *estaminet*. Let's try them all."

I jumped up. "Great idea," I said. "Let's all go somewhere new."

Well, the idea did have appeal. Jim got up. "I'll just go and relieve myself." Edward joined him. After they left, Harry turned to us. "Jim has been telling me the last while: he doesn't want to die a virgin."

Well, we all sympathized with Jim's wish. So it wasn't another estaminet we visited, we wandered down to the first of two Approved Houses (as they were called). But we saw a queue of about ten men outside. Did that mean it was the cheapest? Or the best?

In any case we decided not to wait, and went to a second place, more on the outskirts. On the way, Ralph sheepishly explained that his father had died before the war, and being the eldest, he'd more or less had to raise his four siblings himself, with his mother. His little sister, Jeannie, was a favourite — he even hauled out a picture of her. We had to admit that in certain ways, she did look like that other girl.

But learning of his four siblings, I wondered how they all survived on Ralph's meagre army pay which he sent home like the rest of us: not much use for it on the firing line. We earned so little, though even Ralph's assignment of thirty bucks a month would be something.

When we reached the second Approved House, no queue outside, so the five of us debated: was it the most expensive or the least desirable?

"We can have a drink and wait around while Jim gets satisfied," I suggested.

Inside, the ground floor was much the same as our previous

estaminet: several long tables, one of which contained four or five of the most horrible-looking ladies I've ever set eyes on. None under thirty, one real fat, one skinny like she had TB and the others, well, you'd hardly be caught dead talking to them, much less going upstairs.

But all four of us sympathized with Jim's desire. Indeed, who would want to go to his death at eighteen and still a virgin?

So we sat down at an empty table and began to encourage Jim by extolling the various charms — a hard job, but we outdid ourselves, weaving the most atrocious fibs.

But just as we were reaching our creative peak, down the stairs came one who, if not exactly attractive, looked slightly presentable, apart from a cleft palate.

Harry pointed. "Jim!"

"But she's just come downstairs," Jim complained. "She'll need a rest."

"Nonsense" Harry shouted.

So we decided to split a bottle of wine, but Edward insisted he'd pay — it was still his treat. It ended up being nearly seven francs, but worth it because up Jim went. As he left, we lifted our glasses for a generous toast.

So at least Jim would not die a virgin. And I had to reflect, as we later staggered back to our tents in the rest area, here was another reason for me to hate this last great war for civilization. Something so beautiful as being with a woman for the first time had been turned into an entirely unattractive event, unpleasant, fraught with disease, and for sure devoid of love.

CHAPTER TWENTY-TWO

Passchendaele

Nr Vlamertinghe [Flanders] Oct 21st 1917: The batteries took over RFA [British] guns at the Battery positions. The mud around the Battery positions is indescribable. At the 35th, 38th, and 40th there are some German pillboxes which offer good protection. The 35th Battery now occupies the most advanced position on this front.

22nd: The difficulties in moving the guns cannot be exaggerated, mud "hub high" and the hopeless congestion of traffic making the movement of guns almost a superhuman task. The sight of derelict guns hopelessly stuck in the Flanders mud is almost too common to excite interest.

WAR DIARIES: 10TH BRIGADE CFA

We had thought that the Somme was bad but this was ten times worse. In the middle of the night, I was struggling with our Battery up towards the Front, towards Passchendaele, which meant we were back up near Ypres. Out of the frying pan, as Old Momma used to say, into the fire.

Sure, the 35th Battery had fought in two resounding victories: Vimy Ridge and Hill 70. But, I thought, here we've really met our match.

And we were stuck in the same bowl of soup: men and horses struggling to haul limbers along this plank road. Someone had figured that a horse was worth seven men, so in our efforts to preserve the beasts we were all walking, NCOs and officers. No point in even trying to hitch a ride on one of the limbers, they were continually slipping off the planks, one wheel stuck in the mud, Gunners scrambling to push them back, hauling on spokes, pulling drag ropes, and Drivers heaving at traces — all swearing vigorously.

To make matters worse, the whole route was chaos, just total chaos. Lorries, limbers, and carts lay tipped over on their gaunt, smashed sides and of course, coming back by the score, guys with head wounds or limping on one leg, stretcher carts on big wheels, walking soldiers so covered in mud you couldn't tell if they were shell-shock cases or just staggering because of exhaustion.

I nearly tripped over something and stopped — a fella lying on the edge of a shell hole. When my foot struck an arm, it moved. I bent over. "How ya doing, fella? Need help?"

"Leave me. I just can't go on. I wanna die."

I couldn't do that. "Come on, I'll give you hand up."

"No no, I'm too tired, I can't even stand. Leave me here, leave me to die, I don't care."

I understood, but I couldn't just pass by. I stopped and hauled at him but try as I might, he would not get to his feet. I stood there in the darkness. Men jostled past. Then I saw the shape of a limber coming.

"Okay, soldier, up you get!" I commanded. "Here's a limber."

"No. No." He shook off my hand and rolled back down. I slithered into the hell-hole myself and grabbed his arm but he managed to escape again. This would be a task, I realized.

I clambered up and stopped the limber. "Got a soldier here. He can't walk. Let's get him on that."

Obligingly, probably because he saw my three stripes, a Driver dismounted and we both grabbed at the soldier. He shook us off again, so I gave him a pretty brutal kick and we lugged him to his feet. Together, the Driver and I got him over to the limber and heaved him up on it. "Now hang on tight," I ordered, and left.

I'd been promoted to Sergeant on the 10th of October, but I'd hardly noticed. When they told us, the Major gave us all an extra tot of rum to celebrate. Everyone seemed pleased.

Although still only October, it was damned cold. And rainy. Belgium must be the rainiest country in the world. Since arriving here, I've spent most my life in the rain, wet through. I don't know how I avoided trench foot, but I've always been careful to dry my feet at night. And our firing line wasn't as bad as those trenches where the Infantry stood in water all day, day after day, week after week.

As I shuffled along, others tried to hurry past, cursing the stretcher bearers for being so slow on the narrow board track, flanked by shell holes filled with water and deadly mustard gas, waiting for the splash of any carcass or a living body to drown. I hated Flanders mud, a particularly sticky and squelching kind that could never be traversed without these duckboards. Did I ever bless our engineers, over and over. They had to keep replacing blown-up sections every night. Dreadful job.

Before dawn we arrived at our new set of guns left by the British Artillery; we had left our own at Vlamertinghe. A Sergeant briefed me on this position, ending with, "Bloody good luck, mate." He and his men shuffled off into the night. Now we all just wanted to fall over on a cot in some billet, but of course, there was no billet to be seen. Instead, we faced our next job.

The 35th Battery had been ordered to move these new guns a hundred yards further to the front. Who knows why? But those were the orders.

Sure, I thought to myself, you just try to move a ton-and-a-half gun through this mud — up to your knees the minute you step off the plank road. And here, we were a hundred yards off it. Just as well the night was black, though admittedly shafted with flashes of gunfire and the odd aerial flare. Our officers had come the day before to stake out a new position up ahead. I found Mr. Overstreet in the dark. "How do you want to achieve this, sir?"

"Sergeant Alford, they promoted you for a reason, you know. To command!" So this was not his forte? "Do what you think best."

"Right, sir." Thanks alot, I thought to myself. Righto, the gun has to be moved one hundred yards? Fine. We'll move it one hundred yards.

Well, of course they would not move just one gun ahead — all our Battery had to get forward. I knew our one detachment could never do it alone so I spoke to another NCO in my section, Corporal Browning, and had both guns join up. We got our team hitched onto our gun's trail, then his team hitched on to ours. Now, every man from both guns could haul on the wheels and drag ropes.

Oh-oh, now I could see a rim of light on the Eastern horizon — just great! Haul two ton-and-a-half howitzers forward in full view of the enemy. Earlier in the night I had been blown into a ditch by an explosion, so I was covered in mud, and freezing as well. But I lent a hand as all ten of us heaved on the spokes of the wheels, strained on the drag ropes, and the horses pulled while our Drivers coaxed and cursed. We were worn out, no big farm dinners in months, so our energy was low. But somehow, our combined efforts inched first one, and then the other gun through the ooze and around the craters.

Then the fun started. We heard a 5.9 coming and dove into the mud. It exploded close by. We lugged ourselves up out of the slime and went on pulling. Two minutes later, the next one landed just ahead. We dove again, and this time I saw that the two front horses had been torn to pieces, and one of the Drivers wounded. Two Gunners sprang to his aid. I issued commands, the men undid the traces, the Drivers shot the poor beasts, then rolled them off into a muddied shell hole. On we went with ten horses.

Shells still burst around haphazardly. All through the night, as apparently every night, Heinie had kept up his sporadic bombardment. Seems he'd suspected movement and had registered his guns on these plank roads.

The wounded Driver started to walk out, held up by another Gunner, back to the Brigade Aid Post, not far to the rear. The "no turning back" rule was only a provision for attacking Infantry.

"Thank God Andy works for us and not them!" I shouted over the din of shells exploding, as the light grew.

"Damn right," shouted Red boldly. "Otherwise they'd have obliterated us long ago. Here we are on their target road, and they can't seem to score a direct hit."

Oh-oh, was that ever tempting fate! "I'll pretend I didn't hear that, Ralph!"

With an almighty heave, we got the last gun squelched forward into its position. I turned and looked. The last howitzers were following, a good ways back. But in the faint dawn, all I saw was the terrible morass.

Craters everywhere in the hellish landscape were filled with destroyed guns and corpses. A body floating by itself — when you only see its back — is not so bad; what I hated were the blown-off legs and arms, floating. And the poor horses! Lying bloated, legs in the air, mostly ravaged by rats, tattered bits of hide catching any breeze. My brother had told me about vultures in the Boer War. Would they ever have a feast here! But no vultures in evidence, just millions and millions of rats.

Over on that plank road, stretcher-bearers kept coming back from the front trenches with men moaning, crying out in pain. They'd pause every now and then, putting down their heavy loads, and beg water or rum from us. The last of the night replacements of Infantry kept trudging past, forward into the trenches. What the hell would they do when they got there? Absolutely no way of attacking anything, let alone the village of Passchendaele, ahead on its slight ridge. Strategically important? But just as at Hill 70, just as at Vimy Ridge, the British hadn't managed, the Scots hadn't managed—and now, I suppose they wanted us to manage?

The Jumbo, the recce officer, had found us an abandoned German blockhouse for shelter, so that's why we had moved forward. Now, try to wheel this British gun around, which was in rough condition, having been subjected to hard use. But one thing, rain never hurt a howitzer. Which of course was lucky in this swamp they call Belgium.

So we got the gun deployed, which was almost laughable: we were so worn out trying to tug on the spokes with our last ounces of energy, it was like one of those comedy teams you see in the moving pictures. And beyond caring. Go ahead, hit us with a direct HE, I think anyone would have said. And well they might! All our guns were crowded together, exposed on this one patch of relatively dry, high ground near Passchendaele.

CHAPTER TWENTY-THREE

Passchendaele

Nr Vlametinghe, Oct 23rd 1917: A Gunner, 35th Battery, was killed in action today. Also a Gunner who had won honours for his Battery and his Brigade in the Divisional sports in June was severely wounded and died later in the morning.

25th: All batteries are packing ammunition for tomorrow's fight. Barrages were carried out.

26th: First operation for the capture of Passchendaele Ridge by the Canadian Corps took place today. Barrage kept up well on into afternoon. Our Infantry consolidated a line not far from their final objective. There was no lull, however, and fire was kept up during the night with occasional intense bursts of fire.

WAR DIARIES: 10TH BRIGADE CFA

"Where's Edward?" I asked. He was always one of the first to line up for breakfast, the most enjoyable meal of our monotonous rations.

"I saw him coming over, but he veered to the latrine," Ralph replied. "Poor fellow, diarrhea again. Had to go twice in the night on the way here. So hard in the dark." Ralph helped himself and moved on.

Lots of us had been a prey to diarrhea, as well as other obnoxious diseases. So much filth, rats, and rotting flesh, we were always getting sick in one way or another. I got my serving of bread fried in bacon fat, and then, such delight — jam! Putting my fried bread on top of my porridge, I watched Jason measure out a spoonful of real raspberry jam.

"Where did you find this, Jason?"

"That Jonas, he's some scavenger. Does it to surprise us, I think."

"Where would we be without him, eh?" I moved off to join Ralph where he was sitting, his back against the plain cement walls of the small pillbox looking out over a fresh shell hole and beyond to the trenches, much further away. From where we were, they seemed just jagged slices in the ground. No grass or anything, just earth, mud, the ruined detritus of battle. Any trees were certainly leafless, reduced to limbless trunks. Afraid of lurking mustard gas, we were careful to keep our feet out of water.

"Well, at least Edward got some good news." I put my mess tin on my knees, and started eating.

"You mean about being designated for officer training in Blighty? Yeah, pretty nice. I'll miss him." Ralph scooped up a big mouthful of porridge.

"Oh no, I meant his letter," I said. "It came just before we left the Wagon Lines. Sure made him excited."

"Yeah, he couldn't stop talking about his Katie all the way to the Front last night."

We heard a 5.9 rumbling over and instinctively flopped sideways and covered our heads. It exploded a little ways off. Damn, oatmeal everywhere and mud all over my precious bread. Why couldn't we all have kept up that gentlemanly stance where we never fired till after breakfast. This war was getting really savage. We picked ourselves up as Harry came to join us, also covered in mud. Not so argumentative of late. I saw signs that he was nearing his breaking point. But then, so were we all. Too much and too long. If this war didn't end soon, we all would.

"Yup, I can almost quote from his letter by heart," Ralph went on. "Told us about it so many times. 'Edward forgive me,' she said, 'I just got a bit crazy, but I'm all right now. The old Katie is back and she knows for sure, you're the one.'"

"That's right," Harry chimed in. "Bet you don't know the next line?"

Ralph shook his head.

"She went on, 'I'll be yours forever.'" Harry shook his head. "Corny line. But that's what he kept repeating. I'll be yours forever. You think he believed it?"

"Damn right," I said. I took another bite of my fried bread; Lord, it tasted good, even smeared in mud.

I looked out over the land stretching back towards the Wagon Lines. Just as flat as could be, with black geysers spouting as shells hit the mud and then subsiding. Each one carried its message of death to anyone at that spot. Behind us at the Front, the everlasting din of machines guns and roaring artillery kept thudding against our ears.

"When any girl says to me, I love you forever," Ralph said, "I get suspicious. It never happens."

"Well, from what he's told me about Katie," I said, "she's loyal. For a lady alone, it's not hard to get diverted back there." And for a flash, I wondered how Rene was doing — had she been 'diverted'?

We heard another Jack Johnson coming and all of us fell sideways, covering our heads, letting the food go to hell. Those damn heavy, black German 15-cm artillery shells weighed some two hundred pounds, probably what Mr. Johnson, that heavyweight boxer in the US, weighed himself.

Woosh! It impacted in a bloody great explosion just twenty yards away, enveloping us in black smoke, spraying us with mud, fragments whining past.

My ears were ringing, but I heard screams.

"The latrine!" shouted Ralph in my ear and jumped up. I forgot about my food and followed. Another might be coming but I didn't care. We ran over to the shell hole where the latrine used to be.

A Gunner torn to pieces made me stop in horror. I saw he was dead, but then beyond him, another was doubled over, stifling screams. Ralph reached him first. The body was covered in shit from the latrine and disease-ridden mud.

Ralph bent and put his hand on the shoulder and lifted him. Edward!

Then I saw his stomach. Torn open.

"Ralph," I said. "Get help, the medics, a stretcher... run!"

He was off, I'd like to say in a flash, but the going was so hard he just slogged away through the mud.

Now what?

"You're gonna be fine, Edward," was all I could think to say as I knelt beside him. That's all you ever say to a wounded man. You never say, you're finished, prepare for the Great Crossing.

Edward stared up at me. He shook his head. "Eric, I know, I've seen it before. It's over. I know. And so do you." He looked down and tried to push some of those entrails back where they belonged. Shit clung to his hands. It all smelled even worse than the normal battlefield stench. "Eric, Eric, do something."

"I will, Edward, of course." But what?

"Shoot me, Eric. Shoot."

Shoot him? What was he talking about?

"For God's sake, please..." he gasped. He held up one hand covered in blood and shit and stared at it as though he couldn't believe it was his own. "I don't feel anything. Look," he bent and tried to stuff his guts back in again. "Eric... Eric, tell Katie I love her."

"Yes, yes Edward, of course. I'll tell her. Ralph's gone for a stretcher bearer, we're gonna see you're okay."

"No, no, take too long. Want to see me die like this? Please Eric. Don't leave. Shoot me."

"I won't leave, don't worry, you'll be okay." I'd never leave him. But shoot?

"Before the real pain hits..." He wretched and a gob of black blood shot out of his mouth. He caught it in his hands and stared down. "Why doesn't it hurt?" He looked up at me again like an innocent little boy, then suddenly gave a twist. "Aagh." Not a shriek, a terrible groan. "Spoke to soon..."

I lifted him in my arms, and held him tight.

He grabbed at me. "Hurry, Eric. Hurry. Shoot. Please."

Shoot him? My best friend? Never.

I think he could see the answer on my face. "Eric. Look." He nodded down. His stomach was such a mess. All mixed with the dross of the latrine. No no, he wouldn't last long. Not the day. Maybe not even the hour.

"See Eric. See? Please. When the sun comes up, the heat... and the rats... they'll come, they'll eat... I can't move. Eric, your gun..."

One hand went down to my revolver, and I started to unsnap the buckle. But then I stopped myself. I just could not.

He saw that. "Hurry. You've got to."

Yes, yes, I had to. But how? How could I kill my best friend? I just sat there wishing he would die. But those eyes, begging me. Without thinking, again my hand went to the steel pistol. This time, slowly, it came out of its holster.

Edward saw, and stopped panting. A faint smile crossed his lips. "Oh thank you, Eric. Thank you."

I froze.

"Go ahead," he said, "Right in the forehead. Quick!"

Oh my God. In his forehead? How could I do that?

He looked up at me, waiting. I shook my head.

He grimaced. "Hurry. Hurry up." He groaned again. "I can't take it, Eric."

I looked down at my revolver. How could I? But...

Another faint smile crossed his face.

I stared at him, and he nodded. He tried to keep from crying out. He nodded again, face scrunched up with pain.

I lifted the gun.

"Thank you Eric, thank — "

Before I could force myself to pull the trigger, he gave a lurch, a torrent of breath leapt out of him, followed by blood, and a terrible, terrible guttural sound, and he fell forward.

He was gone.

My best friend at the Front, Bombardier Edward Whitehead, was dead.

***

We were all deaf, deafer than ever, if that's possible. We'd been firing all day, even though our boys had made their first objective early this morning, well, around eight I guess, and here we were — still loading and firing, loading and firing. But one man short. We'd been placed on a bit of high ground, completely exposed in full view of the enemy — well, our Jumbo had such a small area to choose from, with all the flooding everywhere. Sure made the job of the German gunners easy. The trenches lay before us, and then No Man's Land, and beyond, within eyesight, the German trenches. Those enemy gunners would have a field day.

Our gun drill lays down what happens with a reduced detachment so I now set the clinometer and operated the breech, and the loader rammed his own shells home, so that we kept firing. I just wondered how we had gone through the day without another Jack Johnson finishing us off. Heinie was targeting our guns and hitting the plank road, but on the front line our Infantry had dug into their new positions while we broke up counter attacks. The big guns behind us hammered away on counter-battery work. Lieutenant Overstreet was in the telephone pit sending the signallers running out with new orders on slips of paper. No point in talking. All deaf. And what was there to say, anyway?

In between firing, we had wrapped Ed and the other Gunner's remains in their wool blankets to be taken back on ammunition mules to the Wagon Lines, after we were re-supplied that night. We had no time to dig him a decent grave here.

Edward's death weighed on all of us. It dragged us all down even more than the mud. I hoped he would end up in a decent grave. Katie, who had resolved to wait for him, would now wait forever. But most of all, I imagined his elegant mother, in that big Westmount house, having now lost both sons. How ever would she overcome this tragedy? Rich and poor, I guess this damned war got to everyone, us out here at the Front, or them in their own safe beds back home.

On through the night it went, harassing fire, barrages, counter-batteries and SOSs called for by our Infantry. At least in the dark, you couldn't see the death and the corpses all around. But you sure smelled them. You never get used to the stench. Well, a lot better complaining about the stench than not being able ever to smell it again. We had survived. But for how long?

***

"For sure. She bring in conscription, oh yes oh yes oh yes. My father, he write. She not definite, but she comin' for sure." Michel Lavoie, Edward's replacement, seemed adamant. Two days later we had finished our dinners and were grabbing a moment of relative peace; a general pounding still drummed in the air but right here, we'd been given respite. Soon, another barrage, or counter-battery, would be called for. But part of Passchendaele ridge had fallen, an important section apparently, though not the village yet. Another attack in a few days, for sure.

"Why do you say that?" I asked.

"Well, she come in last year in England." Michel had become our political expert. As such, he beat out Harry, who had never been strong on politics, preferring other venues for his sarcasm and attacks.

But Harry, not be outdone, continued, "You know, we Canadians, we're just like sheep. Wherever the Old Country goes, we follow." Harry looked on the dark side of everything. But I kind of agreed with him on this.

"But Borden, he say he never to bring conscription," Michel averred.

"Prime Ministers always lie, didn't you know that?" Harry said. "It's Laurier anyway who's really against it, but he probably won't win."

"So what do you think will happen?" I asked. I must say that politics and elections had never interested me. But I knew I should keep up.

"Well, when we vote in a month," Harry explained, "just before Christmas, we'll be able to put our votes into whatever constituency we want. Of course, they'll tell us where."

Michel went on, "Oh yes. And the wives of servicemen, my father say. She vote for first time, women. Big t'ing."

That was news to me. "You mean, we now have everyone voting in Canada?"

"No," snorted Harry, "only wives, and even mothers, of soldiers. Yeah, soldiers dead or alive. Sir Robert Borden, he knows which way they'll vote, of course. What a way to steal an election! That's how the Conservatives will get in. Stealing. Highway robbery."

"Quebec, by damn," Michel swore, "she gonna revolt. You just watch. Nobody gonna make us French-Canadians go fight if we don't want."

"Why don't you want?" Harry prodded Michel just as he did all our team. None of us resented it; that was just his way. And after he had gotten over his initial fears those first months, Harry could always be counted on. Poor little bugger, his body was covered with lice bites all the time. He was always scratching himself. I don't know why they liked him — he was so skinny, but then, chats like blood near the bone, so they say. Well, wherever they bit him, they'd be near one.

"Oh we want, but nobody tell us we HAVE to."

"So Borden's going to get in," I asked, "and pass that conscription into law?"

Michel nodded. "She gonna come law maybe end of August. Then you just watch the smoke."

I shook my head. I had no idea why Canada needed it. Weren't there enough of us prepared to come and fight for the country?

"So what's gonna happen to you, Michel, when you get home?" Harry asked. "They're not going to like you coming over here to serve His Majesty." Harry always found a way to say the wrong thing.

"Sure. Listen, lots of men from Quebec, they fight, I tell you. Lots of us. You never hear of the Van Doos? Goddam brave. But I gonna move to Ontario anyway," Michel pronounced. "Me, I like the English. For why you think I learn this crazy language? Lots of work in Ontario. You watch. They gonna treat me like hero."

And you know, I believed they probably would.

CHAPTER TWENTY-FOUR

Passchendaele

Nr Vlamertinghe, Nov 6th: At 4:30 this morning the enemy laid down a heavy barrage. It was a nervous time for Infantry and Artillery alike. Our barrage opened at 6 a.m. sharp. The attack went off without a hitch and by 8:15 the whole front was reported as captured. Several counter attacks were attempted but failed to reach our lines. 35th Battery, one killed and two wounded.

War Diaries: 10th Brigade CFA

"Michel! Back on with the mask!" I had to shout loud through my own gas mask.

He complied, but he hated doing it. Frightening, though, this gas. "Damn eyepieces! They steam up."

Michel was right, it was hard to see. "Better blind than dead," I tried to shout. Gas made the work of firing hell.

Michel was our new Bombardier. A nice warm French Canadian, his square, bold face belied a human sensitivity. In spite of his arguing, he showed a welcome concern for others.

We were keeping up a steady stream of shells toward the enemy. I guess we'd been a bit too sharp in our aim and they'd decided to quiet us down. So all our howitzers had been showered with gas shells and although we'd survived attacks before, this one threatened to finish us. I kept checking to make sure no skin was showing. Hopefully, the gas would blow away soon. But every shell hole around was saturated. Liquid chemical in the shells only changed to a gas when the shell burst. Often in cold weather, the mustard would stay on the ground and run into shell holes. We had to be darn careful where and how we walked.

And today, cool still, the mist and the rain made it hard to achieve any real degree of accuracy. But we must have achieved it: why else would our enemy make such an effort to silence us?

In the ten days since we'd lost Ed, the Infantry had attacked again on the 30th of October, and had achieved most of their second objectives. My God, I thought, don't tell me we're going to do it again, when everyone else has failed? Another, and hopefully the last, big attack was scheduled for tomorrow. That would tell the tale. I knew then that we were either going to smash right onto that ridge and capture Passchendaele village, or an awful lot of us would die in the failed attempt. So today we were hitting the last troublesome spots before next morning's big barrage. But their guns were focussed on us and we'd be subject to an onslaught of treacherous gas.

I saw Michel tie his scarf tighter round his neck; the gas had gotten to him. But he was making no complaints, getting shells and putting them in the breech, while I rammed them home.

Harry would shut the breech and boom! Another high explosive shell would wipe out more enemy.

***

I was awakened the next morning by a tremendous crash. A Jack Johnson had landed close by. But what had startled me out of my sleep was the sound of a big rock hitting our pillbox. I sat up.

Fortunately, a stiff breeze and cold temperatures last night had cleared the gas so we were able to sleep without masks. That dreadful day wearing them had exhausted us — so very draining, being covered up, firing under such harrowing circumstances, so we slept well, even though that battlefield ruckus had not stopped for a second. But this explosion woke everyone.

I looked at my watch: five o'clock. Our bombardment was due to start at six, so I thought I'd better get ready. We were all crowded in the little pillbox, but everyone got moving. Someone lifted the entrance curtain we'd hung to stop gas and in staggered a replacement Gunner, face all bloody, his arm hanging down.

"Come in, come lie over here." I ordered Michel to run for the duty signaller to call for medics.

The soldier stumbled to the couch. "Only two of us, thank God." Then he lay back, gasping. "The other... crossing to here... Could have been one of yours..."

An icy feeling rose to throttle my insides. One of ours?

Last night, I had sent Ralph Rideout back to the Wagon Lines for water and to bring up provisions. Jason the cook had asked me because the usual messenger had been wounded the day before.

No, too much of a coincidence, I tried to reassure myself. Jim got up. "I'll check outside." He got his flashlight and I followed him out into the darkness, shells crashing around.

We walked to the lip of a crater and looked down. My God, what a big hole! Jim shone his flashlight into it — already filling with water. So fast. We turned back. "Jim, did you hear something hit the wall of our pillbox?"

"Yes." He turned. "I thought it might be a rock or something." We went to the wall, and he played his flashlight over the ground. A couple of feet from the wall, we both saw something. What on earth?

He bent, shone the flashlight, and then stood abruptly, leaned against the wall and put his hand to his head.

I went up myself and shone my flashlight on the lump.

Yes, unmistakably round, like a rock, but mashed, and a hank of red hair.

All that remained of Ralph Rideout. I stood in a trance. I couldn't move. I felt like vomiting.

Jim shook his head, and then turned and gestured helplessly. We exchanged a look and he went back into the pillbox. Soon, breakfast time. We were to be served before our six o'clock barrage.

I just couldn't absorb this. What should I do now?

I turned to follow Jim and an awful thought struck me: leave this here? Oh no. But how could we ever give Ralph a decent burial? No clergyman around this firing line, that's for sure. Last night, Ralph had said, "I'll bring us back the best feast ever, never you mind. I'll check with our scavenger — he'll find us something." What an infectious grin he wore — a grin no one would never see again.

My God, what was this war doing to us? It got Edward, and now Ralph Rideout — all that was left of the first old team was me and Harry. No doubt, we'd get taken, too. And soon.

I looked down again. Something had to be done.

I couldn't just leave this here for the rats. Not that there were so many: either they were up in the trenches feasting on the dead, or back at the Wagon Lines, because here we hadn't been bothered too much. Too dangerous? Maybe they didn't like all the gas being dumped around. And in any case, they always mysteriously left before a big barrage. Funny.

I stood looking down at what remained of Ralph Rideout, and then I knew. I stepped forward, and tucking my flashlight into a pocket, I bent and picked up the messy head as gently as I could, and breathing a short prayer, I walked over to the lip of the crater.

I stood, looked heavenward, and mumbled another prayer. And I threw. A splash told me the head had landed in the water and sank. With so much death around, I found I could not even summon up any normal feeling. I just turned and went back. But what lingered was the knowledge that I had sent a man to his death.

Nov 9th: Casualties, 35th Battery, six wounded.

12th: The Hun has been making a specialty of counter-battery work and has been pounding away all day.

13th: Heavy strafing of the batteries continues. The weather which has been very misty of late has prevented the accurate locating of hostile Battery positions so that our counter-batteries have been forced to have recourse to area shoots and concentrations; this has so far not proved effective.

14th: The Hun continues to strafe. All 40th Battery guns knocked out, 35th have three left. The plank road running up by the batteries has been shot to pieces, and guns, limbers, and motor lorries have been piled up in hopeless confusion.

15th: The 35th and 40th are working hard to clear their derelict guns for it is rumoured we move out shortly.

WAR DIARIES: 10ᵀᴴ BRIGADE CFA

The great gun slid sideways, righted itself, and then plunged into the crater. Bubbles rose through the murky yellow surface. The barrel still protruded, but now its former platform had been cleared. We stood looking down at its grave with a kind of sorrow. That howitzer had served us faithfully and, before us, the British. Destroyed by a shell, no longer salvageable. Thank heaven we'd not been firing when it was hit. We now were clearing its emplacement for another howitzer from the Wagon Lines.

Demoralizing. We'd been under continuous fire and bombardment for ten solid days. Here it was, mid-November, the 15th to be exact, and I think all of us were at our wits' end. I myself was completely washed out, finished, exhausted, I didn't think I could even walk back along the line of howitzers, facing Passchendaele Ridge, to our little pillbox where we had lived the last month of torment. And what shape would I be in if I ever did get back to safety? My nerves were shaky, my mind barely functioning. My body, well, would it ever recover? How had I made it so far?

"Right men, back we go, no firing until our new gun comes." I was almost too tired to say the words.

We turned and started back to our billet when Lieutenant Overstreet, looking a bit frazzled himself, came to meet us. He held out his arms wide. "Sorry men, we have to go forward and help an 18-pounder Battery. We've been ordered to clear their destroyed guns. Seems the boys need help."

"Mr. Overstreet, my men need rest. The other Battery has its own troops for such tasks." I was stepping over the line in resisting the order, but I did.

"Sorry, Sergeant," he replied, nicely, "but for some reason, their own troops have been detailed elsewhere. They ask if we could pitch in. Not that hard if we weren't so tired."

We looked at each other in disbelief. But an order is an order and we turned and started towards the 18-pounder firing line. I let the men go ahead. Dick Overstreet hurried to catch up and we walked beside each other in silence. Heads bowed, physically broken, we had little to say. But then he spoke up. "What may be a little consolation, Sergeant, is that there's a strong rumour we're being pulled back."

"Praise the Lord," I mumbled. "But I'll believe that when we get the orders."

"No, I was over at the switchboard and heard the Major talking. Seems like the rumour might be true."

Well, that was a blessing, I thought, as we wandered on.

You might think we were crazy, walking so leisurely across this blasted ground in full view of the enemy not far off. But they had no Andy McNaughton. Anyway, Fritz was mostly blasting away at Passchendaele Ridge, which our boys had finally taken on November 10, right after the village itself. And we were beyond caring about their shells now.

"You know, Mr. Overstreet," I found myself saying, for it had been in the forefront of my mind for some time, "Gunner Rideout's death has weighed on me." We walked a few more paces. "You see, I'm the one who sent him back to the Wagon Line to get supplies. If I hadn't ordered him to do that, he'd be alive today."

"Sergeant Alford, responsibility is the price of command. They teach you some of this in officers' training. And I'm not supposed to say anything, but you might find yourself learning about that sooner rather than later."

He was right, I hadn't learned. But what can you learn in officer training that will take away the guilt? You sent a man to his death...

"You see, Sergeant, every command you give might have that result. Think of the Infantry. Their Lieutenant says, 'Over the top, men!' And leads the charge. And as a result of that, fifty might be dead in the next hour. How does he feel?"

Well, Dick did have a point. I guess being an officer involved an awful lot of things you don't think about when you're following orders. If being a Sergeant meant that you had to give orders that involved nasty results, you still did your job. Then and there, I wiped it off my mind. Better to blame the war. Blame Passchendaele.

We arrived at the six 18-pounders, many of which had been destroyed. Overstreet had come along in order to decide which should be removed for repair, and which dumped — presumably to meet the same fate as our howitzer.

We set to work, exhausted though we were. Now an 18-pounder may not weigh as much as the howitzer, but it's still damned heavy: twelve hundred pounds. Enough to give anyone pause. And we had to move a pile of them. We stood looking. Heavens! How many Batteries had been decimated!

And not just the guns. Ten days ago when Ralph got killed, we had two others wounded, and only three days after that, six more. In fact, ten per cent of our Brigade had been casualties, and many units were much worse. Replacements had been sent up, but wouldn't they just go the way of others?

These 18-pounders could fire much faster than ours, easily four rounds to our one. Their shells included a cartridge and weighed under twenty-five pounds. But they wouldn't elevate more than sixteen degrees compared to forty-five with our howitzers, so they shot pretty flat trajectories with less range. I would say the

18-pounder was probably the workhorse. Sad to see so many finished off like this. Closer to the front, they suffered more from counter-batteries. We got one of them that wasn't too badly damaged backed up behind its now empty pit, and then started on the next.

My God, I was tired. Nothing wrong in admitting it: like these guns, I really felt finished. I'd been in action eighteen months. For pity's sake, something had to happen. I was beyond caring. Raine had gone on to a new life, and whatever hopes I had for getting to know Rene were unlikely to work out. Old Poppa had Earle to work on the farm, so I'd be no great loss there either. In fact — and now I was feeling thoroughly sorry for myself — no one would be greatly troubled by my demise.

Well, didn't we all wrestle this damn gun off its sandbagged platform? To keep them afloat on the mud, most guns sat on sandbags. All of us, pushing and lifting, tired as we were, hungry though we might have been, we managed to tip it over into the next shell hole. It splashed in. Another gun gone. The rest, I'm afraid, were a blur.

That night as I lay on the cold floor of the pillbox, I couldn't stop thinking about Ralph's sister, and her brothers at home. Who would look after them now? Who would send them money for food? What would his destitute mother do?

But then as I got even more depressed, I struggled to snap out of it. You've got to keep cheered up, you've got to encourage your men, you must keep going. Don't let them see you like this. Just keep at it. And that's what I did, until a few days later, we finally got word to retire, and we left this hell of death and damnation.

PART FOUR

England

CHAPTER TWENTY-FIVE

February 1918

got off the train at Waterloo and walked down the long platform towards the gate. Finally I'd been brought back to Blighty for officer training at Witley Camp in Surrey. The artillery section, Milford, was on the slope of Rods Hill, surrounded by lots of rolling common land and space for manoeuvres. Good sandy soil, too. Close to London, but we'd been kept busy and I wanted to wait until my nerves quietened down before heading into civilization. So this was the first time I could arrange a meeting with Jack. Unfortunately, the day had clouded over, with rain expected. So like France. Boy, would I be glad to get back to the Gaspe where it's mostly clear.

I was excited to see London after all this time. Had it changed? Would Jack be waiting? If he wasn't, he told me how to get to his offices in Mayfair, but thought he'd manage to come. Since we hadn't seen each other for almost a year, I was hoping he'd come with his favourite drivers, the Gray girls, Leo and Rene.

How long the platform seemed, as long as the darn train ride itself — less than an hour from Godalming, the station for Witley. Funny how time changes according to what you're looking forward to. I was so looking forward to seeing Jack. But more especially, Rene.

Over the past two months in training, the horrors of the firing line were slowly fading. I had been SOS, Struck Off Strength, from the 10th Brigade in early December, still a Sergeant, and transferred to the Canadian Reserve Artillery. These new courses I'd really been enjoying and I had thrown myself into learning with a vengeance. We'd been handed booklets and encouraged to read history. The more I learned, the less my brain was bludgeoned by recurring images from those eighteen months at the Front.

But at night! Far from getting more peaceful, my dreams were worse: Ed Whitehead holding his entrails in his shitty hands; Ralph, well, what remained of him; and Howard, his torso bouncing after me across the chlorine-poisoned ground. I would wake up screaming. Other fellows had the same problems. Our barracks were often wakened by screams. What the war does to a man...

At the gate I handed in my ticket, and who should I see waiting but Jack, and next to him, the most beautiful girl in the world, Rene Gray. I bust out in the biggest smile anyone ever saw. She waited demurely, even shyly, while I grabbed Jack's hand and shook it vigorously, almost to his dismay, and then I turned to her, and she gave me a kiss on my cheek. Then she stood back and looked. "My God, Eric," was all she said. "My God."

I frowned. "Is something wrong?"

She shook her head. "Your eyes... They look so sad. Like the eyes of an old man."

I grinned. "As old as Jack's?"

"Come on, you two, let's get back to the car," he said. "Leo's waiting. I'm going to take you to a good lunch. You see," Jack grinned, "as head of the Chaplaincy Service, I get a bit more money, and I'm going to splurge on my kid brother today, for sure."

We walked over to where the beautiful black and brown Daimler was parked, and Jack managed to deflect Leo's rather too obvious annoyance at having been kept waiting. The trains pretty well run on time over here, Jack explained, but German planes had been sighted. I guess that slowed us down some.

On the way to the restaurant, Rene and I couldn't take our eyes off each other. Hard to explain how much it meant, being in the presence of a beautiful lady after eighteen months. Of course, on weekends, I'd occasionally gone to a nearby pub in Godalming, a nice old market town: plenty of girls hanging around. But I'd paid little attention. I had made sure to reply to Rene's letter, once I'd gotten here. We'd both written again, in fact. Amazing she'd have eyes for me when she could have had the pick of any Colonel around. Of course, those fellows would be a lot older. Rene and I were about the same age.

Leo pulled up at the restaurant and as we were getting out, Rene said, "Listen Eric, we have to drive Father John around all afternoon. He saves up his appointments for the days he gets us. But tomorrow, we don't have to, so I asked my mother for the car. Since you wrote that you have two days leave, if you're interested, I could pick you up in the morning and take you around?"

"Oh perfect! I don't know how I'm gonna sleep tonight, just waiting."

Well sir, that seemed to make her happy.

I went with Jack into this Regent Palace Hotel, with its white tablecloths and smart-looking waiters, some of whom had already been in battle, one limping, one serving us with his shirt pinned over the stump of an arm.

It certainly was good to sit and talk to my brother. I hadn't seen him enough to say he'd aged — well, he always was much older than me. But what I noticed was that so much responsibility these last three years had bestowed on him an uncommon authority — which didn't diminish his brotherly friendship.

We spent the first part of the dinner talking about home. Nothing much changing there, except that Old Poppa had commented on prices going up. Earle was working hard, learning even more about farming; Lil helping, and both sisters away: Winifred nursing and Margaret Jane married to Bert Finnie and enjoying her new home in Montreal.

We ordered dessert. Jack loved Spotted Dick, which he recommended. I agreed, wondering what on earth these Brits would think up next. He ordered two fine glasses of port, a drink I'd never tried. Finally, the talk did turn towards the war, which we'd happily been avoiding.

"And not only do I have to minister to our soldiers at the Front," Jack said as he sat back and our plates were cleared. "I had one poor fellow whose mother was killed by flying glass in that dreadful Halifax explosion at the beginning of December. Two thousand dead, nine thousand injured." He shook his head.

"Oh yes, we were all talking about that in Camp," I said. "Are they really sure it was not a U-boat?"

Jack shook his head. "You can see the enormous power of our explosives. When that ammunition ship blew up in the harbour, it was the worst man-made explosion in history. The poor Haligonians. And you know," Jack went on, "the news from the Eastern Front isn't so good."

Now in officer training, I had been learning something of the Russians who were also battling our common enemy. "We had an interesting fellow come to lecture," I told Jack. "He warned us that his views on the Russians might not be that of the military. Apparently he teaches at some college in London; our regular teaching officer went back to the Front. Anyway, he said this revolution is a good thing."

"I don't know how good it is," Jack replied. "The Bolsheviks will probably pull out — I understand that fellow Lenin, who is now officially running Russia, has sent Trotsky to negotiate a peace with the Germans."

"Lucky them," I found myself saying.

Jack looked up, startled. "Well, I know what you mean, Eric: I suppose, in one sense, they're lucky not to be fighting any more battles. But you know what that means to us?"

"I haven't got to that part in the course, yet," I confessed. "But Jack, those recently liberated serfs have been so badly treated, they had no alternative but to revolt." My eyes widened as the waiter brought us each a plate with an unappetizing lump of pudding and custard. I frowned, and Jack chuckled. "It's good, Eric. Steamed suet pudding with dried fruit, let me look, yes, these are black currents — ."

"Not dead flies? Okay, I'll give it a try."

"The Russian upper classes treat their serfs abominably, but you know the Tsar is the king's first cousin."

"So why wouldn't George V talk him into carrying on? I mean, I've heard he's a prisoner and all that, but — ."

"Look, now that Lenin has taken over, the Bolsheviks are in charge and the one thing they want is to end the war. You know Karl Marx thought the proletariat would revolt sooner in Germany or here, both of us being more industrialized. But what helped was the Russians had the biggest army anywhere."

"And the biggest air force, I heard. But didn't a couple of million men desert? Imagine! That's what our instructor said.

Not enough uniforms or rifles, and not much food. Must be such a badly run country."

Jack nodded. "But you can see what'll happen if they pull out?"

Again, I had to beg ignorance. "I think we get to that part next week."

"Well, Eric," Jack said kindly, "to put you ahead of your fellows: if Russia does reach a settlement, the Hun has a terrific railway system. In no time at all, thousands of troops, fighting the Russians, will race across Germany to the Western Front. I shudder to think what would happen then."

"Oh my heavens. You think it could happen?"

"It is happening, Eric. Trotsky is doing his best to get peace. I have it on good authority from the High Command; they are seriously worried."

"I guess I'd better get back as quick as I can," I said, not without regret.

"We'll need every man, certainly." Jack finished his last spoonful. "How did you like this?"

"Better than it looks, for sure. They do things well at this here hotel — I mean, this hotel," I said. "Thank you very much, Jack."

"We'll take our port in the lounge," Jack said, "where we can light up."

I followed him and we sat in big comfortable chairs, and talked of other things, including Rene. Again he warned me not to be optimistic but I only listened to his warnings with half an ear. All I could think about was my day together with her tomorrow.

CHAPTER TWENTY-SIX

London, February 1918

The next morning promptly at ten, Rene drove up in her gorgeous big car. Just the two of us, all day long. Well sir, was I ever the happiest man in creation — until I saw who was driving: Leo. So they were both coming. Oh well, better than nothing.

Rene had gotten out and caught my look of dismay. She whispered, "The Mater insisted we have a chaperone. After all, it's the first time we'd be alone."

"The Mater?" I got into the back seat of the Daimler.

"That's what we call our mother." Rene hesitated, about to follow me, and then got into the front seat beside Leo. So I had to sit in the back alone.

"And what do you call your father?"

"We used to call him the Pater," said Leo. "But he died when I was eleven." She was not as finely featured as Rene: her round face had a pudding look, accentuated by heavy eyebrows. Not a lot of warmth in those big brown eyes, either.

As we started off, I sank back in the leather seat. "I'm sorry to hear that." I couldn't imagine what it would be like growing up without a father.

"I confess," Rene added, "that the Mater is a bit of a martinet. Probably worse than even the Pater might have been."

I hadn't heard about martinets, but I imagine she meant somebody pretty fierce. We crossed Trafalgar Square and then drove on down by the Thames. I was pleased to see a good few horses, mostly pulling carts. Lots of cars, too, though not many as grand as ours. I guess Rene's father must have left some money.

"You musn't think I wanted to come," said Leo, having seen my earlier look. "The Mater insisted."

"Leo doesn't mean it," Rene added sharply. "She's delighted to help any fighting man tour our city."

"Well," I tried to be nice, "I'm very glad you came, Leo. You must have seen all these sights quite often with others."

"Too often." Take that! I thought. But then she made it worse: "Always with officers; this will be the first time with someone of lower rank, whatever yours is. Should be interesting!" Mean too, I thought.

"Leo!" Rene turned to me. "Leo often speaks without thinking." Leo turned and gave her a look, but kept quiet.

In no time at all, we were at Westminster Abbey. As we parked, I stepped out and gasped. Never seen anything like it! Closest were the ruins of Cloth Hall in Ypres — oh, and the spire of Salisbury Cathedral during training. And while travelling I'd passed some big churches; but certainly, this was the biggest. "And they just let anyone in?"

"Well, it belongs to us all," Leo said, "everyone in the Sovereign's realm to enjoy." Inside we went. Leo threw out: "I suppose you'll take him straight to Poets' Corner, as usual." She slipped into a pew at the back to wait.

"Please don't mind her, Eric," Rene said as she led me down the magnificent centre aisle and turned right into the Poets' Corner. "You just have to get used to it. Someone I like — well, she is bound to be even more mean."

I almost blushed. Someone she liked. That was a start, for sure.

Well, first thing we saw was William Shakespeare's tomb. And there he was, in white marble, life size, one elbow leaning on a stack of books, another hand pointing to a scroll with lines from one of his plays — the most famous poet and playwright in the English language. Amazing what they wore in those days! I had never seen a Shakespeare play, of course, but Rene knew several.

Then by golly, Alfred Lord Tennyson. What a sight to see his bust. "But where's his beard?" The smooth face seemed so young.

"He must have grown it later in life. It's him in his forties, I believe," Rene said, pointing out his slab between two other fellas, poets I guess, John Dryden and Robert Browning.

At school, we'd had to learn *The Charge of the Light Brigade,* and I repeated some now for Rene:

> *Into the valley of Death*
> *Rode the six hundred.*
> *Cannon to right of them,*
> *Cannon to left of them,*
> *Cannon in front of them*
> *Volley'd and thunder'd*

I stopped, a bit overcome. Had I not been there myself? I looked down. Rene reached out and touched my hand. Such a warm person.

I watched her as she went to read Chaucer's inscription on his tomb. Perfect features, Rene, so innocent, young looking, actually, capped by a charming hat, so stylish and just right. In her light flowered frock, she seemed so graceful as if Heaven itself had fashioned her especially for this tour of London.

She paused and looked around. "I always come expecting to see William Blake's tomb here, but I can never find it."

"Maybe he was buried somewhere else? Is he a poet too?"

"Oh yes. My favourite." She sang a line from that hymn, *And did those feet in ancient time, walk upon England's mountains green?* I'd heard that during camp services. "Blake wrote those words."

An awful lot of British kings and queens were buried here, and as we passed them by, Rene told me about them. We'd had to study history in New Carlisle, but I remembered very little; never had interested me. But who could not be overwhelmed by these huge arches, the great pillars bearing this splendid roof?

It was all pretty dazzling: being with Rene in the presence of so much greatness, seeing the actual statues of men I had studied at school and read at home. Jack used to send us books and already the Old Homestead had a pretty good library. Right now, I was the one in the family seen as a scholar. But over here, meeting so many educated officers at training school — damnation, they sure teach them well in British schools. Right then and there, I made a firm resolve: if I ever get through this war, I'll go to Bishop's University.

Getting into the car, Rene announced, "Now for the big surprise."

"Lead on! I'm a great one for surprises."

"We just have time before lunch," Leo agreed as she drove us along the Victoria Embankment and all of a sudden, there we were on what I remembered as Horse Guards Parade. We pulled up, parked, and walked a short way. Of course, my curiosity was mounting.

Rene turned to look at me. "Should be any time now." I could see she was excited. "You see, Eric, the day before their Majesties go on a shopping trip, their route is posted in *The Times*. They travel in an open carriage, and often their subjects line up to see them. Here, there shouldn't be too many."

"You mean, I actually get to see our great King George V? You know he visits the Front with his generals?"

We hadn't long to wait. Around the corner came the royal entourage, followed by a beautiful yellow and black landau, drawn by four horses called the Windsor Grays, Rene told me, trotting merrily away, two footmen up on back looking splendid, and there, King George V with his trim brown beard and moustache, and Queen Mary, so upright and graceful.

As they drove close, I snapped into a salute.

And you know, the King saw me and saluted back — just me. On they went, waving occasionally.

Rene actually jumped up and down and clapped her hands. And Leo burst into the biggest smile I've ever seen.

"B'ys, Leo, you should do that more often," I said. "You sure look pretty when you smile." I thought she deserved a compliment, being so obviously happy that the King of England, Emperor of India, Sovereign over all our British Empire, had actually saluted this lowly Sergeant from a Gaspe farm. Pretty high point in anyone's life, I would have to say.

"And now, off to lunch!" Leo drove us eastward and stopped at the entrance of a narrow thoroughfare, Fleet Street, where we got out. We walked down to the Cheshire Cheese, which from the talk about it being the oldest restaurant in London, I expected something a bit more grand. "Look, sawdust on the floor! That's what we use in the stable when we run out of straw."

I saw Leo give Rene a look. I wondered what was wrong with that. We went into the small, low-ceilinged rooms with their dark wood panelling, long benches and equally dark tables, close-packed. Lots of smoke, for already several army types had arrived, and quite a few journalists, so Rene said.

"So you work on a farm, do you?" Leo led us to a table by a leaded window.

"Our family owns a farm," I replied, trying to be as nice as I could. "My brother Jack was born there, too."

"Really!" Leo sounded surprised. "I'd never dream he came from a farm."

"Leo," Rene said hotly, "there is nothing wrong with that. It's not the way it is here, you know. In the New World, they say that everybody is equal. And the farms, they are big and lavish, aren't they, Eric?"

"Well, not exactly lavish." Frankly, I didn't want to spend the day defending my life in Canada. I think Rene saw that too. But when we looked at the menus, she suggested some really strange dishes: Bubble and Squeak, which she ordered for me, and Toad-in-the-Hole for her. I asked for a nice glass of bitter and Rene and Leo had red wine. I wonder what Old Momma would say to women drinking in public. But everyone else here did: sure a ton of different traditions in the Old Country. And who am I to question that?

A sudden commotion made me turn. A lowly Corporal walked in, but he wore the distinctive crimson ribbon of a Victoria Cross. At once, every officer in the restaurant leapt to his feet, Captains, even a Colonel, and snapped into a smart salute, as did I. The Corporal, who returned it, had gotten used to this, I guess. The others waited until he limped over to a table and sat, whereupon they did, too. Quite something.

I wasn't used to having strangers at my elbow. But then looking into Rene's eyes who sat opposite — it kind of blotted out the rest of the world. I wondered how I'd get her alone, so I could tell her how I felt about her. Instead, I asked about their family, and Leo launched into a description of their house in Brentwood, "The Lions", named after two stone lions crouched on each side of their front steps. I think Rene cringed a little as Leo went on about their butler and chambermaids, and their elderly cook and rather dumb undercook.

"Sometimes I wish we didn't have such a big staff," Rene said. "Don't worry, it's not something... well, although I was born into it, I don't find it necessary. I can get along quite well enough washing and ironing my own under things." She blushed as prettily as I've ever seen.

When the waiter brought our plates, I looked down at my Bubble and Squeak. It turned out to be fried vegetables, mainly cabbage and potatoes, but they had added sausages, too. "Well, one thing I'm going to write my father about is this here Bubble and Squeak." As soon as the words went out of my mouth, I knew I should have kept quiet. Leo suppressed a smile, and went on eating her Toad-in-the-Hole, which I discovered was also sausages, but in Yorkshire pudding and some vegetables, all covered in gravy.

"Your father must be a very fine man, Eric," Rene said. "You told me last time we were together he'd had ten children."

"Well, I guess Momma was the one who had them. She is wonderful. She's proud that her children turned out for the best."

"Father John certainly bears that out," Leo remarked.

"And Eric," snapped Rene. She was beginning to lose her temper.

"How many in your family?" I asked. I already knew, I think, but I wanted to change the conversation.

"We have one older sister, Hilda," Rene explained again, "whom I mentioned before. She's gone off now to Macedonia, and serves with the Scottish Women's Regiment."

"Just as well she went off, " Leo commented. "Her views as a suffragist were getting on all our nerves."

"Not on mine," Rene retorted.

"I thought it was suffragette?" I asked.

"Suffragist is one who believes in the movement, but is not actively chaining herself to railings or throwing herself under horses and that sort of rubbish," Leo said.

I had heard about Emily Wilding Davison who did so at the famous horserace they call the Derby. Terrible to have to go to such lengths just to get a vote. Some of them had been stuck in jail. I hoped we didn't do that in Canada.

"The oldest is brother George," Rene said.

"The less said about him the better," Leo added in her own inimitable way. Boy, I thought, she'll wait a long time before she finds a man.

After we had finished lunch and I had paid the big bill over Rene's objections, she announced, "Next, the Tower of London."

"Oh good. A lot of our officers in training have been there," I said. "And the crown jewels?"

"Funny how everyone from the Colonies wants to see our crown jewels," Leo said with a condescending smirk.

"Yes, but there is more to the Tower than just that," Rene put in gently.

Leo drove over the Thames so that we got a good view of the great square castle with its four towers. Back over Tower Bridge we drove, and entered the famous grounds. Huge, they occupied eleven acres, so I was told. After seeing the crown jewels, we walked on through other enclosures and Leo remarked, "Do you remember three weeks ago, Rene, when we took that handsome Captain around? He was just so knowledgeable."

Rene was watching for my reaction. But how could I react? Of course, they took other soldiers around. That didn't make me doubt Rene's sincerity.

"Let's show him where the royal menagerie used to be," said Leo. "I expect coming from a farm, he'd like that."

With Leo, I'd never live that down.

"That officer was just so clever!" she went on, when we got to the enclosure. "I don't expect you know Blake's poem *The Tyger*, Eric, but he told us the poet saw his only tiger right here."

I didn't know the poem.

Leo must have seen that because she went on, "You know: *"Tyger! Tyger! burning bright, In the forests of the night...?"*

"What immortal hand or eye, Could frame thy fearful symmetry?" Rene finished. They both loved the poem, even Leo.

"And this is where he saw it?"

"He'd never been to India or any jungle, you see," Leo finished.

Well, that sure was something — not picked up in any guidebook, I bet. Yes sir, lots of fun moments sightseeing with these two girls, even though Leo left a lot to be desired. But when was I going to be alone with Rene?

"And now, for the finale," said Rene.

We drove just a short way up Ludgate Hill and stopped in front of the most magnificent building ever. Even bigger, taller, more amazing than Westminster Abbey.

"St. Paul's Cathedral," said Rene proudly.

Well, when we got out of the car, I just leaned back against it and stared. A triple layered dome, huge clock tower on the left, classical columns in front. Almost reminded me of some of the blasted churches on the Continent, but so much bigger. And safe, here. Shame what war was doing over there.

"Masterpiece of neo-classical architecture," Leo said, somewhat triumphantly.

We went in, and I followed the girls who went straight through to where Sir Christopher Wren was buried.

I read the slab slowly, *"Lector si monumentum requiris,*

circumspice."

Rene translated: "Reader, if you seek his monument, look about you."

As I found out, after the Great Fire he had designed thirty-seven parish churches and other public buildings. "Took thirty-three years to build," Leo remarked. Then Rene took us over to a big black sarcophagus in a side chapel.

Leo gestured. "Eric, this is the tomb of one of our greatest warriors ever. You've probably never heard of him, but he won the Battle of Trafalgar, and stopped Napoleon from invading England. Lord Nelson."

I could see Rene beginning to blush — fed up with Leo putting me down. But what could she do? She looked at me, with almost imploring eyes.

"Well," and then I put on an exaggerated Gaspe accent. "This 'ere fella, my grandfather served under." Leo looked up, shocked. "James Alford fought on a 74-gun warship, the *Bellerophon,* the one that took Napoleon, when he surrendered, back to Plymouth." Her jaw dropped; Rene broke into a beautiful smile. "Yep, my grandfather served under Nelson at the battle of the Nile in Alexandria, and then in the Battle of Trafalgar. When the ship came to Canada, he jumped off in Port Daniel Bay — all wilderness at that time." I was pleased at their reactions. "So he became the first settler to carve a home out of what they now call Shigawake. Some pioneer, I tell yez!" I hoped that would put her in her place once and for all.

And you know what? It did.

From then on, she treated me like I was the King of England. These damn Brits, they are so full of their own importance. But not Rene, for sure, she was just delighted.

"Come on you two," Rene said, "I am going to take you both to tea in the Strand."

CHAPTER TWENTY-SEVEN

London, April 1918

"**S**o I shan't be seeing you again for a little while?" asked Rene.

"Not till this blasted war is over, I guess." We were speeding along, probably thirty miles an hour, towards the South Coast on a big outing. Such a beautiful day, the likes of which you don't get a lot in England. Being late in April, flowers were out, hedgerows in bloom — you could even smell them in some places — and cattle cropped their pastures. My brother was preaching to the troops at Shorncliffe Camp today. He had suggested I take the train down so we could have lunch, seeing as how I was leaving the next day, 29th, for the Front. When I broached this in a letter to Rene, she came to Witley in the morning so we could spend the day together.

"Let's make a pact not to talk about the war, Rene," I said. "This is one day I'll remember, probably all my life."

"May I just ask if you're looking forward to going back?"

"Yes, and no. I sure learned a lot being at the Canadian Gunnery School. And I know I'm needed over there. I've almost forgotten, thank heaven, what it's like on that firing line. So I don't want to spoil today with you..."

My Lord! How amazing it was to sail along like this! A car meant you could go wherever you wanted whenever you needed. Imagine if we had a car on the Gaspe! The trip to Bonaventure to get our wheat ground into flour took all day with a team of horses, whereas in a car maybe you'd spend only an hour or two. Imagine how a doctor would benefit, instead of relying on his horse and buggy, no matter how fast. Any accident, he'd be down from New Carlisle in a flash. I wondered when we'd get to see our first car in Shigawake.

I leaned back and watched Rene's dancer's fingers on the steering wheel, and on the beautiful wood knob of that gearshift, listening with half an ear to how much she liked her dancing school. It would take an age to fill in all she knew about the classical Greek dancing she had been studying under Ruby Ginner. "Of course, the Mater doesn't approve. But as you know, when I set my mind on doing something, I find a way to get it done."

"Yes, like getting the car for us to go to the South Coast."

Rene smiled. "Now that she knows your grandfather fought under Nelson, that makes everything all right. I didn't tell her we were going on to Shorncliffe Camp, of course."

We had, it is true, seen each other fairly often the last few weeks. She took me to my first play ever: *The Duchess of Malfi*, by a fellow who had lived around Shakespeare's time. Most other soldiers went to *Chou Chin Chow*, or *Charlie's Aunt*, which Rene classed as foolish comedies. She saw herself as a serious artist, and wanted me to be properly educated.

Such a thrill for me to be invited to a real theatre and see a play for the first time. I can still hear that pretty Cathleen Nesbitt (she'd been engaged to the poet Rupert Brooke, as we all knew) saying, loud and clear, *"I am Duchess of Malfi still."* And later, over her dead body and all that blood and gore, the bad guy, Bosola, saying, *"Cover her face. Mine eyes dazzle. She died young."* That sure applied to what I saw at the Front, I can tell you.

"I might even get into Ruby Ginner's company of Grecian Dancers," she added, "though the Mater would hate to hear of me performing on stage."

"I should think she'd be honoured."

Rene smiled, such nice lips — a perfect mouth for sure. "Oh no, no nice girl ever goes on the stage..." She shook her head. "She wouldn't even support Hilda in her suffragism — another reason she joined up and went off to serve in Macedonia. I do hope she's all right," she added.

We saw a couple of other plays, and then a concert at the Royal Albert Hall, that enormous circular auditorium with balconies and rows of boxes, including the one reserved for the King and Queen. Rene told me that for a small charge, poor people could hear the performance, standing behind the rail.

Rene looked stunning in her evening dress. We went with Leo; the Mater decided at the last minute against coming. So I still haven't met her. I'm pretty sure that she doesn't think a farm lad, albeit a Lieutenant now and grandson of a naval man, would be that suitable a match for her daughter.

Jack's service, at the church of St. Mary & St. Eanswythe in Folkestone not far from camp, was quite inspiring: these young soldiers singing so lustily — including William Blake's *Jerusalem.* The church was hundreds of years old, and of course, with all the trainees about to leave for the Front, it was crammed.

My brother preached a real patriotic sermon — well, what else could he do? I gathered, from the men I talked to, that his coming there to preach was a signal honour. Afterwards, Rene drove us, me beside her this time and Jack in the back, to an old Inn just outside Folkestone.

We went into the cosy dining room with its small coal fire glowing in spite of the warm day. I could tell that Jack had now accepted the fact that Rene and I were, at the very least, good friends. After being given menus, I'm happy to say I saw none of this Bubble and Squeak and Toad-in-the-Hole. Instead, British roast beef, Yorkshire pudding, roast potatoes, and vegetables. Jack even suggested that we all have a glass of wine.

Jack brought me up to speed on the Old Homestead, in which happily nothing appeared to have changed since we talked a couple of months ago. I prodded Rene into telling him about her classical Greek dancing, and then, after we got our sumptuous plates, the last good meal I'd have for a long time, Jack turned to the obvious subject that we could not avoid: war.

"Rene," I said, "You know, Jack always gets the latest from his friends in the High Command." I turned to him. "And the news doesn't seem tremendously good?"

"Tremendously bad, if the truth be known: in the last month, the Germans have taken over fifty thousand prisoners." He said it slowly, to let it sink in. I felt really alarmed. The papers had not told us that, of course.

"Just as I predicted, you remember, those Bolsheviks signed the Brest-Litovsk Treaty in early March, so the Germans rushed their forces across to the Western Front. On the 21st of March, Ludendorff attacked with so much gas and such a terrible barrage that he put our counter-batteries out of action. The Hun was able to penetrate several miles past our front lines. It was almost a rout." He turned to Rene. "I do hope, my dear, you'll keep this under that pretty hat of yours. I shouldn't be speaking out of turn, but then, Eric and I are brothers, and as he's heading back now into that maelstrom, I feel a fraternal duty to describe what he'll face."

"Yes, of course, Father John, I won't say anything."

"Keep on, Jack. I'd better know the worst."

"Well, the Germans are now within shelling distance of Paris, and have actually done so. And only last week — and this I know is bound to depress you — only last week the British gave up the ridge and village of Passchendaele. Before that, the Germans retook most of the Somme where so many of our brave men lost their lives."

Good Lord, I thought, could the news be any worse? I still had faith in our Canadians, but I could see that everyone was sure needed.

"That's about it," continued Jack. "The Germans are on the outskirts of Albert, and are attacking Armentières. Our brave forces are responding and, even though depleted, are engaging in counter attacks. The Americans have arrived and are about to enter the fray; that well help. Let us never forget that right is on our side."

"That's for sure," I responded.

Rene put down her knife and fork; she had lost her appetite. I thought I'd change the conversation. "And how are things back in Canada?"

"Not much better. They tried conscription — only a few hundred at first, but a third of them refused to turn up, so they got arrested. Riots broke out: windows smashed and fires set, so the government backed down." Jack shook his head and went on eating.

"Well, Jack," I tried to cheer everyone up, "you just wait till I get back to the Front. This one new Lieutenant is gonna change everything!" I gave a weak laugh.

Jack looked up, and managed a smile. "I bet you will, Eric. And you feel good about going back?"

The way he said it, I could see that he had been wanting to ask that all along, but had been afraid to do so. Not many veterans who had seen as much action as I had were keen to return.

"Jack, I feel fit as a fiddle and fine to go back!" But dammit, just as I said that, didn't a flight of planes roar over the hotel on their way to France, or perhaps German planes coming to attack, and I found myself shaking. My fork started banging against the plate; there was nothing I could do to stop it. I shook my head. I almost wanted to cry. What was happening? I had noticed recently such reactions getting worse, in fact, out of control. But then, they always passed, as this one did. I took a good swig of wine.

Jack kept eating and Rene picked up her knife and fork in an effort to make everything seem normal. "So Father John, the word is that you have done a splendid job in reorganizing the Chaplaincy Service. Bully for you."

Jack cleared his throat. "Thank you, Rene. Our father always taught us to do our best. That is what I do, and I have every confidence that Eric will acquit himself like a true Canadian hero when he rejoins his Brigade."

***

Rene dropped Jack back at camp headquarters and then asked, "Would it be fun for you to see the ruins of a castle built by William the Conqueror?"

Anything to prolong our time together! As we drove along, from the odd high point I could see black dots of houses in France across the Channel, where I was heading tomorrow. It reminded me of how my dreams had been getting worse. When I heard the cannon fire in training, I sometimes reacted oddly. I wondered if I should tell Rene, but it would only make her worry. Then a passing car gave a loud backfire. I pitched sideways into her lap, knocking her driving arm. I lay there for a moment, my head in her lap. She began to stroke my temple soothingly.

I slowly picked myself up, feeling a bit sheepish. "I'm sorry, Rene."

"Nothing to be sorry for, Eric," she said, eyes filling with tears. "That's what saves your life on the battlefield. Poor soul, having to go back. How many times have I prayed that this dreadful war will soon be over, and you can stay with us in England."

Stay? Well, that had never entered my head. But now, I certainly would think about Rene in my future plans, if I lived through the next long months — or Heaven forbid, years — of war.

Hastings Castle right on the edge of the cliffs turned out to be really just a pile of old walls, but kind of interesting. "Dates from 1066," Rene repeated. On the Gaspe coast the oldest place is where Jacques Cartier planted that cross in 1534. By then, this castle was already five hundred years old. Amazing.

Being Sunday afternoon, there were quite a few visitors. We strolled across the uneven grass and then found, behind one of the standing walls, a small plaque on the Cinque Ports that I stopped to read. Rene leaned back against the wall beside the plaque and looked into my face with her searching, brown eyes. I looked back at her.

And then, as if some force was pressing me forward, I leaned over and our lips met. Hers were so soft and tender, and yet welcoming. Our first kiss.

We parted without saying anything, but continued wandering, holding hands now, through these old ruins. I hated for the afternoon to end.

After going back to the car, we drove off to explore St. Clements Caves, but I'm afraid, after that kiss, everything was a blur.

On the way back to Witley, we did very little speaking. I think we both felt that something had ended and something far more important had begun. When we got to the camp, she said, "I wish we could go to dinner at some little restaurant, but I'm afraid the Mater will be annoyed if I'm too late. I have to drive all through London before I can head out towards Brentwood. So I shall be fairly late as it is."

I was about to lean in and kiss her again, but it didn't seem appropriate. I stood looking at her as she sat in the driver's seat. I wanted to take in everything about her, every feature, and I said so.

"The way you are right now I shall remember when I'm in a Forward Observation Post, beyond the front line." I managed a smile.

But then, I saw she was crying, though trying so hard to hold it back.

"Goodbye, dear Rene, thank you for everything you have done for me. And everything you mean to me." I turned abruptly and strode to the entrance of Witley camp, and my future in the firing lines of France.

PART FIVE

The Hundred Days, 1918

CHAPTER TWENTY-EIGHT

Amiens

Bacoul, [Nr. Amiens] August 3rd: Batteries on detraining were placed in the surrounding woods and kept under cover all day. Absolutely no movement of any description was allowed on the roads. All batteries would march at 10 p.m. tonight to Wagon Lines in Boves Wood.

Aug 4th: Batteries arrived in Boves Wood early this morning after a long march from Bacoul. Owing to heavy rains, roads and tracks were in a very bad condition and the march was made very slowly.

Aug 5th: Battery positions were inspected: these are quite close, up to 1,500 yards of the enemy front line and on the forward slopes. The 3rd and 4th Battery positions are open ones and in full view of the enemy. Ammunition is being hauled up tonight.

Aug 6th: Troops were simply pouring into the area all last night and the roads forward were jammed. Fortunately the weather and observation are very bad. Enemy appears to be getting suspicious and his harassing fire at night has increased.

Aug 7th: The C.O. went forward today and reconnoitred the forward areas for OPs. Owing to very heavy rain, observation was very poor and the reconnaissance was made under great difficulties. Everything ready for the attack tomorrow morning.

WAR DIARIES, 1st BRIGADE

Three months almost to the day and I was back at the Front, and no more shakes, no diving into shell holes unless necessary, and above all, not a jot of panic. Just a few bad dreams: Edward pleading, Howard's torso, the maggot in the nose, and others just as horrible,

It helped that the First Brigade wasn't fighting any major battles. We saw action, oh yes, but nothing compared to Vimy Ridge, or Passchendaele. Well behind the lines, we had sports days and inspections, resting up for some big push. The German advance had finally been halted in heroic manner by the British and French; now in the summer of 1918, both sides seemed to have reached another stalemate. The Americans were landing in their thousands and training; so after the disastrous spring, Allied prospects started looking up.

This night I was sitting in our Forward Observation Post on a slope facing the enemy, waiting for the last glow to leave the horizon behind me before I moved out. My two telephonists and a lineman had established communication with Brigade Headquarters and the Battery switchboard, and they were busy making sure the line hadn't been cut by shellfire. We had brought our two messenger pigeons, rifles for the Signallers, my own revolver, field glasses, telescope and SOS rockets.

We in the Canadian Corps knew something was afoot. We had been stationed up near Arras and made a great show of that. No secret that the enemy knew us to be the finest fighting unit in the war. And our artillery was certainly also declared by both British and Boche to be the best. When we showed ourselves at different points of the Front, the Huns rushed forces there. So this long march southwards to Amiens had been undertaken in as much secrecy as could be mustered: no movement during the day and well hidden at night. Even now behind me, the boys and guns were stationed deep in a partly destroyed wood, forbidden to move by day. And we weren't the only ones who had arrived: masses of infantry were gathering. Our big barrage was scheduled for 4:20 a.m., heralding another big attack in just a few hours.

It had been so damned wet — but what else could you expect from this crazy France? Rain, rain, rain. Right now it had let up a bit, but the clouds were dense, the mist thick, and we couldn't see the flashes of the guns we were supposed to be marking for our boys back at the Battery.

Tim Philpott, our lanky Signals Bombardier, had brewed up some tea and he handed me a mug, which I sipped thoughtfully. I realized that if I were going to get any accurate observing done, we'd damn well better get closer.

"Tim," I said, "I'll have to go, take a quick look forward."

A look of alarm sprang onto their features. "Don't worry, I won't get us into trouble. But we've got to get further under this mist. When zero hour dawns there'll be a helluva ruckus, and we'd better have some decent reports to send back to Battery."

I raised myself over the lip of the shelter. We had taken over an abandoned and thoroughly makeshift dugout. Not fully safe, but deep enough to protect from the machine-gun fire spraying around. The Boche seemed nervous: occasional shrapnel and high explosives had been going off in our vicinity.

I ducked down, took a last gulp of hot tea, and explained the plan to my crew: I would reconnoitre a new O-Pip, then come back to collect us, and we'd all go forward. "Give me one end of that coil of wire. I can't see a blasted thing crawling down the slope and I'll need to find my way back."

With that, I crawled out on my belly over the slimy mud, and then, because it was pitch dark, I got up onto my hands and knees, grabbing the wire in one hand, and felt my way forward.

So many bits of corpses and shell fragments, all in deep mud. I put my hand right onto the face of a mushed-up skull. Ugh! My stomach churned. That fella was once like me, full of dreams and maybe a family back home. Quickly I banished those thoughts and kept on. After a time, I was stopped short by another squishy mess. Oh Lord! Bodies on top of each other like a pile of logs. I manoeuvred around. A star shell decorated the sky and illuminated a black shell-hole ahead, but ugly mustard coloured its surface. Not for me! I started around it and then, as the flare died, I knelt on something else — a dead horse. What was it doing here? The stink! Awful. My knee broke open the hide. I wiped the maggots off and tried to keep on, but a machine gun opened up and I had to drop flat into the squirming mass of putrid flesh and crawling beasties.

Brushing them off as best I could, I wondered if I was getting too close to Fritz's line. Or were these intermittent bursts coming from an unusually advanced machine-gun post? I calculated that it let loose a burst about every five minutes. Timing myself, I got up on hands and knees and crept forward when suddenly — I sensed right ahead: movement! A clink, I heard, some rifle or bayonet hitting a jutting rock.

Should I turn? The sounds came nearer. Not ten feet ahead, I could even hear breathing. A raiding party! One of ours? Guttural whispering — no, an enemy patrol. Now what?

I lay down flat and got out my revolver. Should I just barrel into them and shoot like hell? But what good would that do? Kill a few and then — get killed myself? No, my job was to set up an observation post so that our batteries could wipe out hundreds. So get out of their way? Not possible, no time. I swallowed hard. Closer came the sounds of the patrol. So this was it, then. My last fight.

Silence. I scarcely breathed. They were listening, too. That moment stretched out forever. Then didn't I hear them turn and head back? I let out a big sigh. Too close, that was. Being foolish again? Probably. But we had a job to do when our attack began.

I moved laterally, trying to avoid going closer. Come on, send up another flare, Heinie, show me where the hell I am. No luck. But then, with my hand I felt a smooth edge. An old dugout. Good! I got out my flashlight, shone it down, yes, six or eight feet deep, perfect for our forward O-Pip. At the bottom, well, what else do you expect? Decomposing corpses. I can put up with that, I thought. We'd learned how to rid dugouts of corpses a couple of years ago.

Right now, stake the wire here to establish our new posting, so we could follow it back. I hooked it around a half-buried duckboard and started back on my hands and knees when I heard a whizbang coming and squashed myself deep into the mud. It landed close, too close. Shrapnel showered down.

I lay still, half buried. My first tours of duty had been at the firing lines or even further back in Wagon Lines. Dangerous, for sure, but nothing like this. So why wasn't I now yellow with fear? Well, that's not the way of an officer, I said to myself. I tried to roll, lift myself out of the muck, and all right, I'll admit my heart was hammering and my breathing had quickened. Any minute another whizbang might go off and this time right over me. So in a sense, I was keeping my fingers crossed.

So far so good. But as I was creeping around another shell-hole didn't that damn machine gun open up again? Before I could duck, something knocked me flat.

Damn! I picked myself up but my right hand wouldn't work. I felt it with my left. Mangled by the bullet. Then I realized that my throat was filling with blood. I coughed it up as best I could. I felt with my left hand and my God, my chin was mashed. I'd been adjusting my helmet, I guess, and those bullets got both. Just dandy.

What now? Get back to the O-Pip as fast as you can before you bleed to death! To signal something was wrong, I yanked hard on the wire and it came free. That whizbang must have sliced it. Oh well, there'll be a flare up any minute to light my way back.

I felt dizzy and nauseous, and like I had been burned by hot metal where the bullets struck. But for pity's sake, don't lose consciousness, I yelled at myself. Come on, Eric, stop the bleeding, you idiot! With my one good hand I grabbed my jaw to lessen the blood spurting. By feeling around, I think I got the artery okay. So press there, I told myself.

But how to get back? I was lying on my back. I managed to roll over and somehow kneel up, and hobbled ahead on my knees. And then, another whizbang hit right close? I lurched sideways into the ground, covering my neck as the debris showered around. Brushing it off, I knelt up holding my jaw, but found myself wondering, was this the right way? Could I find the other end of the wire? No, because it would be beyond any shell-hole dug by that whizbang.

Well, keep going. I felt disoriented. I tried to crawl on all fours but one hand was useless and the other held my jaw to stop the blood spurting. So I knelt upright and again hobbled on my knees. Damned difficult.

My knee went down into another shell hole, but I just stopped from toppling in. When I began around it, I asked myself, how far should I go? Might I just be heading back Heinie-wards? Rest a second...

Damn machine gun went rat-tat-tating again. Down I went! When it stopped, I got up and inched on my knees through this sticky, clammy, awful mud. But being upright, I was getting lightheaded. I tried to clear the fuzziness, but dammit, I started going black. I fell forward.

Keep awake, I ordered myself, get up! But my head spun. Hang onto that artery! My hand was also bleeding. So what? Get up and get going or you'll just be another corpse littering this awful No Man's Land. I tried, and then...

Down I went, one knee in a pit. This time, I didn't even want to get up. My bloody hand hurt like hell where I fell on it, and now pain was pouring back into my jaw. What a damn nuisance.

Then as I lay holding my jaw, didn't I hear a sniffing? I lashed out with my good hand. The bloody biggest rat, drawn by the smell of my blood, scampered across my face. Horrid. He'd be back for a meal, for sure, if I didn't get going. So I knelt up and started off as fast as I could. This time, I made headway. I must have even gone twenty or thirty feet. Then, I heaved a big sigh of relief. Voices! So I had made it.

I stopped. Voices? Yeah. German.

So turn around and get going — for a heart-stopping moment, I thought they might have seen me. But after another ten feet, I felt faint again and had to stop. Must be a good long way from the O-Pip. How the hell would I make it. Which way was it? More and more tired by the minute. Losing blood does that, I guess. And I'd been up all yesterday and tonight.

I forced myself onwards, but my head was spinning again. Was I heading in the right direction? I thought so. Another five yards and I had to rest.

As I lay there, I had visions of dawn breaking. Finished for sure — I'd be spotted and a hundred bullets would tear into me.

I tried giving myself commands: don't let that happen; get going. But for the life of me, I couldn't. I lay there and tried to think up the worst visions to drive me on. But no use. Then I thought about the Old Homestead: I had to make it back there. Yes, that did it, and I struggled on a bit more. But in what direction? Completely disoriented, I wondered if I was being wise. Then I heard distinct laughter. I stopped. Not ours. Damn. Wrong again.

All right, just give up. You're finished. Just prepare yourself. Get comfortable. Think about what you could possibly do. One revolver, a few rounds... But even the blackness seemed more black. Death on its way, oh yes. Pray a bit, sure, and ask the Lord for a quick end. I faded...

In my dreams I heard a hissed whisper: "Mister Alford. Mister Alford."

Aha! Angels coming! Whaddya know, I've gone straight to heaven with no pain. "Mister Alford." That whisper again. It sounded real. And familiar.

"Yes, it's me," I hissed.

You know who turned up? Of all people in the entire world? Cecil.

"I been zig-zagging back and forth in the dark. I knew I'd find you. But you got yourself awful close to the enemy here..."

"Cecil I can't believe it!"

He grinned in the dim light, and I saw his buckteeth. "You did good, Eric, back in Gunnery School, getting me assigned to your Brigade. Bet you're glad now!"

"I've always been glad, Cecil, you're the best Runner ever,"

I mumbled, trying to summon my strength. Cecil had been wounded in France, and after recovering he'd been sent for training and re-assignment at Whitely, where we reconnected. I had arranged for him to be posted back to 1st Brigade with me. Thank Heaven!

"Dawn in twenty minutes," he whispered. "Be the end of us." He reached out and tied some sigs [signals] wire around my chest. "I won't go fast."

I don't know how I did it, but having him find me gave me such a burst of strength, I was able to struggle along as he led us right straight back to the O-Pip.

CHAPTER TWENTY-NINE

Amiens

Bois de Gentelles, Aug 8th: At 4:20 a.m. the Barrage opened, and at 5 a.m., the Batteries moved forward to support the Infantry. During the night, Lieut. Almond, 4th Battery, CFA was wounded, 1 Gunner killed and 4 Gunners wounded.

WAR DIARIES, 1ˢᵗ BRIGADE, CFA

Thumping over the lip of the O-Pip, I woke up.

Just as well, because I had been losing a fair amount of blood being dragged these remaining yards by Cecil after I'd passed out. So now, here we were. Though for some reason, I had started to shudder.

In no time at all, Tim Philpott tore open my jacket and got out the field dressing stitched inside. He wrapped it around my head to keep my lower jaw shut, pressing hard. I felt helpless not doing my duty, but nothing for it, because I still felt groggy.

I had to find out what on earth Cecil was doing up here in the first place.

"Right after you left on your reconnoitre, he turned up," Tim explained. "Absolutely no reason for it, but he looked real distressed. Told us he'd been bringing an important document to the Brigade Liaison Officer with the Infantry Battalion near our O-Pip here, but somehow he knew he just had to come. Against all regulations, of course." Amazing, I thought. Good old Cecil. "I tried to send him back before he got into trouble, but he wouldn't go, he just kept looking anxiously over the edge of our O-Pip. Then without warning, he took off."

Strange story indeed. My jaw bandaged, Tim started wrapping another field dressing on my hand.

"After he'd gone," Tim went on, "I heard this great explosion down where you were, and I pulled on that guide wire. Napoo! It had come free."

Napoo we often used: came from the French, *il n'y en a plus*, "no more, gone, finished". Well then, I thought, how on earth did Cecil —.

"Don't ask me to explain any of this," Tim finished, with an odd expression, still patching up my hand that hurt like hell. Obviously bones broken. My saviour, meanwhile, had been sitting, sipping a mug of tea after his exertions.

After Tim finished on my wounds, he suggested, "You'd better be getting back to the ADS now, sir."

"I'll take him," Cecil said firmly.

I was about to object but I didn't feel that good: the shivering was getting worse. The dense mist and overcast kept it pitch black and without the guide wire I'd laid down, my little team would never find the new O-Pip I'd located. Nothing I could do about that now.

I hoped our Heinie machine gunner would not spray more bullets in our direction. We waited for his next burst, then headed out quickly, Cecil holding me, limping as fast as we could up the long, sloping hill. I kept pressing my left hand against my face to stop the bleeding. It was mainly a flesh wound, with the jawbone not broken, I figured.

Well, we made it to our support line, where a Battalion Medical Officer was already tending several wounded men.

"I'll look at you in a moment, Lieutenant," he said.

I sat on an upturned ammunition box trying to calm my shakes, but soon, Zero hour! Our Amiens attack struck with deafening fury: all guns firing, howitzers on one side and 18-pounders on the other. For some reason, the noise so shocked me I leaped up; I just could not take it for one second.

"I won't be long, Lieutenant," said the MO, but I didn't care. I ran for the rear as fast as my shaky legs would take me.

Cecil quickly overtook me. "Mr. Alford, better wait for the MO."

"I'm waiting for nobody," I mouthed with difficulty, regretting my manner. I just had to get away. My stumbling showed me I had no real control of my faculties. Cecil grabbed one arm and held me round the waist, and we set off fast and furiously for the nearest casualty collecting point.

After about half a mile, we caught up with a horse-drawn ambulance and Cecil ran to the Driver, stopped him, and helped me get into it. I thanked Cecil profusely. He had saved my life, and I told him so. He greeted that with the biggest grin, his buckteeth gleaming in the dawn light, and hurried off.

I grabbed on tight with one hand, because I found myself slipping in and out of consciousness, and still shuddering. Not far now, I told myself.

When we arrived at the Advanced Dressing Station, an orderly brought me to a stretcher where I could gather my strength for the next journey, and gave me an anti-tetanus shot, the first thing for a wounded man. I kept clutching my jaw to stay any bleeding, but my arm ached. I didn't know how long I could keep this up. Dammit, I thought, I should have waited for the MO to tape it more securely. But the shaking lessened.

I must have passed out or slept because before I knew it, more wounded began arriving. That opened my eyes! The stretcher cases were crowding in, still in their trench-stained khaki with the clothing roughly torn away from around wounds, stuck by their congealed blood to the canvas stretcher so it had to be cut by the medics. Seeing so many untreated wounds was like visiting a butcher's shop. Men choking for breath, others in anguish begging for attention, still others bore their dreadful, gaping injuries with stoic fortitude.

Eventually, I was led with three or four other wounded to a motor ambulance and was born off towards the Main Dressing Station, or MDS. As we jolted our way along, every lurch loudly accentuated the groans and curses of the more seriously wounded. The accumulated pain in that one little vehicle could hardly be believed, some silent, some seemingly relieved by loud laments, others wracked by smothered crying. I'd never been in the midst of such suffering. Little was I to know that this was just the beginning.

We arrived at the grounds of a building I found out later was the Amiens Lunatic Asylum. The Medics sorted the mutilated and maimed into groups: men who needed immediate attention, men who could wait, and those sad lost causes with devastating head wounds or abdominal contusions who would not be sent back but made more or less comfortable until they died. It seemed I had joined some horrible torture chamber: dishevelled stretchers on the floor, scattered boots and piles of muddy brown blankets turned back from smashed limbs bound by filthy bandages.

Watching more stretchers stream in, I shuddered to imagine what ghastly agony or imminent death lay under each blanket. The more serious cases were seen immediately. In an hour and a half, when my left arm felt about to break from holding my jaw, I was seen by the MO.

He examined my hand first. "It's stopped bleeding for the moment, but bones are broken, so we'll have to get you to hospital. Meanwhile, I think I can tape that face of yours better, to save you holding it."

He worked on the torn flesh, which hurt like hell. Then I waited with others some hours for transport. I found out later that the British 4th Army commanding the Canadian Corps had limited the medical arrangements and transport in the forward area in case they were seen by the enemy. Finally we were loaded into motor ambulances and headed off to the Casualty Clearing Station. One of the men on the stretchers was a badly wounded German. First we try to kill him, now we try to save his life! War is insane.

The journey itself was taking several unbelievable hours, and my thoughts began to wander... How frightened I had been by the sound of our own guns. My muscles had refused to obey my brain. Never happened before. Pray God, I would not be prey to those bizarre symptoms that had first bothered me in England, shaking or ducking non-existent shells. Well, since I had no control over any of it, I had better just wait and see.

This Casualty Clearing Station had been set up near a railhead. I was seen first by a VAD, a sort of voluntary nurse, who told me this Number Five CCS was near Cachy. The first thing she did was douse both wounds with iodine. My God! My brain almost exploded. The pain, which most soldiers seem to bear, set off something in my mind, and I started shaking again like one of those threshing machines back home. No good telling myself to stop, I just had no control. When the MO came over, he saw the symptoms. Nothing new, apparently.

I don't know how I fell on such a sympathetic doctor, but I heard his words, muffled as through gauze: "Son, don't you mind. If I told you what I've seen from men coming here after a battle, your shaking is normal. You'll get over it, don't worry. Let me re-bandage this face, and you could do with a new dressing on that hand..." He worked quickly and efficiently, and soothing away my tremors: "After every big attack, soldiers come in here in all states and conditions: shell-shock, my heavens — they tremble violently, they're terrified, their hearts develop wildly uneven rhythms, even the slightest noise will make 'em jump. I've seen them," he paused as he pressed the bandage tighter, "I've seen them jump up and run away, just like that, searching for safety, I suppose. They'll scream out, or burst into tears just like a child. Some can't even walk without babbling insanely, their legs trembling and giving out. Many just stare silently into space."

Well, I absorbed all that and hoped my shaking wouldn't get worse. But the cries of so many delirious patients and the ravings of the five or six who were coming round from anaesthetic kept this Clearing Station in pandemonium. Beneath each stinking wad of bloody gauze, I wondered what new and obscene horror awaited these overworked doctors and nursing sisters.

He finished. "We'll get you off to the Field Hospital in Rouen, where they'll X-ray your hand and do a proper job of setting the bones, don't you worry." With that, I got up and the next wounded man sat down to receive attention. I was then bathed and given a hospital uniform to replace my bloody rags.

I rested a bit, and found my dreams replaced by a reality even more gruesome: convoys of haemorrhages, of delirium; I saw one man with a gangrenous leg wound, slimy and green and scarlet, with the bone laid bare. Horrifying.

That evening, Thursday the 8th, as dusk began to fall, I was loaded onto a train with a number of others, but it was all becoming a bit of a blur. I was so fatigued that during the first part of the trip, I dozed. Then I saw bright moonlight and heard aeroplanes over the low thunder of guns. I drifted into more nightmare visions of ambulance trains jolting noisily, gassed men on stretchers clawing the air, dying men reeking of foul bandages, shrieking and writhing or as still as the death written in their fixed, empty eye sockets.

I tried to stay awake, and when a bright-faced young nurse came lurching past, I smiled at her. The train gave a jolt, and she grabbed onto a seat-back for support, and shook her head. Exhausted, of course. I motioned for her to sit, my companion officer having gone to the bathroom; it was one of the few seats vacant. She hesitated, then gave a weak smile and flopped down.

"Must be a tough job," I said. "No man knows how tough. Am I right?"

She nodded. Too worn out to talk.

"Did you just get on with us?"

"Oh no. I live on this train. A week or more at a time."

I frowned. How could that be?

"Most of our hospital trains have a live-in nurse. But just one for this whole long train." I frowned. "They gave me a place up in the first-class compartment. That's where I do my washing — we have to be bright and clean, no matter whether we've walked through the mud to help soldiers onto the train, or tended others who vomited, and..." She shook her head. "Up there, when I get a moment, I sit and check my clothes and comb out my hair to find any lice you fellows bring in. So many train trips... Load after load of desperate, dying men... I don't know how much longer I can take it."

She made to get up.

"Sit a while, Sister," I said. "You need a break."

"They need me more," she sighed. "Sorry to have spilled it out, but you know, sometimes I..." She turned and went on with her struggle to dispense mercy to the trainload, heading some forty or fifty miles to Rouen.

CHAPTER THIRTY

Rouen, August 1918

The Red Cross train arrived at the platform in Rouen in the middle of the night. One by one, the carriages disgorged their loads of broken humanity. Stretcher cases were taken off by bearers who had quickly assembled. Those of us who could walk made our way painfully along the platform, limping, hobbling or lurching forward in great streams of agony. I was one of the luckier ones, no doubt, but was my mind all right? My muscles weren't. As we jostled one another, some alert, some biting their lips to avoid crying out or making a scene, others stoic with large staring eyes, what a stream it was — flowing like the damned into some dark region of Hell.

That mass exodus remained so vivid, blotting out exactly how we reached this Number Two British Red Cross Hospital. We were the first train from the Amiens slaughter, so we were processed rapidly, some into immediate operation rooms, others into wards with beds, still others onto chairs to await attention.

I found myself beside a soldier who had lost his arm at the elbow, and another whose head had been swathed in bandages through which one bleak eye peered. And all the time, crowding out these horrors, inner visions kept torturing my brain.

Don't worry, I kept telling myself, it's normal, remember what the doctor said, it's not our fault, no, we can't stop them, it will pass — oh yes, pray God, it will pass. But not right away, because whatever my brain could not supply, there in front of me passed and repassed images of such mortal stress, such indignities, such shattered hulks of men, hobbling or being wheeled by bleary-eyed Sisters and orderlies.

Finally, I was assigned a cot in a ward with severely wounded men until I could have my hand X-rayed, only a first assortment. In the next bed, the soldier had half his buttocks shot away, the fleshy part. In her haste to attend to him, the nurse hadn't pulled his screen fully around so I watched her cleaning the raw flesh, not red as I expected, no, yellow with pus, absolutely suppurating with pus. She couldn't do much, just apply those gauze things wetted with iodine to disinfect it.

On my other side, a young lad had had his genitals blown off. When the nurse came in to dress him, I wondered how he stood it. I saw him watching her, dreading the moment she'd arrive. The hole — it was just a hole — was packed with gauze and a tube — the catheter that led into his bladder. She started and I jammed my eyes shut, but they opened again. All the packing she had to pull out, bit by bit, clean the hole then pack it back in. Such agony. He started to cry; he couldn't help it, so she covered his face with a handkerchief to save him embarrassment. After it was over, and I felt almost as badly as she did, she returned with a drop of brandy that I could've used myself.

Across the ward, another officer had half his face blown away. How hard it was for the young VAD to look him straight in the eye. He watched intensely to see how she was going to react, dressing his wound. Pretty hideous, he looked! His face was raw, though no worse than such horrors on arms or legs, but much more unpleasant because his breath, mingling with stale blood in the mouth and passages, smelled just so foul. The poor girl worked hard to sustain a smile during her adjusting of his drainage and feeding tubes.

And with it all, sharp pains from my own tiny wounds stabbed me, filling me with despair that I might be confined here forever, that I might never escape. My whole world was filled with misery. But was I not as guilty as the Hun, for had our guns not filled the German hospitals with just as much suffering? Had I not, by commanding a howitzer, laboured to produce the same, if not more, suffering? What was all this about anyway? Why were we really fighting? For what were we dying? Worse than that, had we been handed so much torment because we ourselves had inflicted even more across a few yards of No Man's Land? Was this not therefore a just retribution?

I found myself crying out in rage and frustration, but so many other wounded also allowed cries to escape their lips. So many groans, and even, yes, I hate to report, volumes of blasphemy coming from the wounded that no one paid attention to my sudden bellow of despair.

Finally, I did drift off. But had I not just come from the train? So what were these hordes of broken beings striding along in a black mass, like a vast army of damned, dark-suited souls all marching down, down, down.

We reached the gates of the Underworld, black and threatening. We crowded against them, trampling each other underfoot. Then with a thunderous boom, they opened. Gates of Hell? Or some vast subterranean cavern of descending circles at the bottom of the universe?

With the surging multitude, I faced new, great black gun barrels spouting flame and death right at us. But somehow we remained untouched by the avalanche of shrapnel and searing bullets, and pushed on. Was I now trapped in a nightmare from which I'd never, ever escape? I must have been screaming for I felt myself roughly shaken, and some orderly jabbed me with a needle, causing the images to subside.

But their place was taken by a kind of icy emptiness... a dead mass of black blood that had congealed like treacle, like the mud of Passchendaele, yellowish, greenish, black, from which nothing could emerge. The deadness of a void. Would I float or would I drown?

No, because it turned out this was a field of actual ice, like Chaleur Bay when it freezes: flat, torpid, lifeless. This horror became intensified by the frigidity, so deathly quiet, so different from the steaming battlefield. It struck me: did I feel like giving up? Oh yes, my footsteps that had been pounding along, thump thump thump, as I staggered always forward, had become less certain. Below me, macabre shapes formed in the ice to freeze the blood in my veins. I knew I must not look down, these clutching fingers of corpses craved my body and my soul, tempting me to join them.

But I continued, shakily, step after step, until there, at the very end of the ice field, stood a huge, horrific figure, waiting. As bad as what I had been through? No, worse than anything I'd ever seen.

But something told me I had to deal with him if I were ever going to escape this icy prison of pain. I paused in a kind of bewilderment, and again felt the putrid, white, crystalline substance beneath tugging at me, trying to absorb me, pulling me in! If I stayed, I knew I'd become like the others, stuck forever, so I made myself stagger on, yes, towards that indescribably menacing figure, the personification of War, like Satan himself.

But I could not face him yet. I could not. I woke up. I was being wheeled into an examination room.

***

By noon my chin wound had been repaired by a worn-out doctor in his mid-forties staring through large bifocals. He had deftly stitched my flesh in place and bandaged me. Then my hand. My shuddering was so bad that when they placed it in an X-ray machine, two men had to hold my wrist to keep it still.

Once they got the X-ray back, more pain stabbed but I kept calming myself — it will all soon be over, my hand will be set and flesh stitched and bones in plaster, so healing would surely begin.

But what terrified me most was that another night was fast approaching. Would I not be assaulted by images even more horrible? Would I have to again face that dreaded monster at the end of the ice field? But luckily, no, out the hospital windows in the setting sun, I saw Sisters coming to move us off, making room for more trainloads arriving from the Front. "Our troops have been so successful," one was saying. "We advanced eight miles yesterday. The furthest advance since the war began. The Canadians did it!" Well for a time, that held at bay any blackness crowding round.

Then I thought of "the terrible Boche" being subject to the same merciless pain in hospitals probably staffed, as the word was going around, by nurses even more worn out. I had heard discussed in the corridors that the Germans were down on their luck, little food, poor uniforms, not enough ammunition — they had thrown everything into their spring offensive and it had been halted. So at last, the tide had turned.

CHAPTER THIRTY-ONE

England, August 1918

The Fifth Southern General Hospital at Portsmouth was a fine sunny place. Having been among the first surge of wounded, those of us who had shared the trek to Rouen were now safely across the Channel. We had been moved quickly back to Blighty to make room for the waves of casualties flooding into the Advanced Dressing Stations, the Casualty Clearing Stations, and the hospitals in France.

I was still a prey to tortured visions — made worse, no doubt, by being in the company of so many suffering from gas gangrene. This, by the way, was not caused by chemical warfare but by bullets or shrapnel driving bacillus microbes from the soil deep into a wound. In the absence of oxygen, the microbes quickly multiplied in that hothouse of crushed bone, tangled blood vessels, and shredded flesh. The infection created a septic swill that soon bubbled up like gas, sometimes within as little as twenty-four hours. The smell would make anyone vomit, even experienced medical men. I shall never forget that smell: a sort of chlorate of lime odour, as if the stench of the wounds themselves was not terrible enough.

Gas gangrene made your death so agonizing because you were eaten away from within. Since the infection could only be eradicated by oxygen, the doctors had to expose it to the air. So they cut away living flesh from around the wounds, both where the bullet or shrapnel went in and came out. Then they punched a hole through to allow oxygen to enter and kill the infection. You just would not believe the smell of the drainage holes I glimpsed during dressings, some the size of clenched fists. It might have controlled gas gangrene, but surely made for other challenges, nearly killing soldiers with pain. Every day a nurse had to pull a piece of sterile cord through the wound from front to back, leaving it overnight, then pull it out again and stick in another one. Imagine! And with this going on around me, I was trying to forget the war and blank out its horrific visions.

The worst of it was watching poor young fellows awaiting phlegmatically the approach of their own death. A doomed lad lay in the next bed, his pale, once-handsome face now yellow, his cheeks sunken, his lips bitten out of restlessness and agony. He asked me in a courteous whisper if I knew how long he had to wait before he died. Not long; the next morning they brought in the screens round his bed. So many gas cases doomed from the start — I'd see them watch the nurses with fear-darkened eyes, afraid to ask the question to which they already knew the awful truth.

Three days after I arrived, I was out on a balcony when who should arrive but my worthy brother, Jack.

"Eric! My! You don't look so bad after all! The telegram said, *wounded face and hand — severe.* I expected to find you much worse. You only have a bandage across your jaw." But I could see in his face he'd been really concerned.

I got to my feet, and we embraced. "You shouldn't have bothered to come all this way, Jack," I said, sitting down beside him. "I know you have your hands full in London." Just words — I was really glad he'd come.

"Don't be silly, Eric, Momma would skin me alive if I hadn't. And I made sure that I found business to do while here, checking our Canadian chaplains at these hospitals — I hope one of them visited you?"

"Not so far, Jack. A lot of fellas are soon heading for the Almighty, and they need the chaplain far more than those of us left in the land of the Ungodly." I cracked a smile, and yelped because my jaw still hurt.

"You brought that on yourself Eric — no more cracking jokes while I'm around. Otherwise we'll both be laughing ourselves silly, and you'll need another operation on that jaw!" Then he reached into his pocket and handed me an envelope with Rene's writing. "Well, I brought this."

I looked at it and then put it away. "Now Jack, please make sure she doesn't come down." I didn't know quite how to tell him, because he was such a fighter himself. "You see, Jack, it's not just the face and the jaw."

A look of alarm crossed his features.

"No no, it's not, you see, physical. It's just that you never know when these terrors are gonna grab a-hold. When they do, I could shout, scream, dive under tables, I get shaking. I'm not really well enough to see anyone. And I have these Satanic nightmares. They call it shell-shock."

He nodded. "It's something we're all struggling to understand."

"Jack, they say I'll get over it. I haven't yet, that's for sure. And there's nothing I can do about it. They give me warm baths. I've seen a doctor fellow who specializes in this sort of thing. Lots of cases are worse than mine." I leaned forward. "Fellows who can't actually stand, although there's nothing wrong with their legs. Some can't even speak — they try hard, but they just cannot."

He shook his head. "I haven't been visiting the hospitals as much as I should. You wouldn't believe the officialdom I deal with every day." He sighed. "I do believe faith and prayer can somehow help our soldiers deal with their terrors. But listen, here's what one Major of the Royal Medical Corps does in treating men who cannot speak: he lashes them to an operating table, puts a constrictive gas mask on them, and lets them suffer in near suffocation. Then he comes back and asks in a soothing voice, 'If you speak the words, *Take it away* I shall do so.' Can you believe it?"

I shook my head and sighed. No doctor here like that, I thought.

"Oh yes, other experts," Jack went on, disgusted, "employ electric shock therapy. They'll electrocute tongues, eyelids, even genitals, to brutally shock these poor fellows out of their catatonic states, brought on as you know by the horrors of constant bombardment, so they can send them back into the same hell."

"Well here, I'm told by this doctor I'll get over it. I'm soon off to a convalescent hospital for Canadian Officers."

Jack nodded. "Yes, at Matlock Bath, in Derbyshire, I know of it, and have been up there, visiting."

"I'm told that with rest, with peace and quiet such as I shall get, these terrors will disappear. I earnestly pray that is so."

"I'll tell you what I'll do," said Jack. "I tried it once in the Labrador. In fact, I did it several times. A form of exorcism. Not really sanctioned by the church. But if you will allow me, we'll do a little ceremony together, and it might help. Needless to say, no one knows how the Holy Spirit works, whether He can be summoned at will, or whether He takes His own sweet time. But why don't we give it a try?"

We walked down the steps of the hospital off into the grounds and found a sunny bench. I closed my eyes while Jack said a few prayers. Then, didn't he smack me on the forehead with the flat of his hand? I was never so surprised all my life.

"Well," I said opening my eyes, "maybe that will knock some sense into me, even if it doesn't get rid of the terrors." And then in spite of myself, I started to laugh. And dammit, that jaw hurt like hell all over again. But it was worth it, to have my spirits raised.

***

I soon found my physical ailments healing and off I was shipped to Matlock Bath. Our convoy of ambulances arrived at St. Pancras Rail Station for the trip north and the wounded were wheeled, assisted, or carried across to the station. A group of little boys surrounded us with cries of delight.

"Coo, look, here's one with no arm!"

"This one here, he's got no legs, come quick, look!"

"There's a man coming out with only one eye! Look, lost an eye."

"What's that one on the stretcher like? Sister, let us look at him, I bet he's real bad."

Of course, the orderlies were quick to chase the urchins away and bundle the more severely wounded into the station. I was trying to suppress my annoyance when one of the lads came up and said, "Excuse me, sir, can you bring us some more to see tomorrow? We've been waiting all week."

I turned, without giving the lad the cuffing he deserved and, suppressing my natural anger, went off to the train.

When we arrived, I found the Officers' Convalescent Hospital nestled in a rather wide, flat hollow surrounded by interesting hills, one of which rises abruptly out of the town, called High Tor. I was told these hills made for wonderful hikes and, in a way, the scenery reminded me of parts of the Gaspe Coast. Exactly what I needed; I really felt at home. If anything was going to cure me of disabling visions, this might be it. But then, inevitably, night would fall and I would be wracked by horrors once again.

I joined several walking parties on trails that led out into the countryside so that I could familiarize myself before attempting any on my own. Then one morning I awoke after a particularly distressing night. I had once again found myself on that icy plain, facing the dreadful fearsome barrier of the devilish Angel of War. But the sun, not known for its regular appearance here in the Old Country, came out in all its Gaspesian glory, if you will forgive the analogy. Today, I determined, I would go off on my own.

At the base of the tor I found some inviting pastureland, with sheep nibbling the verdant April grass. So like the Gaspe in many ways. I sat on a rock, and then I moved off and just lay back, gazing up at the wisps of high cirrus strung out across the cavern of sky. And then, I slipped into sleep.

***

I should never have allowed myself to do that. Because once again I had slipped into another electrifying dream. I was on an ice field, facing the same War Devil.

I stood wondering what to do when I saw the figure make a gesture of judgment. He didn't speak, he just grinned and pointed downwards. Oh no! Was I now, with the rest of humanity, being condemned to an everlasting nightmare?

But you know? His grin seemed a bit uncertain — like a trickster, as if he were not in a position of spiritual authority and, in a way, had no real power behind his gesture. Was he only trying to persuade me to accept this hell of icy petrification? That hint of uncertainty was all I needed. Summoning up all my strength, I kept on walking straight at him.

And do you know, the image began to shimmer. I walked still closer and then didn't the figure begin to dissolve into a ghastly clammy mist, like the ones from a gas attack? Was I now seeing that image atop Hill 70 — the Angel of Mons, the Angel of Mercy, shaping itself? I braced myself, and ended up walking right through that mist.

I staggered forward, still shuddering from the effects of the deadly chill, and headed towards a dark opening in a precipice wall. Within this cave I glimpsed what seemed to be a stairway cut into the rock. I started to climb it and found myself mounting circular stone steps with no railing. I kept my body pressed against the dank wall. I had to keep looking up, for above I caught sight of a tiny spot of light. No longer hindered by these supernatural terrors, I continued round and round, step after step, always looking up. If I slipped, I would hurtle to my death.

The higher I went, the more certain I became. Something was calling, softly out of a dreadful void. A faint hymn wafting across the waters of death below? Or the loving whispers of my mother at my bedside when I was a little lad? Or somehow, as Jack once explained it to me, the words of One who had himself gone down into the void, into the maw of Hell itself and in three days wrested a victory from Death?

But it was none of those celestial sounds, no, it sounded rather like a female voice, but whose? I listened, and yes, possibly

Rene's, or rather her laughter, bubbling and tingling the air, and beckoning. Whatever it was, I calmed slightly and developed a regular rhythm in my progress. After an age of exertion, I did reach the top.

I opened my eyes. Here I was, collapsed, once again on this verdant pastureland, at the foot of High Tor. There above, the cirrus still drifted gently across the blue sky. I lay, exhausted, knowing I'd been given a kind of blessing.

I rose up after this vision, or still in it, and moved across to a rivulet running down from on high. I knelt and splashed the cool water on my face. Was I not washing off the grime of the Underworld? And of my frightening ascent? My terrors melted in this cleansing, living stream.

Follow the rivulet upwards, I thought, let the breezes dry your skin. And so I began again, this time an altogether different ascent. I hiked upward and this lovely little stream became somehow energizing, splashing from rock to rock. I found the pastureland giving way to a steeper and rockier terrain, working in me a unique spiritual abrasion.

It had begun softly and gently, but as I climbed higher, I felt the challenge intensify. I knew somehow I had to shed those deeply imbued fears and anxieties from my wartime experiences. Oh yes, this curative process was stripping away at my mental or spiritual states and replacing them with Higher Virtues. And as I climbed, I felt lighter, my step more purposeful, more secure, even as the hill became more challenging.

Reaching the top of High Tor, I stood in the strong winds and breathed deeply. Yes, now having achieved this conquest of the hill, I realized I was in fine shape to leave the war behind and encounter the world once again. And I'd make sure that world included Rene, for her call had awakened me on the grassy pasture: she had been beckoning me up the hill. Now I could meet her when I got back to London, and be at her side in a way that was not possible before — had I not gone through these visionary and physical experiences.

As someone who has passed through the hell of the battlefield, both real and spiritual, I could confront anything. This Aristocracy of the Warrior, so much more than just written a phrase, enveloped me like a mantle. As an ancient knight and ready for anyone or anything, I had somehow been crowned monarch over myself.

THE RETURN 1919

I stood looking down at the white wooden cross I had made as a younger man. Fifty years ago, maybe a bit more, James Alford, 1778-1863, and his wife, Catherine Garrett had been put to rest in this New Carlisle cemetery. I don't know how long I was lost in my gaze, but suddenly I fell on my knees and grabbed a-hold of the cross in both arms.

You'd understand it all, James, I thought, my fighting forerunner, my sailor ancestor. You'd know what I went through. You'd know what war was like. And Catherine, did you understand it, too? Did James tell you about it? Because now, you see, I know him better. I know what he went through on that there great big ship-of-the-line. We both fought, yes, and know that nothing, nothing we can say or do, will ever make others understand. No one ever understands. I see that now. But why was I crying?

Three weeks ago, when Poppa and me in the buggy reached Momma's large English flower garden and turned up our steep driveway, I could feel my heart just bursting. There, unbelievably, was the Old Homestead, with its black tarred shingled roof, its whitewashed walls and its wrap-around veranda, where we had spent so many Sunday evenings looking out across the bay, and over to the new wharf. Lillian waved from the window and came rushing out, calling Momma who burst out the back door in her apron, Earle came on the trot from the barn, my cousins, playing on the grass by the shed — they all gathered round as Poppa pulled Lively to a halt after our fast trot from St. Godfrey station. I was home at last.

But they all just stood there, looking. What did they see? Had I changed so much? I started to get down, and at last Momma ran forward. I grabbed hold of her and the tears poured down my face. I hung onto her so tight I nearly killed her. I couldn't let go. But when I did look up, the others were watching me, kinda strange. Well, I don't blame them.

I wiped my eyes, tried a smile or two, and then shook hands with everyone. But I could not get their look out of my head. I was like some guy from Africa or Zambesiland. Hey! I'm your brother, your relative, your son, I felt like yelling. But they still looked on me as someone they'd never known.

Earle told me later, he'd gotten such a shock. He'd never seen no one age that fast. And that look in my eyes. Another fella, Will Wiley, he'd come back earlier, Earle saw it in his eyes, too.

I guess Jack had written. He'd warned them to watch out. I had been through so much, maybe I wasn't going to be what they expected. The army doctors told me I'd better rest for a good long time. But since I arrived back, I feel a bit better: nothing like sleeping in my own feather bed and Momma making me breakfast, maybe going to sit on the veranda for a smoke, a bit of a read, and the war followup in the *Family Herald*. A couple of times I even walked back over the hill. Didn't get back as far as the Hollow yet. Though they told me no one had heard of Raine for a couple of years. Last anyone knew, she was in Montreal and doing pretty good.

Matlock Bath had sort of cured me, and I'd gotten thrown back into action at Arras. Then after only two weeks I was invalided again to Blighty, ten days before the end of the war. First I'd recuperated at a French hospital and then in England stayed at different hospitals. That's when I got to see a fair bit of Rene. Finally, they put me on a ship that reached Halifax on the 14th of May, a month ago now. I'm real glad I didn't persuade Rene to try and make it here, or follow me soon. I mean, after London — the Old Homestead? Oh no. And she knew it. When we said goodbye, we knew it was for good.

Well maybe not. I'm going to write to her by and by. She said she's going to keep training as a dancer, even though it annoys the Mater. Jack wrote that he'd had a lunch with her after I left. So nice of him. We'd gotten to know each other real good in the three or four months before I left. Listen to me, I no sooner get home than I talk like a Shigawaker. I'll have to smarten up again. Specially if I intend to get to University, though the doctor warned it might take a year or two before I'm ready to do anything much. Funny, Earle don't — I mean doesn't — make me do anything round the farm. They just sort of leave me be. Which is just as well. I guess the shell-shock never leaves, though I sure was hoping it would.

In New Carlisle, I let go the cross and got up off the grass, wet from yesterday's rain. Today, Sunday, they didn't need Lively, so Poppa let him bring me to the cemetery. I walked over, untied him, and got into the buggy. I paused a while, looking around. I guess I'd better make myself shape up, drive back to the Old Homestead, and take another go at this different life in Shigawake, after that Great War for Civilization, the war to end all wars.

AFTERWORD

After Amiens, when Lieutenant Eric Almond (on whom this story is based) was wounded, the Imperial forces, in what became known as the Hundred Days, pushed the Germans back some eighty miles up and down the Western Front. They put up stern resistance, but the morale and social order within Germany began to crumble. Their fleet was ordered out to sea but the sailors mutinied, and armed groups began to spread throughout Germany in open revolt. Fearing another Communist revolution, the Allies were happy to sign — with an extemporized German government (the Kaiser having been sent into exile) — an Armistice at the eleventh hour of the eleventh day of the eleventh month of 1918.

The *Guardian* newspaper recounts that between 8.5 and 9 million soldiers perished. Indeed, some 10.5 million soldiers were killed and wounded on the Western Front alone. Tim Cook of the Canadian War Museum writes, "The statistics are staggering in their horror." In all, some 50 percent of mobilized soldiers were either killed, wounded, captured, or declared missing. At least 80,000 British soldiers were shell-shocked, though some experts think this estimate far too low.

In spite of intensive research by historians, there is not now — and never will be — a definitive list of casualties. Soldiers were wholly obliterated or instantly buried, and casualty records were often inaccurately kept, distorted for propaganda, or destroyed by the war.

Canada and Newfoundland enlisted more than 645,000 people, two thirds of whom served overseas. Of these, Canada and Newfoundland suffered over 68,000 dead and some 140,000 wounded — a casualty rate of approximately one half. By comparison, in the Second World War the casualty rate was roughly 9 percent of total enlistments, yet that too was a terrible and costly conflict. What is more, *civilian* deaths in all countries during the Great War are estimated at ten million, a significant proportion due to the terrible famine and disease that war brought in its wake.

Original Writing

My father, Lieut. Eric Almond, left no specific writings on his war experiences. I was guided in my fictional account only by the fierce but understated reality of his battalions' diaries. He did leave a looseleaf with some stories that I finally read fifty years after his death. I have chosen from among them some excerpts to illustrate here his involvement in that mighty conflict.

Major Eric Almond, Shigawake, Bonaventure County, Quebec

I wish to state that I wrote these stories in the autumn of 1926 during the time I was attending lectures and carrying on with all my work as a university student in Third Year Arts. They are rough and ready like the scenes I have depicted for I have made no attempt to polish them. But they are human true, because all these events actually happened, although I have changed a few names and places.

Reminiscences of the Great War

Six old soldiers were gathered together in a large upper room in the Windsor Hotel, December 31, 1921. They had assembled to watch the old year out and the New Year in — a solemn time. It was a typical reunion of old soldiers, a bottle of Scotch, pipes, cigars, and cigarettes were soon sending up a gas cloud like the Germans put over Ypres but such friendly gas. It was more like an incense rising to heaven.

There was quiet in the room for a while, when someone proposed "The Silent Lost," everybody busy with memories of friends who had gone west out in Flanders. But the Scotch whisky did its work... They pointed a finger at me and I seemed to be back in France...

"Did I ever tell you boys about the Black Cat, OP?" All right, here goes:

Our infantry had dug in the old German lines in front of Arras. The trenches were fairly close together — about forty yards of No Man's Land. The First Canadian Brigade Artillery were supporting the Third Divisional Infantry and I was shooting officer for the Fourth Battery and Forward Observing Officer for the First Brigade.

I had gone up the trenches this night with the full outfit — you fellows know — two Signallers, two Linesmen, two pigeons, rifles for the Signallers, my own revolver, field glasses, telescope and SOS rockets.

The OP overlooked No Man's Land and the German country, just behind our old front line — one sheet of corrugated iron over our heads and just below was an old forty-foot German dugout.

Everything in the Front was absolutely quiet. The Infantry Intelligence Officer had no news for me worth anything. All there was for me to do was to watch and wait. That everlasting watch, how many nights have we stood looking over No Man's Land, the eyes of the Artillery waiting for dawn? It seemed selfish to keep my Signallers up in the OP for everything was almighty quiet, so I sent them down into the dugout directly below, with the kind order to try to get a little sleep. You fellows know that it is a court-martial offence punishable by death to leave an OP when there is an attack or under any other circumstances. And I suppose you know that I'm not usually "yellow" or shirk my duty.

All Roman Catholics have Guardian Angels, so they tell me. Well, my Guardian Angel was with me in that observation post, or something like it. Yes, everything so very quiet not a single shell. Away on the left a machine gun rattled once or twice. The Germans were not sending up any planes for a wonder. It was such a perfect moonlight evening.

Poor old Colonel Dorothy — he is pushing daisies now, God rest his soul — called me up about 11 o'clock to enquire about the Front.

"Everything quiet, Sir." I said.

"All right, Eric, I will turn into my sleeping bag. Goodnight!" answered the old Colonel.

About 12 o'clock I was dreaming wide awake when suddenly, boys, I felt somebody in the Observation Post beside me. No, don't laugh, I am in deadly earnest. My flesh started to creep — it was not a view of physical death, because I have been scared blue often before. I know what it is to face rifle and machine-gun fire and dodge whiz-bangs. It was a supernatural fear, as if all the ghosts in creation were beside me. My hair stood straight on end. Then somebody seemed to throw me headfirst down into that forty-foot dugout.

I picked myself up at the bottom after frightening my Signallers to death, and started to climb back, when suddenly the whole earth seemed to shake above me, mud, clay, and stones came down on my head with the fumes of the gas of an exploding shell. I pushed my way to the top through the debris to find — where my OP had formerly stood — only a shell hole about six foot deep. It was a direct hit of a German 5.9. The only shell the Huns fired that night. I was thrown out of the OP by my Guardian Angel while the shell that should have killed me was coming on his mission of destruction through the air. The rest of the night I watched our front from the shell hole.

The next day, I was up before Colonel Dorothy. "Well, Eric, my lad, I see Black Cat OP has been destroyed by an enemy shell. Why ever were you not blown up also? You know, my boy, this is a court-martial offence. What have you got to say?"

So, fellows, I told the old Colonel this story that I am now telling you. He smiled and said, "There are strange experiences nowadays. Have a drink my boy and forget about it."

But this is the mystery, old-timers. I never breathed about the experience to a solitary soul, but three weeks afterwards — you know, Harry had been invalided back to the States, on account of his smash-up at Vimy. Well, I had a letter from the old swamp adder in New York, congratulating me on my sudden dive into the dugout from Black Cat OP. Now how in thunder did that man of mystery know about this, I ask you?

A Dugout in Flanders

"No, it is no use to carry him back to the dressing station for he would die on the way," the field doctor said. "He has been terrible hit by an exploding shell in the stomach and legs, so he will pass out in a few hours. Let his friends stay here with him and see him across in peace."

"Are you afraid to die, Billy?" his friend asked.

"No, old man, this war is over for me. And if it wasn't for mother I would be happy to go, but you know, I am her only son, and she is old. There is a girlfriend, too, but strange to say, I don't feel so badly about her. My one thought is mother."

"Never mind, old man, God will help her," his friend replied.

"Yes, I know. Could you say the Lord's Prayer with me? And tell mother, for it would please her so. My legs feel funny, they are so numb and there is an awful blackness before my eyes".

"You are all right, Billy boy, I have my arms right around you. Trust in God, and go to sleep."

And this was death.

The Hero

After we took Vimy Ridge from the Huns, I was ordered in charge of some of our battery drivers, with about fifty men from the Divisional Ammunition Corps to carry shells on the horse's backs up to the guns. It was impossible to get wagons over that hell-accursed ground, just one sea of shell holes after the terrific battle, where all the big guns on the Western Front had been massed for the attack. We overcame the difficulty by tying ammunition on the saddles, riding one horse and leading the other.

The Germans put over a gas barrage so I ordered the drivers to wear their gas masks, which made the going very difficult, as a matter of fact. The divisional men, not being accustomed to gas shells, dumped their ammunition in the mud and galloped back. However, my own battery men stayed with me — true soldier hero hearts, God bless them! We were forced to go through a huge railway culvert under a big embankment to get forward to the guns. And we were ordered to make about four trips so our artillery would have lots of ammunition in case of a German counter attack. All at once the Boche artillery registered on that culvert with 5.9 shells and fast 4.2s, at the same time putting over bursts of shrapnel. They kept firing all night at intervals to prevent the passage of our troops through the embankment. It was one hell of an obstacle for you did not know what moment that quiet culvert would turn into a wall of fire with exploding shells.

The first time through, they caught us nicely. Three of my drivers were killed, two wounded, with their horses only mangled heaps piled up on the side of the road.

We were all loaded up with shells to go through that culvert a second time when a young boy, one of my drivers, with white face and shaking limbs, rode up to me. He looked about sixteen, God only knows how he ever got into the army, I suppose he lied about his age. This was his first time in action.

A hell of a baptism of fire from that mere child.

Sir!" he said, saluting me. "I am frightened, I don't think I can go through that culvert again."

I said, "Tommy my lad. You must not show cowardice in action: it is punishable by death. It is better to die, than be a coward. However, the greatest hero of the lot is the man who will face the enemy when his legs want to run back. I expect you to go through that culvert even though you're frightened to death."

He replied, "All right, Sir! But will you go through by my side?"

We went through together four times that night. It was surely nerve-wracking business, even for old soldiers, that was one rough passage: twice the Boche shelled us again, one caught the front of our column killing one man, then the rear of our party wounding two others, eight casualties in all, almost half our original outfit. The boy was trembling all over, but he did his duty like a veteran. Tommy never went into action after that but what he was still yellow with fear. However he stuck it just the same and did his duty with trembling knees.

I tell you shell fire is no picnic! When you can hear them come whistling down on top of you! — even the bravest will duck and take cover. I would still rather be under shellfire than face rifle fire in the open — it takes all your nerve to stand up to those droning bees: zip zip.

We buried this young lad at Hill 70 where he fell under rifle fire but with his face to the foe — Thank God.

I had to write his mother. That was one hard letter.

Yes — a real hero scared to death but too brave to run away.

I have no fear. What is in store for me shall find me ready for it, undismayed. God grant my only cowardice may be: afraid — to be afraid!

The Monument

At the present moment I am thinking of monument in Sherbrooke Que which represents the Canadian Infantry in the trenches, looking up to the figure of Victory on top of the parapet. To me, where the sculptor carved in granite the essential truth — God's own truth, was this:

That in spite of the lice, mud, hunger, cold, wet, gas and shelling, those Canadian boys are still looking up. Not down, mark you, but with eyes forgetting the misery of soul and body, were looking up straight through the blue.

And we who are living in the Paths of Peace, when sickness or suffering with disaster almost overwhelms us, may we seek an inspiration and catch the vision from that soldiers Memorial in Sherbrooke and "look up!"

Notes on Organization, Ranks, Guns and Ammunition in the Artillery

Gun Detachment: consisted of a gun, three limbers, two ammunition wagons, twenty horses, ten Gunners and nine Drivers commanded by a Sergeant. Two guns (a Section) commanded by a Lieutenant.

Battery: two or three sections (three for most of the war) with a large headquarters and support component commanded by a Major (approx 6 guns, 195 men and 165 horses).

Brigade: two or more batteries (generally four) with a small headquarters commanded by a Lieutenant-Colonel.

Ammunition Column: (to which Cecil was assigned) approx 590 Artillerymen and 666 horses commanded by a Lieutenant-Colonel.

Division: two or more field brigades, three heavy mortar batteries, an ammunition column and a small headquarters commanded by a Brigadier-General.

Canadian Corps Artillery: five division artilleries plus units from

Army Artillery commanded initially by a Brigadier and later a Major-General (approx 240 field guns, 84 heavy guns, 80 heavy mortars, 14,400 men and 10,000 horses).

THE WOUNDED: Eric was evacuated after being wounded via the:
CCS: Casualty Clearing Station; and the
ADS: Advanced Dressing Station

ON RANKS

Commissioned Officers (Second Lieutenants to Field Marshals) held a King's Commission, a personal contract between the officer and the Sovereign. On being given/granted a Commission, a soldier was recognized as being His Majesty's "good and trusty friend". Commissioned officers were referred to as "Sir" by subordinates and were saluted as a mark of respect for the Commission.

Immediately below the Commissioned Officers were the Non-Commissioned Officers (NCOs) (Warrant Officers and Sergeants). Warrant Officers (for example "Battery Sergeant Major" or "BSM") also held a King's Warrant and were addressed as "Sir" by subordinates. Sergeants were addressed as "Sergeant". NCOs were not saluted. NCOs and officers formed a "command team" although final authority and responsibility rested with the officers.

Below the NCOs were the ORs, Other Ranks ("rankers" because they stood in ranks on parades). Most were Gunners and Drivers. Next came "Bombardiers" (Lance Corporals), and above them, Corporals.

Thus, each small group of soldiers was led by a Corporal or Sergeant who supervised, trained and disciplined them. Daily life, meals, washing, and pay all happened at this level. This was the soldier's "family". His extended family was the battery and the field brigade. Levels of command above this were quite remote from the soldier's experience, except as sources of tasks and orders. To most soldiers, the ways of the higher levels of organization would always seem rather distant and foreign. They would tend to be forgiving of their unit leaders while often complaining of being "buggered-about" by commanders higher up.

ON GUNS AND AMMUNITION

The Canadian Field Artillery was equipped with the 18-pounder, a flat-trajectory gun (mostly shrapnel and smoke rounds), and the 4.5" howitzer, (mainly High Explosive and gas) which fired a larger projectile on a much higher trajectory in order to reach beyond obstacles and into trenches.

Shrapnel rounds expelled hundreds of small lead "balls" in a lethal cone which extended up to 200 yards in front of the projectile, making a greyish-white cloud of smoke. A soldier was safe as little as 25-yards behind the burst. High Explosive rounds caused the projectile to disintegrate in a black cloud of smoke, sending out a lethal shower of metal fragments, dangerous within a radius of 150 yards. Smoke rounds simply hid our troops or blinded the enemy.

A vast array of heavier guns lay further behind our lines, but they figure little in our story. Eric and his comrades were regularly on the receiving end of the whole gamut of German artillery, and they, like all the front-line soldiers, came to know — and name — the different German shells by the sounds they made in the air and on arrival. Those nicknames are:

"**Jack Johnson**" the High Explosive rounds fired by German heavy Howitzers. Jack Johnson (1878-1946) was a popular black American who was world heavyweight boxing champion from 1908-15 and renowned for being a hard hitter. Large caliber HE Howitzer rounds (including the often referred to 5.9s) rumbled through the air and on impact made black smoke, hence the nickname "Coal Box," which reminded soldiers of dropping a coal box.

"**Whizbangs**" were shrapnel shells fired from high-velocity relatively flat trajectory guns such as the German 7.7 cm. They made a whizzing noise followed by a loud "bang" when the shrapnel was expelled. Shrapnel often gave off sparks which reminded one of fireworks. "Whizbangs" put on a better visual show, so the nickname was more light-hearted.

ON CANADIAN GUNNERS

Few people know that of all battle casualties in WWI, the artillery killed and wounded about 60% — a crucial element in the war. Our guns became more accurate, more technically reliable and much more lethal throughout the conflict. Canadian Gunners were leaders in technical and tactical innovation, and this was perhaps attributable to some curious social reasoning.

The 3% or so of British society that ruled the empire, and who were in charge of the war, looked down on tradesmen. As an example, they would want to own a watch, but they would never want to know how to repair it: that was a tradesman's job. Gentlemen were not tradesmen. Officers, especially the most senior ones, were, above all else, dyed-in-the-wool gentlemen. They resisted, and thus delayed, many innovations during the Great War because delving into that level of detail smacked of being reduced to tradesmen — beneath their station in life. Certainly not all British officers had this crippling social viewpoint, but enough did to cause real delays in improving things.

The Canadians, not having this hangup, were able to think creatively about ways to improve artillery fire and so they embraced change. When General A.G.L. (then Lieut-Col) McNaughton devised new ways to increase the accuracy of counter bombardment (CB) fire, as outlined in this book, many British officers frowned on that; in fact, he had a hard time of it at first. But statistics show that during the Battle of the Somme in 1916, CB fire (the greatest test of accuracy) was only about 30% effective. However, only six months later during the Battle of Vimy Ridge, after Andrew had made his improvements that were adopted across the Canadian Artillery, Canadian-directed CB fire had become 83% effective. Thus Canadian Gunners lead the way among the artillery of the Commonwealth forces.

BOOK SIX ACKNOWLEDGEMENTS

The battles, equipment, daily weather and actions of the men who served in our distinguished armed forces during the First World War (and more particularly, the battalions mentioned herein) are accurate. My military friends and historians have checked and rechecked the manuscript. My characters, however, are entirely fictitious. Out of respect to the brave soldiers who actually served with the battalions, other than my father (Eric), my uncle (Father John as he was known) and other specific historical figures, I have described no real personages.

Ted Wright, my cousin, being a formidable student of history, knows something of army ways. He helped me cull through a hundred plus books amassed on WWI: novels, histories, diaries of batteries (see list on my own and the Red Deer Press website). There is no room to acknowledge all the authors here, but they certainly gave me a feel for the Front. I have chosen their spelling and nomenclature in most cases. All of the books are accessible through libraries and from that great internet resource, Abebooks. Ted found time between building fences for our two goats, Fran and Marie, and overseeing the making of crab-traps at *La Fine Mouche* in St. Godfrey, to do all my research on Internet and guide me through the war, enlightening me on the historical background and helping with scenes.

Now, as for the splendid Major (ret'd) Marc George who runs Canada's National Artillery Museum in Shilo, Manitoba, words can not fully express my admiration for his unique knowledge: no one in Canada, I can confidently say, knows more about a howitzer and the gun batteries in the First World War than does Marc. He has been beside me, metaphorically, every step of the way, contributing to the manuscript himself by adding superb descriptions. If I diverged from his advice from time to time, then the errors are all mine. He tells me his staff looked up material we needed and covered for him while he worked on my book, so I thank them too. I'm most grateful to both General Christian Barrabé, whom I met at the BCS Cadet Corps Review, and to his Lieut.-Col. Dany Fortin, for finding Marc for me.

My wife Joan and I were fortunate enough to be invited by His Excellency Jeremy Kinsman, then Canadian High Commissioner to the European Economic Commission, and his wife Hana, to their impressive ambassadorial residence in Brussels. Jeremy gave me his knowledgeable driver, Jean Saint-Pierre, for a tour of the battlefields. Rather than visit cemeteries, we focussed on the actual museums: the In Flanders Fields Museum with its realistic muddy trenches, then on to the Passchendaele Museum in Zonnebeke, followed by the Hooge Museum and its trenches, the Albert tunnels, and some really good trenches at Sanctuary Wood and a local museum there. Then we went to Essex Farm, where John McCrae wrote his poem, *In Flanders Fields*.

In the gloriously restored city of Ypres (Wipers) we stayed at Old Tom's and attended the evening sounding of "The Last Post" at the Menin Gate with some three hundred onlookers (and this was not during a school holiday). I'm happy to see that the great interest in WWI continues. Afterwards, Joan and I spent a liquid evening at a café with British veterans on pilgrimages of their own — some do this annually, in fact. The beautiful Cloth Hall, restored at immense expense and now a museum, provided pictures and examples of life at the Front in that Great War for Civilization, as it was known at the time.

At Newfoundland Park, near Beaumont-Hamel, we saw a fine trench layout showing how close the enemy lay across No Man's Land. The Newfoundland Regiment had attacked and within half an hour more than 90 percent became casualties. Their very human Newfoundland museum we liked best of all; certainly it outdid the impersonal one at Vimy, obviously put together by bureaucrats.

As to my chapters on the wounded, rather than rely on my imagination, no matter how vivid, I borrowed phrases and descriptions, rearranged of course, from those who knew and saw such misery: Vera Brittain's wonderful *Testament of Youth*, and some of the actual descriptions recounted in Lynn MacDonald's, *The Roses of No Man's Land*. Tim Cook's splendid history, *At the Sharp End*, manages to encapsulate the horror of gas-gangrene wounds so well, I have with his permission borrowed some of his language also. His second volume, *Shock Troops* is equally engrossing. We should all of us revisit what mankind actually went through during that terrible period, and thus do our part to prevent future wars.

The dialogue in the Canon Scott scene I adapted largely from his own definitive book, *The Great War as I Saw It*, published by F.D. Goodchild Company, Toronto in 1922. He too suffered shell-shock after his wounding at Amiens. Lois and Carl Hayes again provided me with details of genealogical backgrounds, and another cousin, Elton Hayes, checked my Shigawake chapters.

The main sources of written material are, of course, Library and Archives Canada and the Canadian War Museum in Ottawa, both of which helped on my annual spring visit. But in my research,

I was shocked to find that many European historians ignored Canadian successes. Thank goodness for Pierre Berton's *Vimy*!

Leslie Ann Ross, Psy.D., an old family friend and senior director of a Child Trauma Centre in Los Angeles, works with combat veterans at the Veteran's Administration there. She gave me a thorough analysis of Post Traumatic Stress Disorder, helping me with my father's "shell-shock". I must also pay tribute to Prof. Paul Piehler who helped me with Eric's descent and rebirth, as patterned after Dante's *Divine Comedy*. Duff Crerar, author of that stunning *Padres of No Man's Land*, has continued to be a warm supporter of my writing, and I cannot thank him enough for the extra time he took guiding me in Uncle Jack's footsteps, and even reading the manuscript.

My desire to keep this book short is running amok here, as I insist on thanking my many readers who have so often offered more elegant phrases, new ideas, minor corrections and important changes: writer Rex King from her houseboat on the waterways of England near Nottingham, textbook whizz and novelist Diana Colman Webster whom I met sixty years ago in Oxford, as I did the fine director, Peter Duffell, who also helped prepare my battlefield trip with many references. Rev. Susan Klein has read all six books so far and encouraged me ceaselessly; Captain Timothy Winegard, still in the military and then working towards a DPhil at Oxford University, gave valuable input. Retired diplomat Nick Etheridge has scandalously sharp eyes in spotting anachronisms, and is a faithful critic. British writer David Stansfield, a new friend, went through the whole book painstakingly adjusting bits of prose. The grandson of my own English teacher at Bishop's College School, Louis Evans, himself now teaching English on the Gaspe Coast, followed in his ancestor's footsteps by helping, and even my son Matthew took me to task on an earlier version, causing me to rewrite the first chapters furiously. I thank them all.

I would also like to acknowledge the contributions of Corel's Canadian Word Perfect, the superb word processor by which I wrote all six books, and Dragon Naturally Speaking, which permitted me, during daily walks, to talk these stories into a tape recorder and then on its own type the results out as I prepared my coffee.

A couple of personal notes: I was delighted to see that Uncle Jack's burly roommate in *The Chaplain,* Harry Burstall, in this war become Commander of our Corps Artillery and later of the Canadian Second Division. And also my old metaphorical chum, EWB (Dinky) Morrison, the Boer War correspondent whose book *With the Guns* was at my side during the writing of that previous manuscript, followed Harry to be General Officer Commanding the Royal Artillery Canadian Corps, and then was largely responsible for the barrage at Vimy Ridge that broke the Germans back. He was knighted 1919. I'd like to add that Edmund Blunden and JRR Tolkien fought in the assault on Regina Trench, and Saki, the great short story writer (Lance Sergeant H.H. Munro) was killed by a sniper there.

While I wrote in the Old Homestead, Francine Senneville tirelessly prepared our noon dinners. Joan came to Shigawake from time to time to encourage and inspire me; she is the force behind this series of books. Her love and kindness has nourished me through the periods when I had no idea how to start, and then worse, how to get it all finished. These books are dedicated to her, but I would be remiss without placing special emphasis upon her help and encouragement. And of course, my new friend Richard Dionne, of Red Deer Press, who works under the umbrella of Fitzhenry & Whiteside, deserves my undying thanks for having rescued The Alford Saga, and who will publish the next two books as well.

In conclusion, I found this the hardest to write of the eight volumes in The Saga. To read, as I did, one hundred plus books, and to learn that so many thousands of young men, all "flowers of their nation", were wiped off the face of the earth, their rich lives wasted, often their last days spent in the most horrific conditions of lonely pain one could ever imagine. I tried not to let these feelings overwhelm my writing as I endeavoured to recount with honesty this story of my father and his friends, dead or alive, who did their best for what they believed in at the time, and to show, as well as the devastation, a few bright spots in their brave lives.

Paul Almond,
Shigawake, Quebec

THE DESERTER

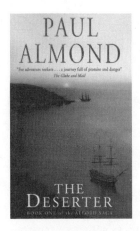

Imagine you're in a swaying hammock on a British man-o'war around 1800, riding out a harsh spring storm in a deserted estuary. Behind those high red cliffs lie a hundred miles of uncharted wilderness. If you jump ship and are caught, you will be branded a deserter — subject to death by one thousand lashes. What can you bring to help you survive? Within minutes, the ice-strewn waters will freeze your body and claim your soul. Even if this were your one chance for a life in the New World, would you jump?

Thomas Manning did, and his leap into uncertainty begins the epic tale of a pioneer family, one of the many who built our great nation. Through his and his descendants' eyes, we watch one small community's impact on the great events, which swirl about them and bring conflicts they must face in their struggles to create homes and families.

Absorbing, touching and full of adventure, *The Deserter* is Book One of the Alford Saga, a series chronicling two hundred years of Canadian history as seen through the eyes of one settler's family.

THE SURVIVOR

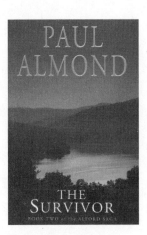

Thomas Manning, branded a deserter from the British Navy, is forced to change his name to James Alford to avoid the death penalty.

Determined to forge a new life on the Gaspé Peninsula, he struggles to survive the harsh landscape and win the hand of Catherine Garrett. After working in harsh sub-zero woods, he saves the life of an orphan working in a sawmill, and so gains crucial lumber to build a homestead out of intractable wilderness. But first he must battle murderous brigands to rescue a starving bull calf he hopes will be the first of the oxen he so desperately needs to clear his land. Finally, heroically surviving Canada's worst-ever famine, he faces down implacable bureaucracies to keep the farm he has been fighting to bring under cultivation.

A captivating and fast-paced adventure, *The Survivor* is Book Two of the Alford Saga, a series chronicling two hundred years of Canadian history as seen through the eyes of one settler's family.

THE PIONEER

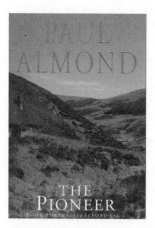

The riveting Alford Saga continues with James Alford, the Deserter, battling old age and ferocious winters, but even more crippling, the departure of his son and only heir, Young Jim, who sets out on snowshoes for Montreal, seven hundred miles away.

Arriving at last in Montreal, Jim is driven by starvation into a back-breaking job constructing the Victoria Bridge. Jim finds lodgings with an Irish widow in Griffintown, and falls in love. After being deceived in this romance, he rejects the bitter realities of urban life and returns to the Old Homestead and its community of pioneers. His ageing father recruits him to rally recalcitrant neighbours to found a school for their children and a church for their worship in Shigawake.

Enthralling and adventurous, *The Pioneer* is Book Three in the Alford Saga, a series chronicling two hundred years of Canadian history as seen through the eyes of one settler's family.

THE PILGRIM

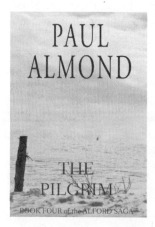

In 1896, young rector Jack Alford is sent to the implacable, granite shores of Labrador on the vast St. Lawrence River. Hazards imperil his life as he travels this harsh 450-mile coastline by boat and dogsled to visit his far-flung parishioners. Jack also manages to rescue a cook from the crew of a schooner to keep him company on his travels.

In this fourth book of The Alford Saga, his zeal for the welfare of Labrador's hardy parishioners diverts Jack from romance. Through summer storms that menace his tiny mission boat and fierce blizzards that almost annihilate his dog team, Jack brings succour to stranded families, care and leadership to villages perched on the windy granite and, finally, inspired teachings in hill-top churches that stand as beacons of hope among the seal-fishers and rugged pioneers of Labrador.

THE CHAPLAIN

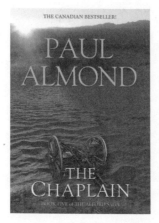

The Prime Minister gives permission for John Alford, *The Pilgrim*, to board a tramp steamer crammed with a thousand young enlistees bound for adventure in the Boer War. They steam across a stormy Atlantic into a year of dusty, disease-ridden battles in South Africa — the first engagement by Canadian Forces on foreign soil. He and his courageous comrades endure freezing night-long marches and thirst-ridden days as they mount dangerous attacks on Boer commandos under a blazing sun, turning the tide of war in the great battle of Paardeberg Drift. He falls in love, but as Chaplain, he must first comfort the dying, tend wounded friends, and with his troops assault the impregnable Thaba 'Nchu, the Black Mountain.

This enthralling tale of bravery and self-sacrifice is the fifth book in the Alford saga and is the first romantic adventure novel set in the Boer War for over a hundred years.